The Boy from the Island

By
William Miller

Grosvenor House
Publishing Limited

This book is published by
Grosvenor House Publishing Ltd
Link House
140 The Broadway, Tolworth, Surrey, KT6 7HT.
www.grosvenorhousepublishing.co.uk

This novel is a based on a true story and real events,
drawn from a variety of sources. Some events, details,
characteristics and people have been changed, added or removed.
The names have all been changed, and the dialogue has
been recreated.

A CIP record for this book
is available from the British Library

ISBN 978-1-83975-168-4

Preface

Just before starting my final year at school, my parents sent me on a three-week language and sports course in the south of Germany to brush up my German before taking the A-level. It was there that I met over fifty Italians, among them was the protagonist for this novel. When I was at school, my dream job was to become a writer or a script writer, and I made plans to read media studies at university, but this all changed once I came back from this trip. I was curious to learn Italian, and the protagonist became a very close friend of mine, so I changed direction and decided to study languages at university. I visited him and the lady who had taken custody of him many times and, as I got to know them better, I soon discovered that both of them had radically different histories, and came from different cultures. One thing led to another, and I ended up not becoming a writer, but working in business. Just before the millennium, I moved to Italy, and I lived there for fifteen years. Given that I had an original story to tell, I attempted to write something and saved it on a floppy disk somewhere! Then I abandoned the whole project, probably because I was busy with work, and maybe I wasn't ready. It wasn't until 2012, that I finally decided to realise my dream and write the story. I was catching up with one of my colleagues from Ireland in an Irish bar in Florence, and got talking about the story I wanted to write, and she encouraged me to put pen to paper. So, in 2013, I spent Saturday afternoons conducting research in the library and, in September, I went to São Nicolau, Cape Verde, which is where the protagonist is from. And in 2014, I started to write the story.

The Boy from the Island is based on a true story, and here I want to stress 'based on'. In the interest of storytelling, I have added purely fictional events and characters, removed certain events that I considered inconsequential to the essence of the story, and changed some of the details.

Whilst there are several themes explored in this story, such as racism, escapism, identity, women as victims; I would say that the core theme is cultural adaptation. Neither of the two central characters, who end up living in Milan, are Italian (Miguel is from Cape Verde, and Maria is from Romania), yet through extraordinary circumstances, Maria takes Miguel into her custody: one of them adapts, and the other one doesn't. To fully appreciate these two people living together, I felt that it was important to understand their backgrounds, hence the novel is divided into three parts.

Part One takes place on the island of São Nicolau, Cape Verde and introduces Miguel, the protagonist. The introduction gives a summary of the archipelago's history and geography. Part Two addresses the story of Maria, before she meets Miguel. And Part Three is about them living together.

Introduction

The first part of this story takes place between 1960 to 1971 on São Nicolau, one of the islands belonging to the archipelago Cape Verde, which is situated in a remote part of the Atlantic Ocean, several hundreds of miles from the African continent. It was given its name by the Portuguese, who had reached the green and verdant African coast twenty years before the islands were discovered, and so they decided to name them Cape Verde because of the proximity to where they had landed. Cape Verde is indeed a misnomer as the islands are dry and barren for most of the year, and the rocky, volcanic terrain together with the little topsoil have significantly impeded agriculture. As a result of the dearth of precipitation during the long dry season, most of the population's staple diet came from mackerel or tuna fish rather than crops. Luckily the cassava root could last many years without rain, and it was often turned into flour and stored for long periods.

It is not clear who were the first visitors to Cape Verde. It is claimed that the first settlement from Portugal and slaves arrived in the 1460s. The Portuguese had established a durable relationship with the Phoenicians and Moors, which helped them to navigate using modern maritime inventions in the fifteenth century, especially when there was conflict over ownership of the islands with northwest Africa. Subsequently, the infamous slave trade in Cape Verde was developed into a slave plantation economy by the sixteenth century. There were various alliances and conflict between Portugal and Spain; and numerous attempts at invasion from England, France and Holland. The feudal system continued, and the abuse of slavery became a habit. Several criminals, which included *degredados* (convicts), *lancados* (outcasts) and prostitutes were exiled to Cape Verde.

In 1866, an influential seminary was opened on São Nicolau. The Cape Verdeans became more educated for the first time, and a new culture formed called Crioulo, which enabled them to express themselves in words, culture, language, literature, customs and music. The lingua franca has different dialects and comprises a mixture of African and Portuguese syntax. It is not considered an official language, especially in its written format. Many words are derived from Portuguese, but there are stark differences in the grammar. The *lancados* (outcasts) had primarily contributed to the crioulizing of the Portuguese language on the ships, and the *badius* (descendants of runaway slaves) had played a role in the evolution of Crioulo society and civilization, by maintaining some of the cultural aspects of African heritage (folklore and beliefs). They believed that the essence of the soul is in the music, such as the *batuka*, an erotic dance accompanied by songs of a political or sexual nature. A group of women formed a circle, and one or two other women would dance inside it, wearing short shawls above the thighs. The *batuka* dance was disapproved by the Catholics for being too African.

The political influence in the years leading up to the independence of Cape Verde in 1975 is complex. The New World refers to the names of countries in the western hemisphere, especially the Americas. Slaves were transported to this world by the English, French and Portuguese, and on their return, they would bring goods, such as gold, rice and further slaves. Unfortunately, many died during their journey to and from these islands. At the same time, social systems had been created to segment slaves for import-export, general labour and domestic purposes.

Further segmentation was introduced based on African ethnicity, and this would determine the type of work they would perform as well as their treatment. Slavery became an accepted and profitable practice, and it contributed to the social infrastructure and economy of the islands. With a mixture of African slaves and Portuguese government and military officials on the islands, a new race, often referred to as *mestico* or *mulatto* (mixed race) emerged, which formed the basis of the identity of modern Cape Verdeans. It was not until the early nineteenth century that slavery was abolished due to moral and ethical concerns despite initial resistance from the Portuguese government and slave traders. Many slaves were returned to Africa. Slavery continued to linger in Cape Verde because its concept belonged to colonialism, and therefore it had become the norm; others from pure African descent identified colonialism as the core problem. The US navy sought to strengthen the need to remove slavery from Cape Verde by forming an African squadron, which would reduce the slave trade. Before the independence in 1975, the *brancos* (whites) from Portugal had control and power over the islands and consequently, those who advocated slavery decided to integrate Portuguese culture and abolish African heritage and history by giving Portuguese names to Cape Verdeans and introducing the Catholic religion and Portuguese language.

After 1962, the Hart Cellar Act permitted increasing migrants into the US, which enabled remittances to be sent back to the islands to partially sustain the economy. The population was entitled to a Portuguese passport, which facilitated entry into Europe and the New World. Rotterdam became a popular place for Cape Verdean men, as the shipping industry there was prosperous. Young single mothers followed the trend, many going to Italy with the increase in demand for domestic work. The number of females on Cape Verde exceeded the number of males, and men had lower life expectancy than women; consequently, polygamous relationships burgeoned and were tolerated, even though it was formally disapproved. In the 1960s and 1970s, there was still a culture of racial discrimination. New arrivals from Cape Verde tried to show association with Portugal and not with Africa; however, their dark skin colour gave them an appearance of being African. The first wave of immigrants worked in the cranberry bogs, docks or the textile mills, and they received low wages and were treated poorly. They did make more progress with Brazil as they shared culture, a legacy of Portuguese colonial rule, and a following of the Miguel evangelical Church.

Efforts have been made to gradually improve irrigation and the import of food, but with poor economic conditions, the population had to rely on their resourcefulness to conquer famine initially. Today, international food aid has made a difference to the Cape Verdeans, who are no longer dependent on local resources. The local people provided repair work and supplies for ships, whose sailors and traders used Cape Verde as a stopping point before proceeding to the Americas. The environment had driven men to become skilled sailors, whalers, traders and merchant mariners.

The Cape Verdeans now have their own identity, and many currently reside in Europe and the Americas. With a new age of multiculturalism, it is easier for them to "fit in" in other regions of the world. Whilst poverty is still prevalent on these islands, the Cape Verdeans have received significant help from other nations, and some of the islands have become popular tourist destinations.

Part One

São Nicolau, 1960 – 1971

One

São Nicolau, Cape Verde
1960

Ana had always liked time to herself. On one afternoon, five days after her thirteenth birthday, she went for a long walk and got lost in the fog and long blades of grass. She collected some small thin leaves from a dragon tree and skipped through the foliage, humming a merry tune. She found a rock and sat on its rugged surface, and pierced the leaves in the middle to make a necklace.

Her stockiness made her look determined and feisty, yet her bulging cheeks and shell-like eyes gave her face an innocent and soft appearance. She loved bright and colourful clothes, and today she was wearing her favourite sun yellow blouse and red shorts. From afar, you could see a happy-go-lucky girl lost in a world of her own, with unblemished skin and an immaculate outfit, but if you took a closer look, you would see three dark bruise marks on her right arm.

She was not allowed to stay out for too long otherwise her father would come looking for her, and that was the last thing she wanted. When she was alone, she would either make up her own stories of mythical creatures or just stare into space. Her favourite story was about dragons.

There was a good dragon and a bad dragon. The good dragon had a friendly face and looked after all the families on the island, and protected them from the bad dragon. The bad dragon was much bigger than the good dragon and had a mean and cruel face. He hissed like a snake as he trod through the grasslands, looking for children to eat. The children were afraid of the bad dragon, so they ran away. The good dragon told the children to sprinkle some rice around their homes to keep the bad dragon away. When one little boy forgot, he could hear the roaring, snarling and hissing of the dragon outside his home. As he was about to snatch the little boy with his claws, the good dragon leapt on the bad dragon and stung him with his poisonous tongue. The sting made the bad dragon fall into a long sleep. The bad dragon is still on the island, but no one knows where he is.

Immersed in her story, she was startled when a boy appeared out of nowhere. He was much taller than her, had broad shoulders, a big chest, and black curly hair. He was wearing a brownish-red t-shirt with loose, blue short trousers.

"Hello, little girl! What are you doing here?"

There was something about him that made her feel uncomfortable. Maybe it was his size, but his smile reassured her, so she gave him the benefit of the doubt and let him talk to her.

"Nothing. Just playing," she replied.

"Do you mind me talking to you?"

"I like time to myself. I like being alone."

"Come on, just give me five minutes," he said teasingly.

Ana continued playing with her leaves, and the boy sat cross-legged opposite her.

"What's your name?" he asked.

"Ana."

"Ana's a beautiful name. Where are your parents? Shouldn't you be with them?"

"They're okay with me being alone. They're used to it."

"So here we have a beautiful girl with a beautiful name!"

"Where do you live?" she asked.

"Not so far away. What are you making with those leaves?"

"I'm making a necklace."

"Is that for you or someone else?"

"Maybe for myself, or one of my sisters. I haven't decided yet."

"I think you must love dragon trees. There are some wonderful leaves on them."

"Yes, I do."

"There's one near here. Let's go and have a look."

The boy took her by her hand and led her to the dragon tree.

"It reminds me of an umbrella. You can find these in the New World. They're used to stop the rain from falling on your head," he said.

"Why would they want to do that?" asked Ana.

"I have no idea to tell you the truth!" he laughed.

"They must be very strange people."

"Yes, they are!"

"I like the rain," Ana said. "Do you like the rain?"

"Yes, very much."

Hundreds of knotted sturdy branches sprouted from the short thick trunk, leading to an array of thin oblong leaves.

"They look like stars!" said Ana, looking at how the leaves were displayed.

"Yes, they do!"

The boy got on his hands and knees, crawled towards the tree and touched the bark on the trunk with the palm of his right hand, and she followed closely behind. He gently took her hand and placed it on the tree trunk."

"How does that feel?"

"I don't know. It feels like bark."

It was a dumb question, but she thought it was best not to confront him as he didn't look the type you would want to argue with.

"Shall we go for a walk?" he suggested.

"Okay, why not?" They stood up, and she followed him.

"So, tell me about your family."

"I'm the eldest of two sisters and a brother. My father goes fishing every day and my mother stays at home to do the cooking. My brother spends most of his time outside, playing football. My youngest sister is always crying. Every time she eats something, she throws it up over my mother."

"That's funny!"

"Do *you* go fishing?"

"Yes, sometimes."

Ana remembered the boy talking about umbrellas in the New World.

"What is the 'new world'?"

"They are other lands, much bigger lands, far far away from these islands and they're very different."

"I see. Have you ever been?"

"No. I just heard about them from friends who've been there."

"Would you like to go?"

"Yes, I would. What about you?"

"I think so."

"Well, let's go together," he said cheerfully.

There was an awkward moment. Ana didn't know what to say to him, and she wondered why he wanted to talk to her. He was too familiar with her, so maybe it was time for him to leave. She moved away from him, sat on a rock and took the leaves out of her pocket. The boy followed her, sat opposite her, and admired how her delicate hands made tiny punctures in the leaves and wove them into each other.

"You've got beautiful hands," he remarked tenderly.

"Thank you," replied Ana politely.

"May I see?" asked the boy, pointing to the neckless.

Ana gave him the necklace, and he looked at it in amazement. He smiled at her.

"You're a very clever girl!"

He took her hand and rubbed her palm with his thumb.

"Do you like that?" he asked.

Ana didn't reply and didn't look at him either.

He then moved and sat next to her. He held her right hand and caressed her thigh with his fingers, initially in slow motion and then slightly harder. He put his hand inside her shorts and near her waist. Ana didn't like his face and breath being so close to her and felt helpless as he forcefully placed his hand on the back of her head and pushed it towards his face until their lips met. He closed his eyes and stroked her hair, put his arm around her and took her right hand and moved it under his trousers. Ana froze. It suddenly dawned on her that something terrible was about to happen. She was in the middle of nowhere with a stranger who she had mistakenly trusted.

"I can hear someone," she whispered.

"It's just the wind. Don't worry, no one's coming," he replied.

The boy became restless, picked her up, and walked to a clearing. He removed his clothes, hastily ripped off her shorts, pushed her onto the ground and climbed on top of her. She tried to wriggle away, but the boy was too strong.

"What are you doing?" she cried.

The boy smirked and put his mouth next to her ear.

"It's all right," he whispered.

"Stop! Stop! I don't like it," she pleaded.

Tears welled up in her eyes, and the boy's friendly expressions became cold and cruel, just like the bad dragon. He put his left hand over her mouth to mute her muffled screams.

When the boy finished, he stood up and saw blood on his legs and around his groin. He quickly put his clothes back on and ran away, leaving Ana in the grass bruised and bloody. Ana sat up, feeling dizzy and confused, and as she was about to put her shorts back on, she saw the blood all over her thighs and legs. To avoid telling this shameful episode to her family, she decided to find a stream to wash the blood off. As she stood up, she heard her father's familiar slow and heavy footsteps. Domingos was a large, muscular man whose complexion was much darker than Ana's. Her heart beat rapidly when she saw the thick stick he was carrying.

"Papai," she wailed. "A boy, he …,"

She coughed and looked up into the air.

"I know exactly what has happened!" he shouted.

"It wasn't my fault," Ana said feebly.

"Do you think I'm stupid? You let him! You let him!" Domingos boomed. "This wouldn't have happened if you hadn't gone into one of your daydreams. Always going off alone. Maybe this will be a lesson for you."

He pushed Ana onto the floor and raised his stick and thrashed her repeatedly until her back bled.

"Get cleaned up before you come home. I don't want your mother seeing you like this!" he said, before leaving her.

Ana never saw the boy again. He was probably a visitor from another island. How much had her father seen? If he had been there when she suspected that someone was watching her, why had he not gone after him?

São Nicolau, Cape Verde
1969 - 1971

Two

"What about José? Whatever happened to him?" asked Afonso.

"Nothing. I don't want to talk about him. He's a liar, and I don't trust him."

Ana's eyes darted around the cooking area, looking for the rice.

Earlier that day, she had been to visit her brother, Angelo, who worked in a grocer's shop. Inside, the walls were painted ocean blue, and there were three lopsided shelves behind the wooden counter, on which stood bags of rice, sugarcane and grogue, a strong alcoholic drink. On the table, there was a small plastic tub for the money.

She eventually found the bag of rice, lying on the bed amongst some of the clothes. At that moment, she saw Domingos burst into the kitchen area with a small plastic bag of fish. When he saw Ana, he grunted and threw the bag at her, and it landed with a thud on the ground right in front of her. She sighed, picked it up and watched Domingos as he lay down on the bed and propped his head on the sugar flour-filled pillow. He was wearing a sand-coloured shirt and some lime cotton trousers, held loosely around his waist. She could tell by his tired eyes and irregular breathing that he was consumed by the exhausting daily fishing trips to Ponta de Vermelharia. He lay on his back, motionless, no doubt listening to the children playing outside.

"Why don't you try and get some sleep?" asked Ana, knowing that he wouldn't reply.

Ana knew that he only really spoke to her mother. She showed him respect just because that's what a daughter should do, but deep down she hated him, and she had become good at veiling her disdain. She turned away from him and went outside, where her mother was standing next to the fire.

"Shoo!" exclaimed Ana, as she almost tripped over some children, who were playing *mancala*, a hide and seek game. After pouring the rice into the pan, which sat lopsided on the stones surrounding the fire, she wandered back into the kitchen area and waved away an army of flies, which were bouncing off the bag of fish. "Dinner will be ready soon," she said to Papai.

Ana went outside again with the plastic bag along with even more flies following her. Using a stick, she spread the tuna fish evenly on a pan over the fire, and once it was ready, she scooped the rice out of the boiling water onto six cracked plates. Her mother put aside more food for her father and helped him to eat it using her fingers. Outside, Ana, Angelo and her two sisters, Leticia and Olivia, ate the fish and rice around the fire.

As the sun was setting, Ana could see the silhouette of Afonso, who was playing football with two children. He often appeared behind the door of her house, and teased her about José, it was none of his business, and she preferred to put José to the back of her mind. She thought how much José had hurt her with his lies and broken promises.

The house was made out of concrete, and there were blotches of mould and small holes on the exterior. Outside, you could see the corrugated iron roof, and two large squared apertures, boarded with blue-coloured wood because glass windows would have been too expensive. Inside, there was a small kitchen area and a bedroom – there was one bed for Ana's parents, and one for Ana, Olivia and Leticia. Angelo slept on the floor. There were similar looking houses scattered haphazardly amongst the unruly foliage and trees.

Ana's mother woke up to the blinding sunlight piercing its way through the doorway. After waking her children up, she turned on her side to face Domingos, who was in a deep sleep.

"Domingos!" she said in a hushed tone, prolonging the vowel sounds of his name. She knew he was unwell, but the family depended on him going fishing, or there would be no food for the family.

"Domingos!"

His wife always used the smell of food to wake him up, so she placed a ball of left-over fish and rice under his nose until he half opened his eyes and ate it.

Ahead of him was the arduous journey from Faja Baixa to Ponta de Vermelharia where he would board a bottom trawler with other fishermen and spend the day catching fish. He no longer needed to guide the mule, as she was accustomed to going there and back. Many mules had died en route because of a lack of food and water, and he often wondered how long she would survive. A successful fishing trip would depend on the wind and current of the sea so, whilst he was riding, he would pray that the weather would not be so ferocious. On this day, he was fortunate as the weather was calm, and they chose an area where there were schools of tuna fish.

On his return to Faja Baixa, he could see his wife, Ana and Leticia waiting for him. The mule stopped, and he climbed off slowly carrying heavy bags full of fish.

"We could make this last three days," he said.

Ana and Leticia attempted to help him to walk to the house by letting him lean on them and looping their arms.

"Get off!" he snapped. "I'm okay on my own!"

His wife took the fish back to the house.

"This won't last three days. Maybe two days if we're lucky, but not three," she muttered.

Still, two days was good enough, and it would let Domingos rest the following day. In the distance, they saw Elena, Ana's cousin, balancing a container of water on her head.

Domingos went straight to bed and drifted in and out of sleep as he waited for his food to arrive. He opened his eyes and saw his wife preparing the fish, and not Ana, so he suspected that something was not right, and he thought it was strange that his wife was not enlightening him on the comings and goings of their friends, as she usually did. She seemed to be in deep thought as she gutted the fish without saying a word.

Afonso was playing soccer with his two sons. They would play for hours, using sugar cane leaves and sticks as goalposts. They always wanted Afonso to be the goalkeeper and asked him to stand next to one of the sticks so they could easily score. Unlike many of his friends, who had left São Nicolau to work as cleaners or painters in Holland, he had remained on the island to work on the maintenance of the trawlers. Ana, who was watching the game, laughed at his big black shorts, which were far too big for him. He asked the boys to play by themselves and went up to her.

"You still think about him, don't you?" Afonso asked, turning his head towards Ana.

"I should be in Holland now. He promised me a better life, and I don't hear nothing from him."

"You know, I don't think that place is as good as you think it is. Maybe he can't write to you. How long has it been now? One year? Why don't you go and speak to his family? You know where they live."

"I told you. He's a liar, and I can't stand him."

He knew that José had a reputation for being a womaniser and he was probably enjoying himself with some Dutch girls.

"Why don't you come to mine tomorrow?" Afonso suggested. "Then we can talk about this. Rita is visiting relatives in Tarrafal tomorrow, and the kids are at school."

Ana laughed.

"What will people say if they know that you and I are alone in your home? What will your wife think?"

"She's not my wife. You know that. Anyway, it's up to you. You know where I am."

Ana returned home and saw her mother cooking the fish outside.

"You're wasting your time with that one," she said sternly.

Ana gathered the plates from the kitchen area and brought them outside. Leticia and Olivia joined them, and they ate the fish watching the flames.

Three

Five days later, sometime after sunset, a mysterious figure emerged from the fog in Faja Baixa. The dimly lit oil lamps inside and outside the houses revealed a man wearing a smart beige suit and balancing a small vase with some flowers on the palm of his right hand. No one saw the grin on his face as he walked with confidence towards Ana's home.

When he arrived, the door was half-open, so he called Ana's name and added, *"Mi N krê falá má bo!"* – I want to speak with you!

Ana, who was busy preparing fish, recognised the voice straight away.

"Bá fóra! Mi N (s)ta ukupóde. Txó-me in paz!" - Go away! I'm busy. Leave me in peace, she responded aggressively. *"Mi N ka kre nada ma bo"* – I don't want anything to do with you.

The man didn't take any notice of her harsh tone.

"Mi N krê oió-be, nha amor. Dó-me sinku minute pur favor!" - I want to see you, my love. Just give me five minutes, please.

Ana's father, who was lying in bed, listened carefully. He recognised the man and knew that Ana would succumb to his charming words. It was just a matter of time.

"Ka bo txemó-me bo amor mo mi N ka ê bo amor!" –
Stop calling me your love. I'm not your love, she
replied fiercely.

Uninvited, José went inside and placed the flowers
next to the fish on the table. Ana caught sight of them
in the corner of her eye but did not display any
appreciation. Instead, she continued to prepare the
fish, whilst José sat down. There was a brief silence.

"You promised me you would send me the papers!"
she hissed.

"There were problems," replied José solemnly,
looking up at her.

She hurled some rice into his face and faced him
with a deadly glare and pointed finger.

"What problems? You didn't even write to me.
And how long have you been away? Almost a year!"
she exclaimed angrily.

"I can explain," José said calmly. "I've been working
day and night, seven days a week, just for you."

"Really? So why did one of our neighbours see you
with another girl?"

"These are all lies, my love. You know what people
are like. They like to gossip."

"It's you who is lying. Lies and excuses! You
promised me a better life in Europe!"

José thought carefully about how he would reply.

"I thought about you every day. You know that
you are my only one. This is why I came back to see
you."

"I don't believe you. I waited and waited and
waited!"

"Please, my love. Give me another chance to show
you that I mean what I say. I'll be leaving for Holland

again soon, and I will get the papers. It'll be easier this time. Less red tape. But I don't have much time, and I want to spend it with you. Just you and me."

"I'll think about it," she said nonchalantly.

"All right." José got up slowly and kissed Ana lightly on the cheek. She didn't look at him. José then left, singing, "*Mi N sta mi so na munde pa bo*" – I am alone in the world without you.

Four

Three days later, Domingos insisted on going fishing again, even though he wasn't feeling well. The strong wind coming from the Atlantic Ocean would make the fishing trip a strenuous one, and it would take a miracle for them to catch any mackerel or tuna.

In spite of the mule's old age and battling winds, which almost pushed Domingos down the steep slopes, he proceeded on his laborious journey to Ponta de Vermelharia, hoping that his fellow fishermen would not retreat because of the weather. When he got closer to the harbour, he could tell by their animated gestures that they were deciding whether to go fishing or not. He left his mule by a tree and went to greet the other fishermen who helped him onto the boat before setting off across the bumpy sea.

Domingos made himself comfortable at the rear of the boat with his fishing line. His irregular breathing made him feel tired, and as he was about to fall asleep, a huge wave swept over him, causing him to lose balance and fall over.

"Domingos!" shouted one of the fishermen.

There was no reply.

"Domingos! Are you okay?"

"Of course, I'm okay," he mumbled.

"What? I can't hear you!"

Domingos closed his eyes and then opened them again and raised his voice.

"I'm okay!"

Half an hour later, the sea became increasingly volatile, and as they moved forward, more waves splashed onto the boat, causing the other fishermen to fall as well. Some of the sails collapsed, making it hard to manoeuvre the boat back to the harbour. Lying in icy seawater, Domingos wondered if his friends had caught any fish at all. Luckily, they made it back and helped Domingos off the boat and laid him on the ground. He turned on his side to see them gutting the tuna and then looked at his mule by the tree. He stood up and hobbled towards her. His fellow fishermen looked round to see where he was and saw him sitting next to his mule and stroking her.

"You've had a rough time, haven't you?" empathised one of them.

Domingos nodded.

"You shouldn't have come today at all," he continued.

"I know," said Domingos.

"Well, we'd better get you home. Mateus is also going to Faixa Baja, and he has a couple of mules so he'll look after you. He'll be along in five minutes or so."

"Thank you," said Domingos.

"Don't worry about the mule. It happens all the time. And by the way, we'll make sure you get your fair share of the fish."

Mateus helped Domingos onto another mule, and they rode back to Faija Baixa together.

When Ana and her mother saw Domingos, they ran up to him,

"We've been so worried. Where have you been? It's so late," said Ana's mother.

"He's not a well man. He really shouldn't have been with us today. Anyway, I've got you some fish. This should last you a week or so," said Mateus, as he lifted off three bags of tuna fish.

Ana took them and rushed back into their home.

"Thank you. I'm Francesca. You didn't tell me your name," said Ana's mother.

"Mateus. Don't worry. We'll bring some fish back for your family. Just make sure Domingos gets some rest."

"I don't know how to thank you" she replied.

"It's no problem. Be seeing you!" Mateus rode away.

Domingos returned to his habitual position in bed and watched Ana preparing cachupa probre, a fish and corn stew. She took it outside and cooked it over the open fire, and when it was ready, she passed a dish to her mother who fed it to her father with her fingers. Francesca looked apprehensive as her husband's breathing was notably erratic.

The following morning, Francesca prepared some cachupa and a fried egg and tried to wake Domingos up with the smell of food, but it didn't work this time.

"Domingooooos!" she said gently in his ear.

There was no sound, no breathing. She put her head gently on his shoulder.

Five

The family accumulated in the church for the funeral and the priest led a thoughtful service with prayers and hymns. Afterwards, Domingos was swiftly buried in the same area. Ana wasn't sorry that her father had passed away but pretended to be distraught and mournful, especially in front of her mother. The only thing she was worried about was how they would get fish without him.

Ana was torn about José's visit. He was insidious, spurious, yet she yearned for his warmth and charm. The day after the funeral, José visited her to offer his condolences and was unusually quiet. He realised that Ana must have found his narcissism distasteful and displeasing, so he changed tactics by proposing that they go for a walk. When they reached one of the inclines, they spent an hour silently gazing at the flavescent landscape. He was a chatterbox and most of the time, he could not stop talking, and he knew that, so he didn't talk about the bright lights of Europe, nor the fact that it was not as luxurious as he had thought. His hours in Holland were spent cleaning and maintaining the ships at the harbours, and the accommodation was uncomfortable. He didn't disclose that he had spent most of the little money he earned on gambling and frequenting nightclubs.

"So, how have you been?" he asked.

"Same old boring life, waiting for my father to come home with the fish. Well, when I say father, he's not been a father at all."

"Well, he always went fishing for you."

"I know. I know. But he wasn't a good man, and he's been horrible to me. I've had so many nightmares about him."

"I'm sorry to hear that."

"Anyway, it's over now. Otherwise, I've been cooking, going for walks, eating and that's it."

They admired the beautiful glow of the sun sinking below the horizon, leaving the sky bleeding purples and reds. They looked at each other. He rested his hand on her shoulder, and she embraced him tightly and rested her head on his chest.

"It's getting dark," he said softly.

After several minutes, they held each other's hands, and he took her to the comfort of his own home.

Six

The following morning, Ana washed her hands and face in the water container, whilst José prepared some rice and egg for breakfast. She had no idea how she would explain her absence to her mother, who doubtlessly would know precisely where she had been. It wasn't the first time she had spent the night in someone else's home, and each time, her mother fiercely reprimanded her for the shame she brought on the family. There were eyes everywhere, so as soon as José reappeared out of the blue, people started to talk about how she had visited Ana, and now everyone would know that she had spent the night with him.

Ana didn't care what people thought. As soon as she finished breakfast, she walked with José, hand in hand, towards her home.

"You know I'll be ..." began José.

"Yes, I know you're leaving again tomorrow," Ana interrupted.

"I promise I'll organize the documents this time and then you'll be with me sooner than you think", he said.

"I hope so," she sighed.

She withdrew her hand, walked the rest of the way to her home and turned around near the entrance to see José still standing in the same place. She waved at him, and he blew her a kiss.

Her mother was busy in the kitchen area and didn't look up when Ana arrived.

"I know what you're thinking, Mamãe," Ana said.

"It doesn't seem to matter what I think. Anyway, you don't need to worry about what I think. Everyone is talking about you and José. What's the matter with you? Can't you see he's trouble?"

Ana didn't want her to bad-mouth José. After all, he had looked after her and comforted her after the loss of her father.

"He's changed, Mamãe. I think going to Holland has done him some good. Didn't you see the way he treated me yesterday? Anyway, he said he's going to get me the papers this time, so that I can be with him."

"And you believe him?" her mother replied. "He's a notorious liar! And you've been taken in by his charms and good looks once again."

She laughed at her daughter's lame attempt to see anything good about José's character.

"The point is that you stayed the night with him and in doing so, you have disgraced our family once again. I daren't go outside. People will be giving me looks and talking with each other," her mother said.

"I think he wants to marry me," said Ana.

"Marry you! Marry you!" her mother shouted, rattled even more by her naivety. "Of course, he wants to marry you! And then what? Do you really think he will stay with you?"

"And do you want me to stay here with no hope for the future? Shall I never have a husband? In Holland, I can earn money and send it to you."

Ana was fighting a losing battle. Her mother didn't reply, and there was a brief, painful silence.

"What's done is done," said her mother. "Time will pass, and everyone will find something else to talk about, as they always do. All I can do is advise you not to see him again. Don't listen to his promises. You're a grown woman, so you can do what you like, but mark my words, if you stay with him, you're going to get hurt. Badly hurt."

They avoided talking about José again that day. Ana wanted to say goodbye to him at the harbour before he left for Holland. There was no harm in saying goodbye.

On the following day, Ana went to José's home. He came out with a small bag of clothes and helped Ana onto a mule. As they travelled to the harbour in Tarrafal, they chatted joyfully about the future, dreaming about better lives together with money, good food and a better lifestyle.

"And we'll have an enormous house with a garden and ten bedrooms and a huge kitchen and our own bathroom!" said Ana.

"We'll go to the finest restaurants in Europe, drink champagne in Paris, drive around London and visit Buckingham Palace!"

"And I want to go to Italy to visit the Pope and visit the beautiful beaches!" she said.

The oppressive clouds erased all colour, leaving a black and white picture of the stationary boats and grey sailors, who were talking against the backdrop of the shiny black ocean. Wives, children, lovers and friends had come to bid farewell to those who would be leaving. Wives and mothers were sad about the imminent departure of their husbands or children. For some of them, this was the first time they would be going abroad for a considerable amount of time. Husbands and fathers were excited about meeting their friends and embarking on an adventure to another world with promises of wealth, luxury and freedom. The noise of the engine from the boats drowned some of their words. Husbands and fathers said reassuring words about their return, and sending money back to their families. Wives and mothers reminded them to be careful and to come back soon. José pointed at the boat he would be taking to Sal, and from there he would take an aeroplane to Amsterdam and then go to Rotterdam.

Ana held José's hand for a few minutes before leaving.

"I'll miss you," she said softly. Convinced that José was the right man for her, her heart sank as the moment arrived when he had to leave her.

"I'll miss you too," he replied and kissed her on her lips.

"I'll be back. Don't worry. I love you," he whispered.

Ana remained at the edge of the harbour and waved goodbye as José boarded the boat. He stayed at the back of the boat, so that he could see her for as long as possible, and he kept waving at her. She didn't leave until the boat was completely out of sight, and then she returned to her mule.

When she returned home, she met her mother at the entrance.

"Why do you never listen to me?" Francesca was exasperated. Protecting her daughter seemed a lost cause. She no longer had the will or the energy to be angry. Sooner or later, she would lose her daughter for good.

Seven

One afternoon, two months after José left, Ana was sitting in the washing area outside, looking into the air thinking about him. She thought about him every day and yet she still hadn't heard from him and thought that he must be busy trying to get the papers and working on the ships. Since he had left, she had become noticeably lethargic and more pensive, so Olivia took over helping with the washing and preparation of food. Everyone kept asking her if she was feeling well and she would either ignore them or inaudibly mumble that she was well or feeling nauseous.

That afternoon, they were all in high spirits, because Mateus had brought them plenty of fish and Afonso had brought some grogue. Olivia and her mother started cooking whilst Ana sat on a rock a few metres away, replaying José's words just before he left. After they had eaten, the sky gradually became a rich dark blue, so Angelo lit two oil lamps next to the dying fire.

"I often think what it is like out there," said Angelo.

"Where?" replied Leticia, "You mean the other islands?"

"No, I mean the New World. I've heard it's very different from here and so many people have gone there to find a better life, just like José," said Angelo.

"It can't be that good," said Olivia, "Someone told me there's a lot of noise and the people aren't very nice."

"Well it can't be much worse than here, can it? Here there's no food and no money. Anyway, there are lots of jobs all over Europe, not just the ones José is doing on the ships. I've heard that they're looking for cleaners and people who can cook," said Angelo.

"I don't know. I'd be nervous about leaving here. It might be dangerous in Holland," said Olivia.

"It doesn't have to be Holland. You can go anywhere: Portugal, France, Italy, Germany. The door is open for us. It's thanks to the Portuguese that we've got the freedom to go wherever we like," said Angelo.

"I think it all sounds wonderful!" Leticia exclaimed.

Afonso had been drinking the grogue, and he offered some to Elena.

"Oh no! I couldn't. I know what that stuff does to you!"

"Come on, just try a bit. It won't do you any harm!"

Afonso poured a bit of undiluted grogue into a mug, and Elena drank it, as though she was performing a magical circus act. She stumbled, fell on her back and laughed. Regaining her balance, she started to dance the *batuka*, and the others formed a circle around her. Leticia sang, Elena danced, and Mateus, Alonso and Angelo used their knees as drums and their hands as drumsticks. Elena was a slim and sturdy woman, had an oblong face and large preying eyes. Her seductive moves enticed Afonso and Mateus whose eyes became fixed on her. As the drums and singing increased in intensity, Elena increased the rapidness of her erotic moves. Olivia went inside and saw her mother standing near the entrance of the house, looking in despair.

Francesca caught sight of Ana and went up to her.

"What's wrong?" she asked

"I'm feeling a bit ill. Don't worry. It'll pass."

"Have you been sick? You've hardly eaten!"

"Yes, I was sick earlier. But I feel better now. I don't feel like eating much at the moment."

"Why don't you go and get some rest?"

"Okay, I will."

Francesca told Angelo and his sisters not to disturb Ana, who went inside and lay on the bed. Something was amiss, and it was not just about José leaving.

Eight

One day, three months later, a letter arrived, which would change their lives forever. They had cold fish and rice for breakfast and then went about their usual routine: Leticia and Olivia tidied the exterior of the house by removing the crawling grass leaves, Francesca cleaned the dishes, Elena went to get the water from the pump, Mateus and Afonso went fishing, Ana went for a walk and Angelo went to work in the shop.

Angelo was tall, had small eyes and always wore a contagious smile. His mother had always said that he was born smiling, and many people thought this was the reason he had so many customers. He was practical and was the one who would repair roofs when the rain damaged them. He had often contemplated becoming a fisherman, but he had become used to working in the shop and besides, he liked working with his friend and he earned money to buy food for his family.

When Angelo arrived in the shop, his friend was scrupulously looking at a piece of crumpled paper, desperately trying to decipher the words.

"Good morning!"

"Good morning, Angelo. Sorry I was a bit distracted. I got a letter this morning from one of my cousins, who's living in Italy. Can you do me a favour and read it for me?"

"Yes, sure."

"I think I've understood some of it. His writing's not very good."

Angelo took the paper and read the letter.

"This is a letter from your cousin, right?"

"Yeah, he's in Italy. Milan to be precise."

"Well, he says that there's a family, which might be looking for cooks and cleaners for their apartment in Milan. He goes on to say that there are quite a few opportunities for domestic work there."

"I see."

"You know, this is exactly what we were talking about a few weeks ago!"

"Are you thinking about going?"

"Not sure yet. I mean I'd love to go, but we lost Papai and don't know how Mamãe would take it." He paused, and then another idea struck him. "If we do go, why don't you come with us?"

"I've got the shop. I can't leave it. I too have a family, and the shop helps us make ends meet, and so does your smile!"

They stayed in the shop and talked with regular customers. They asked each other about their families, and eventually, Angelo's friend left to visit his grandmother.

Angelo took his friend's letter with him and showed it to Leticia when he returned home.

"That's brilliant! When do we leave?"

"Leticia, calm down. It says, 'might'. It doesn't mean that they will take us on."

"That doesn't matter. It says there are a lot of opportunities. We can just turn up, and we'll get something. I'm sure others have done the same thing," said Leticia.

"How are we going to get there? We haven't got the money. It's not as if they will pay us to fly from Sal. They haven't agreed to anything," said Angelo.

"What's the matter with you? You usually like adventure, and now you're being pessimistic. In any case, I think it's worth the risk. And I know that you do too."

Angelo laughed. "I'm just being cautious."

"I'm just being cautious", she mimicked, "You've never been cautious! I can't wait to tell Elena when she gets home," she said.

She crunched the letter up, held it to her chest and danced around the house.

Ana was lying in the middle of the bed with her eyes closed and she was sweating. Her mother was next to her with a damp cloth, which she pressed on her daughter's forehead. When Angelo and Leticia excitedly came into the house, their mother motioned them to be quiet with a finger on her lips.

"What's the matter with Ana? Has she got a temperature?" whispered Angelo.

"We think she's pregnant," said Olivia.

"I can't believe it," Leticia squealed, cusping her hands around her mouth.

"How did this happen?" asked Angelo.

"José," said his mother. "He promised her a new life and Ana was taken in by his charm. As you know, he's now in Holland, and we haven't heard from him since. I warned her time and time again, but she never listened. Mind you, your father didn't exactly help as he kept asking her about him, and Afonso kept teasing her."

Nine

Nobody liked the long dry season when the lush green foliage morphed into hay. The dragon tree was one of the few signs of life, as it was almost impossible to grow crops and engage in any kind of agriculture. Along with the plant life, many animals and people died because of dehydration and starvation.

Miguel was born during this season, and he was a such a noisy baby that anyone living nearby could hardly sleep. Secretly, Ana had been hoping for a baby girl, but she now looked happier than ever before, as she swayed him in her arms. And he took her mind off José, who she had been brooding over for the last nine months. Leticia came in, picked him up and sang him a nursery rhyme, accentuating some of the words and, to her delight, he smiled at her. When he started to gurgle, she gave him back to Ana and said that she would come back a bit later.

Outside, the neighbours' children were playing *mancala* and Angelo was talking with Olivia, who was sitting on a stone stitching some panos, untailored textile, to make a new garment for Miguel.

"I still think we can go. Merchant ships leave all the time. What are we waiting for?" interrupted Leticia.

"What about Ana? We can't leave her here by herself!" said Angelo.

"She can come with us! She'll love it, I know she will."

"But she won't come without Miguel."

"Our mother and Olivia can look after the baby. Elena and Mateus will also be here. Mateus has been a good friend of the family since Papai died," said Leticia.

Angelo surveyed his surroundings. It was useless playing devil's advocate with Leticia.

Since Miguel was born, Ana had never left him alone, but one month later, she started going on walks by herself again. Angelo spotted her trundling through brittle hay stalks and thought that this was the right moment to talk to her about emigrating to Italy, but he didn't want to push her. He stopped a few metres behind her.

"Ana, can I speak with you for a minute?" he asked.

"So, you're leaving us," she said, without turning around.

"Not yet. But yes, we're planning to go to Italy. I know it's a risk, but there really is a need for domestic work there, and we can send some of the money here." Angelo paused. "Listen…"

Ana raised her left hand, signalling him to stop talking, and like a soothsayer, suspected what he was about to say.

"You want to know whether I will come with you," she said and turned around to face him.

"You're also thinking that I'm dreaming about José and wish to see him again."

Angelo didn't know what to say. He had always been wary of Ana's sudden change of personality. Sometimes, she was fun, informal, casual, spontaneous and reckless, and other times, like now, she was formal, decisive, assertive and condescending.

"I've given up on José. He's worthless, and you were all right about him. I haven't even put his name on the birth certificate."

Angelo imagined her at the town hall, glaring coldly at the officials who would not have dared to confront her. It would have been a quick and easy operation, and she would have left the town hall with what she wanted.

"José is in Holland, and not in Italy, so I wouldn't see him. I have given it some thought and would like to come, but I'll come back for Miguel when he's a bit older and can manage the journey." Ana smiled at him.

"Well, that's settled then!" Angelo said with relief.

She held onto his arm and walked back to their home so they could tell their mother all about their big plan.

"So, we, that is Ana, Leticia and I, will leave for Italy to become domestic workers so we can send money back here and you and Olivia can look after Miguel until he gets older. Then Ana will come back for him," said Angelo.

"Well, so be it! You've obviously made up your minds. There's nothing more to be said on the matter," said Francesca.

She stood up and went to collect the plates, which had been left outside. Angelo, Leticia and Ana looked at each other, bewildered by her mother's reaction. Did she approve it? Had she given up on them all together?

Ten

On the morning of their departure, they approached the harbour in Preguiça with excitement and trepidation: excitement because their plan was becoming real, trepidation because of the unknown. Angelo had given his sisters a rough idea of what lay ahead in the following three weeks. They would spend a day travelling from São Nicolau to São Vicente on a schooner, named Sonny Maria, then two weeks on a steamer to Lisbon, and a further week on another steamer from Lisbon to Genoa. The night before, Angelo had packed bags with clothes, canned food and water.

Clusters of heavy fog swirled through the air impeding visibility of shape and form, making it hard to distinguish the boats, which were frantically yo-yoing on the sea. The swollen charcoal clouds merged with the darkness of the sea. The howling wind accompanied the crashing of the waves, which engulfed the passers-by. The crew was on board, making last-minute preparations. Angelo was talking with Leticia, whilst Ana looked at the Atlantic ocean's volatile and terrifying waves. Francesca embraced her children and wished them a safe onward journey. Olivia looked at all of them disapprovingly and kissed each one, appealing to them to return soon.

As they boarded the Sonny Maria, two of the crew helped them balance themselves on the jetty before jumping onto the schooner, Leticia nearly fell over with the constantly moving floor. Ana looked down at the white wooden floor and then at the grand white sails, towering above her. When the crew removed the anchor, Angelo instructed Leticia and Ana to sit close to the tack in the middle of the boat. Ana turned around to wave to her mother and Olivia, but they were no longer visible.

After they set off, Ana moved to the side of the boat and stared at the ocean and Leticia laid her head on Angelo's shoulder. The harsh sounds from the wind and sea prevented them from talking to each other. Once the island of São Nicolau disappeared, they fell asleep on the floor and dreamt about their new life.

In the middle of the day, Ana felt a trickle of water on her face and woke up to see a crooked streak of bright light in the sky and, moments later, torrential rain fell from the heavens. The strong gusts of wind pounded onto the sea, causing the waves to increase their size and momentum and the boat bounced off them like a galloping horse in distress. She saw one of the crew mouthing, "Hang onto something," but it was too late as a wave crashed onto the boat drenching everyone in icy seawater. Leticia let go of the grab rail and slithered ferociously towards the stern. Luckily one of the other passengers grabbed her arm and pulled her to safety. Another strike of lightning appeared, and the winds pushed the tide into a fury of wild manoeuvres, and a colossal wave immersed the boat again, shooting pools of water onto the deck.

Their bags split open, cans of food rolled out, and their clothes stuck to the floor. Ana shouted into Angelo's ear that her feet were cold, so he did his best to rub them and wrapped his arm around her. He looked at Leticia who was being looked after by other passengers, and he glanced at the crew who were desperately managing the sails, mast and rigging.

In the early afternoon, the sun emerged through the soft white clouds and dried the boat, the clothes, the passengers and the crew. The waves became gentler, and there was a pleasant breeze which was ideal as Angelo and his sisters were tired, and they spent the rest of the time asleep on the floor. When Mindelo port and its small harbour came into view, Ana woke up and tugged Angelo and Leticia and pointed at the steamer.

"Is that the boat we'll be on?" asked Ana.

"Yes, that's the one," replied Angelo, "and we'll be on that boat for two weeks!"

"Well, at least we can stay inside if it starts raining again," said Leticia.

The boat pulled into the harbour, and the crew dropped the anchor into the water, helped the passengers off the boat with their bags and wished them luck with their next voyage.

"How long do we have to wait?" asked Ana.

"Not long. Let's have a sit down over there," said Angelo. "Leticia, are you okay?"

"Yes, I'm okay."

"Just think! In three weeks, we'll be in Italy!" exclaimed Angelo.

Part Two

Maria's story

How can I describe the house? Well, it's more of a villa with a cellar and an attic. It's situated on the outskirts of Bucharest, and it's one of ten identical houses, which are separated by an array of small plants and trees. I was born on the twenty-second of May, 1928, and I live there with my parents, Daniel and Izabela, my older sister, Iona, my younger brother, Ben as well as our French nanny, Stephanie. Tomasz is employed as the chef and waiter.

Iona and I share one of the bedrooms on the right as you enter. On the wall, you can see the artwork from school, and like any child's bedroom, there are toys scattered around: coloured plastic trains, dolls, a magician's play-set, and a puppet show with soft-toys replicating a mother, father, two children, a policeman and a dog. Ben's room is next to ours.

After school on Saturdays in spring and summer, we go for a walk in the city centre. The city looks so busy and alive. We look at the modern white office blocks with their black rectangular windows on each storey. The large polished black cars have a sense of grandeur as they intersperse between the trams, the horses and carriages and the pedestrians. Everyone's looking so happy as they go about their business. They're dressed formally in suits and dresses and aimlessly wander around, stopping to look at shop windows, and then sipping coffee outside the cafés. The market sellers carry large oblong baskets of fruit, strapped to each shoulder, and we taste the grapes as we pass by. A woman balances a basket of different flowers on her head with her left hand. In the market place, I'm impressed by the size and intricacy of the large hand-made carpets and rugs which hang on a line, gently swaying in the wind. The market is full of stalls, selling beautifully embroidered shirts and blouses, and everyone enjoys the bartering. The customer laughs at the proposed price, then the seller looks surprised and marginally reduces it, then the customer starts to walk away, then the seller gives him another price, and after much animation, they come to an agreement and everyone's content. The horse riders read their newspapers and wait for the shoppers to finish.

We go and look at some of the sturdy monumental buildings with their arch-shaped openings and shutters. The King's Palace's bright white façade beams on the surrounding buildings and the guards with their immaculate dress and posture, sword in hand, look minuscule against the enormous pillars.

As we walk towards the park, we come across the Metropolitan English with its bell towers protected by ornate umbrella-like covers. In the lower half of the building, there are narrow arches, which are separated by pillars, and above there are religious portraits squeezed next to each other.

We walk through the park, past the stocky trees and large ponds, where people bathe and take boat rides. There are packed outdoor swimming pools, where people race with each other, splash, and dive. Nearby there's a pole with swings around them, and a line of people waiting to have a go. There are plenty of musicians to keep the city cheerful and upbeat. Some of them play alone on street corners, winding up their music boxes, and others play together using the violin, pipes, percussion and cello.

Owning a successful sportswear shop, my father comes across many of his customers with their wives on our journey. He embraces and kisses each one, pats their children on their heads and makes polite conversation about family, the weather and current affairs. He's proud of us and always introduces us to them. We know how to greet customers respectfully with a smile. Most customers have become trusted friends, and my mother frequently invites them for dinner.

Winter is a different story, as it's often too cold to go outdoors. After school, we go straight to a restaurant and then to the cinema to see films with famous actors and actresses, such as Stan Laurel and Shirley Temple. When it snows, Iona and I sit on a sledge and our neighbours pull us along the pavement. My father is a big supporter of the Maccabi football team and we have an exclusive cabin at the stadium. My mother often accompanies him there on a Sunday, in spite of the freezing weather. We seldom go with them, but when we do, we're covered from top to toe with layer after layer of clothing. On Sundays, Stephanie teaches us how to sew and how to make toffee, or we produce theatrical plays using blankets as curtains. When friends visit my parents, their children join us in the kitchen, and we sit on the floor with a glass of homemade lemonade and some biscuits and listen to Stephanie reading us stories. At the same time, the men play cards in the sitting room, and the ladies continue talking in the dining room.

On one Saturday in the summer of 1940, we go to one of the swimming pools in the park. My mother is in the pool holding Ben. He doesn't stay still, and Iona keeps tickling his feet to make him laugh, and then she dives into the water. My father is wearing light grey trousers, a white shirt and a dark grey waistcoat. He's standing a few metres from the pool talking to a couple I recognise being Marcario and his wife, Sabella, who emigrated from Greece to Romania before I was born. Marcario, in his early thirties, is taller than my father and he's a very handsome man: he has deep-set brown eyes, a smooth and slightly tanned complexion, thick curly brown hair and a fashionable beard. Having worked for my father in his shop for many years, he and his wife have become loyal friends, and my father talks fondly about them. With the noise from the pool, we can't hear what they're saying. My father frowns and keeps touching his forehead. Marcario holds onto my father's shoulder and then embraces him before walking away with Sabella.

Marcario and Sabella come for dinner on one Sunday afternoon two weeks later. Tomasz, who's about forty years old, has a tall, slim build and a warm face, is in the kitchen cutting up vegetables and preparing the beef. He goes into the large dining room on the right of the entrance hall and places the cutlery, placemats, wine glasses and candles neatly on the table. My mother asks me to go and wash my hands, so I go to the downstairs bathroom next to my father's large study. His door is ajar so I have a quick peek, hoping he won't notice me. Inside, there's an enormous antique oak desk on which his papers are organized tidily, and there are some shelves on the back wall, with ledgers, folders, books and journals, which are kept in immaculate condition. He has a separate bookcase for his contracts, receipts and bookkeeping. In front of the desk, there's a small round table with four chairs which is where he has meetings with suppliers and customers. My eyes look upwards to see four original water-coloured paintings of landscapes with thick golden frames on the walls. My father, sitting behind his desk and wearing his round reading glasses, studies a document and then takes his fountain pen, signs the paper and blows on it.

Stephanie startles me and asks me to check the sitting room, as this is where they retire after the meal. I check to see if the small side tables are neatly placed next to each sofa and armchair. Near the window, there's a pianoforte, which Iona and I have started to learn how to play and Hanna, our private tutor, comes to teach us on Monday and Wednesday evenings.

Whilst Tomasz is making a raspberry pie, Iona Ben and I eat a casserole in the kitchen. My mother puts Ben to bed for an afternoon nap and goes to her room to get changed.

Just before half-past two, my mother comes downstairs, and she's looking as elegant as ever in her deep purple dress, pearl earrings, sandy make-up, hair brushed back and a slight scent of lavender perfume. She's stunning, and it's hard to not stare at her beauty. Half-way down the stairs, she stops, takes her hand mirror out of her handbag, and looks into it to double-check her lipstick. She confidently goes down the remaining stairs and walks into my father's study.

At three o'clock, we hear a knock on the door. Iona and I stand next to our parents as they open the door and greet our guests. Marcario ruffles Iona's hair and asks her how she is and how her piano lessons are going.

"Maria's also learning!" gleams my mother. "They're enjoying every minute. Iona has started to play Beethoven. She has real talent."

"That's wonderful," praises Marcario. "I'm expecting big things from you." He turns to me. "And who's this? Another musician! Enough to make an orchestra!"

My father looks pleased with all the compliments about us. Sabella kisses Iona and me, and thanks my parents for their generous hospitality.

"Well, dinner's nearly ready, so let's go into the dining room and have a drink first," says my mother.

She walks towards the dining room, and my father and their guests follow her. Before reaching the door, she looks at us.

"Thank you, girls. No mischief. Understood?"

The dining room is a museum, art gallery and library. There are antique tables and chairs in each corner of the room. On the right wall, there are shelves stacked with dusty books, and on the other three walls, there are numerous floral drawings. In the middle, there is a beautiful large oak rectangular dining table.

It's times like this that we play hide and seek and other games. The house is spacious enough to allow us to hide from each other in the various wardrobes and cupboards. The attic and the basement provide the best hiding places because of the dim light and the crooks and crannies amongst all the old furniture, which have been in a permanent state of storage with old woollen blankets thrown over them. Ben has just turned four. He often wins the card games, and we pretend to be happy for him. If Iona or I win, he grabs our hands and bites them. He's a bad loser. But when Iona or I look sad, he runs to us, wraps his arms around our necks, and gives us a kiss on our cheeks.

After being bitten twice, we decide to eavesdrop on our parents and their guests, who are now in the sitting room, so we stealthily go down the stairs and stand next to the door.

"We've been loyal friends and business partners for many years. I just want to make sure that it doesn't get into the wrong hands. I'm not saying it isn't without a certain degree of risk. But I'm trying to create an agreement which will be in both our interests and allow my family to survive if the worst happens," says my father.

Sabella adds, "Yes, I'm afraid it looks as though it will."

"They hate us. God knows what will happen to us if they come here," says my father.

"We've got a contingency plan," says my mother softly. "We've already been through a scenario in case it happens. It's not foolproof, but it might work."

"We've also decided that we'd rather go into an everlasting sleep using a coal solution I have prepared. Better than being taken to those places," says my father.

Iona puts her finger on her lips, indicating that we should not make a sound. It's hard to hear what my father is saying because he mumbles, so we don't know what they are talking about. All we know is that something bad is about to happen and that some people hate us. At that point, Stephanie sees us speaking to each other sotto voce, and ushers us to come and play with the toy trains upstairs. On the way up, I think they must have been talking about the same thing as they were when they were in the park.

The following morning, we get up and go to the kitchen for breakfast, and as Stephanie prepares the porridge for us, I can't resist asking my mother some questions.

"Will everything be all right, Mamă?"

"Of course, sweetheart! Where has all of this come from?"

She bends down and touches my nose affectionately.

"Who hates us Mamă?" I ask.

"No one, darling. Now hurry up and eat the porridge or you're going to be late for school."

As I'm eating the porridge opposite Iona and next to Ben, my mother turns away and washes some dishes. She sighs. Iona gives me one of those looks, which means that I should stop asking her questions, but I ignore her.

"Have we got a plan, Mamă, if someone bad comes to see us?"

Even though I can't see her face, I imagine that it's one of those moments that she collects herself, closes her eyes briefly and prepares what she's about to say. When she does turn around, she realises that we've heard part of their conversation at dinner.

"So, you were being naughty yesterday, listening to me and Tătic talking with our guests! Did you not have anything better to do? Anyway, there is nothing to worry about. Tătic was talking about business with Marcario, and we've sorted everything out."

My mother isn't good at lying.

"Will we sleep in the attic?" I ask.

"If the bad people come, yes. We will hide in the attic where no one can find us."

We put our blue uniform on, and Stephanie takes us to a prestigious English private school, which is a large white building with some trees dotted around the exterior. We start the day at nine o'clock and finish at four o'clock. I don't contribute much as I'm afraid of the very strict teachers, not that they have any reason to pick on me, as I'm a good all-rounder. I develop a keen interest in biology, which helps me when we eventually move to Tel Aviv.

****

I'll never forget what happened on the third of October 1941 and in fact, it's one of the last days we stay in this beautiful home. It's eight o'clock in the evening, and we're having dinner in the attic and I look out of the window. The constant gentle raindrops give the surrounding houses a shiny greenish-grey colour, and the few people in the street rely on the glimmers of light from the lamps to see each other. Ten minutes later, we hear the increasingly loud sound of marching towards our street. My mother quickly snatches me away from the window, blows out the candle and takes us all into the basement. The marching stops, and we hear a sudden thudding sound of our neighbour's front door being kicked open.

"Please don't shoot!" a woman begs.

A baby starts to cry.

"Raus!" shouted one of the soldiers. "Schnell!"

The soldier shoves the woman and her baby downstairs and outside.

"Wo ist Dein Ehemann?"

"Ich weiß es nicht," she cries.

"Kein problem. Wir werden ihn finden."

After five minutes, the marching, crying and shouting fade into silence.

I see my mother and father whispering to each other, and I can tell that my father is proposing something to my mother, but it looks as though she doesn't agree with him. She stands up, leaving my father looking disconsolate.

"Why don't you go and play with your trains with Ben? It'll soon be time for bed," she says to me.

With the advent of the bombing, we put beds into the basement for overnight sleeping and welcome our neighbours to use it as a bomb shelter. If a bomb does land on us, we would be blown to smithereens, as the house isn't strong enough to withstand such a powerful explosion. We have to be cautious about everything we do, which means starting school at eleven o'clock instead of nine o'clock, not staying near the windows during the day, and sleeping in the basement as soon as it gets dark. My father formalizes the shop going under Marcario's name not long after he and Sabella came for dinner, and he deposits most of the revenues into reserves in Switzerland and England.

For some reason, which I still don't comprehend, my mother and father host a party to celebrate the wedding anniversary of two of their friends on the day after the soldiers took away our next-door neighbour and her child. There's the usual smorgasbord of food, wine, beer, cocktails lavishly placed on the table in the dining room, and relaxing jazz music comes out of the gramophone. After lunch, my father gives a speech, congratulating the couple on their anniversary and this is followed by dancing and drinking, as though there's not a care in the world. At four o'clock, my mother dismisses the cooks and additional waiters, giving them the following day off and asks them to come back the day after to clean everything up.

The next day, we go about our normal business: school, piano and French lessons, and we go to bed at nine o'clock. Three hours later, we wake up to the sound of violent pounding on our front door.

"Öffnet die Tür! Schnell!" booms a voice from outside.

My father opens the door, and ten soldiers dressed in SS uniform burst into our house. One of them grabs my father and pushes him forcefully onto the floor. Another soldier comes into our room and switches the light on, making us squint. We sit up, speechless with fear, as the soldier menacingly comes towards us and points his hand pistol in front of our eyes. I look at his stiff greyish-blue, slim-fitting jacket with bold golden buttons and badges and the neat silver metallic belt around his waist. I'm frightened of the bright red band at the top of his left shoulder with a white circle and a black SS sign in the middle. I look up to his neck and see a beige shirt with a pea green tie between two large lapels with silver badges. His cap has the same colour as his uniform and has two rope pieces at the front, and the SS symbol underneath.

"Don't move!" he shouts.

His cold narrow eyes terrorize me. We hear the other soldiers frantically going around the house, opening the doors with their boots, in search of other residents. When they discover Tomasz, Stephanie and my mother in the kitchen, they drag them out and push them into our parents' bedroom. As they're about to stand up, the soldier loads his pistol and points it as them

"Don't move! Stay exactly where you are," he shouts.

At this point, I believe that we're going to die or be taken to one of the camps. So much for my father's plan to send us into an endless sleep. To this day, I still shudder when I see anyone dressed in military uniform, whether it's the army or the police.

"Kommt her!" calls one of the soldiers enthusiastically from the dining room.

When the other soldiers discover the leftovers from the anniversary party, they seem to forget the reason for coming to our house in the first place, and they feast their eyes on the treasure of food and drink in front of them. It must have been half an hour later when we hear glasses being broken, one of them falling over and the others laughing uncontrollably. This doesn't ease our terror at all, and my thoughts turn to what they'll do to us when they're drunk.

I guess it's after half-past midnight when they consume the last drop of alcohol. I'm not sure where my father is, but I assume he's been left on the floor in the hallway near the front door. I'm right as, after a few minutes, the soldiers lift him and escort him outside.

"You will come with us!" screams one of them.

"No, please!" he begs.

"Don't worry. We'll take you somewhere nice!" says another soldier.

The soldiers are so intoxicated that they stumble into the two cars outside the guardrail. My father tries to resist two soldiers, who are leading him to one of the vehicles.

"You will come with us!" repeats the soldier.

My father opens his jacket and stretches his arms.

"Shoot me! Kill me now! Just don't take me to the camp."

The soldiers are still trying to find space for my father and, on realising that there's no room for him, one of the soldiers lowers his gun and gets close to him.

"You will report to our office at ten o'clock tomorrow morning. If you don't, there will be consequences for you and your family. Clear?" he asks.

My father nods and says, "Yes, it's clear."

The two cars vanish.

My father staggers into the house, and we meet him in the hallway and embrace him. My mother is crying.

"I need to make a call," he says out of breath.

"What? At this time?" asked my mother.

"Yes, at this time. The guards want me to report to them tomorrow morning at ten o'clock. We don't have much time. I need to make two calls. One to your brother and one to Anton."

"Anton, the lawyer? What can he do? And why my brother?"

"Your brother has useful connections, as you know. With a bit of money, I can hopefully cancel our meeting tomorrow. Anton has a property. We need to move away from here."

My father picks up the telephone receiver in the hallway.

Even though it's late, we aren't tired, and when my father finishes his calls, he summons us to my parents' bedroom. We sit on his bed, and he looks at us with a faint smile.

"I don't have to report to the authorities tomorrow,"

My mother puts her head in her hands, relieved.

"However, we're going to need to move house. I've guaranteed some transactions of money, and we'll be moving to a villa in the Catholic district."

The following morning, I wake up early and go downstairs and see my father's study is ajar, so I have another peek inside and see him sitting in his armchair, staring into space and he's wearing the same clothes as the previous day. There's an open book on his lap, but he's not reading it. When I knock on the door, he quickly puts on his spectacles and pretends to read.

"What's wrong, Tătic? Is it something to do with last night?"

My father sighs, puts the book down and looks at me.

"You must never forget that your mother and I will always love you," he says. He stands up, goes into his bedroom and closes the door behind him.

Two days later, Anton arrives in the morning. He slips through the back door, removes his hat and hands it to my father.

"Thank you, thank you so much for coming."

"Yes, yes, I am deeply sorry to hear about your experience. It must have been terribly worrying for all of you, especially the children."

My father pats Anton on the back and leads him to the basement.

I'm disappointed that there's no school the following day. I watch my mother and father going around the house on tiptoes, selecting the most essential items they need to take to our new home. I go upstairs to the attic and play cards with Iona and Ben, and then my mother comes in, sits down and starts weeping. My father comes in shortly afterwards and holds her in his arms.

"How can they do this to us? This is our home! We built all this from nothing, and now we are throwing everything away," she says.

"Sshhh, my darling. We have no option. You know that. This is to keep all of us safe. Living here is becoming more dangerous every day. We could, of course, try and move to Tel Aviv," says my father.

"No, I think it best to go to the villa as arranged. The children are too young to make that journey."

"Is everything all right, Mamă?" asks Iona.

"Yes, dear, everything will be fine," she sobs, drying her eyes with a small handkerchief. She stands up and continues with the packing. Clothes, cosmetics, jewellery, bed linen, blankets, pillows, towels, kitchen utensils, ledgers and books are squeezed into bulky suitcases and deposited near the front entrance to the house. A separate lorry has been arranged to take the pianoforte, pictures and furniture.

Over dinner in the basement, my father talks to us with a serious expression on his face.

"A van will arrive at the front entrance sometime tomorrow. Regardless of what we are doing, when I give the word, I want you all to leave and get inside as quickly as you can. I've just bought a large villa in the Catholic district from Anton. It's relatively safe there, and you should be able to play outside again."

The next day, the driver faintly knocks on the back door and helps my father to take the luggage to the back of the van, and we clamber inside. Once we depart, I look out of the window at the familiar streets and shops, as we leave our lovely home for the last time. After twenty minutes, we enter suburbia full of enormous villas, gardens and trees. I do feel a sense of relief when we finally reach our new home, a modern white villa with lots of windows, just because I want to be safe and I'm tired of hiding all the time. The driver takes the luggage out of the back of the car and brings them to the front door, just as Anton appears with two Doberman dogs.

Inside, my mother touches the oak table in the hallway and swipes some dust with forefinger on her left hand and tuts. Iona and I run around the house, counting the number of bedrooms.

"Mamă! Mamă! There are ten bedrooms!" Iona tells her.

"I don't think anyone has lived here for some time," remarks my mother, no doubt thinking about the dust, which is still on her finger.

Stephanie starts preparing rice and chicken and then helps my parents to unpack everything. I leave Ben and Iona to play trains in the sitting room and go and read my book in my bedroom. When the food is ready, we all eat in the kitchen and Anton joins us.

"I'm going back to work tomorrow," says my father.

"Are you sure? It must take at least twenty minutes by tram from here. And is it safe?" asks my mother.

"Yes, I'm sure. Remember that the shop's name is under Marcario. Besides, I want to keep earning a living."

I'm so happy that we can go back to school again, but we need to take the tram because it's no longer within walking distance. In my class, there's a new boy, Richard, who's plump and has a mass of curly blonde hair, and lives with his mother and two younger brothers on the same street. His mother befriends my parents and invites us for dinner on several occasions, and my parents reciprocate her generosity by inviting him to play cards with us and go to the football matches with my father. He flirts with me a lot and keeps trying to win my affection by sending me flowers anonymously, but I don't find him attractive. I do admire him for being bright because he passes all his exams with flying colours, but he seems cold and remote. I later discover that he witnessed his father being shot by Nazi soldiers which probably explains why he is like he is, so I do feel sorry for him.

****

The next two years pass quickly. Ben starts to help my father in his shop on Saturdays. When I finish school, I learn how to type and earn some money as a laboratory assistant. I work hard to obtain an additional qualification in biology at night school, and I am delighted when I am awarded a diploma with distinction. Iona finishes school and becomes a lady of leisure and eventually marries Samuel, who was in the same class as her at school, and they move to another home.

****

Although we don't fear for our lives, the invasion of the Russians along with a new communist regime does have an adverse impact on us. We're no longer allowed to go to school, which doesn't affect me because I finish school shortly before they arrive. Ben never finishes his secondary education, and since we are not sanctioned to work either, we stay at home doing very little, which frustrates me so much, because I like to keep busy.

My mother welcomes the Russians by preparing tea and pastries for them and gives them clothes as gifts. They seem very friendly at first but also naïve and ignorant as I recall one of them wearing a watch on his left leg and another wearing a t-shirt back to front. The friendliness soon dissipates as they force us to sell some of our possessions, such as the piano and branded watches for a pittance. Then my father loses his business and Marcario loses his job. My father is so worried about our cash being discovered, that he hides it under the dogs' sleeping cushion in the garage. With not much left to do, we play with our neighbours' children, pick weeds in the garden, go for walks with the dogs and read.

Even though we feel safe to play outside, something happens which unnerves me to this very day. It's a typical summer's day: families are sunbathing on deckchairs in their front gardens and couples are going for walks. Iona and I are cycling when we see a tall man slowly coming towards us. When he gets closer to us, we stop cycling and stare at him. He's wearing a uniform, a woolly hat and shiny black boots with a pistol attached to his belt. I feel trickles of sweat falling down my forehead, as he looms over us, casting an intimidating shadow. I don't know whether to run or stay where I am. Finally, he speaks.

"Where did you get these bicycles?" he asks in a quiet and monotonous tone.

My mouth is dry with fear, and I'm too scared to reply. I just hope Iona says something, but she's probably feeling the same way as I do, so she doesn't speak either.

"I asked, 'Where did you get the bicycles from?' Are you both deaf?" he asks.

"They're ours. They are a present from Mamă," Iona replies quickly.

The man glares at the villa behind us and then looks back at us.

"Give me the bicycles," he orders.

We obediently hand the bicycles to him, and he walks away with them.

"Did you have a nice time, girls?" asks my mother.

"A nasty man took our bikes," I tell her, tearfully.

"What happened? Who took your bikes? One of the neighbours?"

She kneels next to us.

"Shh shhh. Don't worry. It's all over now. Come on. Why don't you help Stephanie in the kitchen?"

****

My father makes plans for us to go to Tel Aviv, but another confrontation with the Russians almost impedes us from leaving. I suspect that the soldier would tell his superiors when I saw him glancing at the villa. Everything depends on my father and me being able to tell the same fabrication of the truth but in different rooms.

One afternoon, when Ben and I are drawing and painting, two soldiers knock on the door, and my father lets them in. I watch them taking a good look in the hallway and noting the enormous and opulent interior. They're probably wondering why our family possesses such a large property as they venture into the dining room and sitting rooms, their eyes like cameras, taking snapshots of every single artefact. By now, I know all about the Russian's communist ideology, and I'm worried that they're going to confiscate all of our things, some of which have sentimental value having been passed down through generations, such as the jewellery and the antique desk. We follow them until they return to the sitting room.

"We need two separate rooms," requests one of the soldiers.

"Yes, of course," says my father, as he gets up to lead the way.

The same soldier looks and points at me.

"You too will come with us."

My father and I walk ahead of them. My father shows them my parent's bedroom and my bedroom. We are then separated. I'm with one soldier in my bedroom, and my father is with another soldier in his bedroom. The soldier takes a chair and sits down opposite me. At first, he doesn't say anything, he just stares at me, and then pulls out a clipboard and pen from his small bag, ready to begin a fusillade of questions. He takes my name and other details about my age, where I live, and the school I went to.

"You live in a very nice house," he remarks.

"Yes, we're very fortunate. We enjoy living here."

"So, I assume you finished school. How did you find it?

"I liked it very much."

"What did you think of the teachers?" he asks.

"They were strict. There was no messing about. We had to study hard."

"Really. And which was your favourite subject?"

"Biology."

"I see. I also enjoyed science at school! Surely you must have some sort of qualifications!" he exclaimed.

"No, I didn't do any exams."

I look down, avoiding his eyes. I don't know whether he believes me or not. I keep telling myself to be strong, and in my head, I'm busy conjuring up credible falsifications.

"So, a bright, motivated girl like you goes to school, has a favourite subject, studies hard, and finishes school with no exams and no certificates. Come on, I wasn't born yesterday. Don't be afraid. I'm just curious."

"I became a bit lazy at the end of school. I didn't think I would be able to pass the exams, so I decided not to take them."

"Well, I don't believe that! What did you get, a merit or a distinction? There's no need to be modest."

"I told you, neither of them. I really didn't take any exams."

"Well, that is strange because I read a report from the school, which clearly states you have a diploma."

"It's not true. They got it wrong. You can search the house. I don't have a diploma. I wish I did, but I don't have one."

I remember my father explaining to Ben and me that it would be harder to go to Tel Aviv if the Russians find out that I have qualifications, as they are eager to keep graduates from school and university and put them to work with meagre salaries. In fact, my father already attempted to get Ben and me into Tel Aviv by offering to pay a princely sum to the authorities, and for some reason, this falls through.

"So, you and your family are Jewish! That must have been tough in the last few years."

"It was indeed tough, but we got through it."

"I wonder how you managed that. Most Jews were taken to the camps. How did you and your family survive?"

"We just did. We were lucky, I suppose."

"Very lucky! Well, I'm glad that you and your family made it. Have you always lived here?"

"Not always. We used to live closer to the centre, but still in the outskirts, and then we moved here because it was safer."

"I see. Much safer than in the Jewish quarter."

"Yes," I confirmed.

"What would you like to do with your life, Maria?"

"Nothing much. I'm happy to become a housewife."

He nodded his head in disbelief.

"What about going to Tel Aviv? That's your real dream, isn't it?"

"No, why would you think that?"

"Well, you're Jewish, you have a high school diploma, and you're clearly a bright girl. So why wouldn't you want to go to Tel Aviv and get out of Romania?"

"I didn't say I have a diploma. You're putting words into my mouth. It hasn't even crossed my mind to go to Tel Aviv. In any case, I want to be close to my family."

He shakes his head again and puts down his clipboard.

"Listen, you have an extraordinary house. Your father must have money, and I have intelligence that your father has bribed officials so that you can go to Tel Aviv with your brother. In addition, you have a diploma in biology, which will make getting a job easier for you once you arrive in Tel Aviv. One moment, please. Stay where you are," he says mechanically.

Ten minutes later, he returns to my room, sits down and sighs.

"It's useless going on like this. You know that lying to us is a criminal offence. I've just spoken with your father, and he's admitted to you having a diploma and bribing officials to gain entry into Tel Aviv."

Instinctively, I know that my father would never reveal any of this, even under pressure. I might be wrong, but I think that they're just making assumptions based on the house we live in and that I have been to school.

"Then my father is lying. I'm telling you the truth. I don't have a diploma, and my father would never bribe anyone."

"So, you're calling your father a liar."

"I don't think my father lied. I don't believe that he told you I have a diploma and that he used coercion to get us to Tel Aviv."

The solider folds his arms and looks at me one more time. He leaves the bedroom and goes to talk with his comrade. I'm relieved to hear them leave the house. I go into the sitting room with my father, and he recounts a similar cross-examination to the one I have had, even though it sounds that he had a tougher time than me. My father tells us that his interrogator said that I have admitted to him bribing authorities and having a diploma, but realises they were trying to play us off each other.

I am relieved to hear the soldiers leave the house, but I shouldn't have been. I think that the whole point of them visiting us is to expose my father's bribery and my lies about my qualifications. But it isn't the only reason. I have almost forgotten them surveying the whole house so it shouldn't have come as a surprise when they decide to take over the villa and confine us all into one bedroom, even though we are allowed to use the kitchen and the bathroom. To make matters worse, Iona and Samuel are no longer able to afford to stay in their rented home, after Samuel's salary is halved, so they move in with us. I don't know how many Russians are staying in the house as we don't dare to go into the sitting room. It's hard to sleep at night because they stay up late, drinking vodka, laughing and singing. When they do see us in the kitchen, they say something to us in Russian and throw eggs or tomatoes at us. Sometimes, I think this is worse than concealing ourselves from the Nazi soldiers in the basement in our previous house. My father, always the pragmatic one, looks to the future optimistically and has a master plan for Ben and me.

"It's time you went to Tel Aviv. I've agreed this with your mother, and I've already made the arrangements. Iona and her husband will stay here with us, and we'll follow in a couple of years," announces my father.

"But Tătic …" I want to stay with them, but my father doesn't like interruptions.

"No buts, Maria. You have to go."

****

My father makes all the arrangements and books first-class cabins for Ben and me. We pack two small bags full of clothes, toiletries and cigarettes, as Ben has started to smoke. I'm very apprehensive and try to mask how upset I am to be leaving my parents and Romania behind. When we get to the harbour in Costanza, I'm shocked to see the sheer number of refugees who are clambering aboard. Once we reach our luxurious cabin, we give one of the beds to an elderly gentleman, and Ben and I share the other bed, rotating every few hours. We're frequently woken up by the commotion from the deck and the corridors, as passengers are squeezed so tightly together, that they start to fight with each other when someone treads on another's foot.

After the ferry docks, there's a mad surge of passengers going onto the harbour, and we're amongst them, being pushed and prodded from here and there, as though it's a race. When we're assembled at the entry point, I see that our bags are open and look inside and panic when I see that the cash is missing. There's no time for us to think about how we'll survive without money as we're immediately ordered to go to a camp, which makes me feel that we are being quarantined. I don't know what food they give us as it smells, looks and tastes disgusting but we have to eat some of it as we are so hungry. We sleep in aluminium boxes, that's the best way I can describe our accommodation. It dawns on me that we are refugees like everyone else even though I would never have thought we would be labelled this way. There are so few facilities for washing given the hundreds of people in the camp that we have to go without bathing for several days.

On the sixth day, I'm feeling hot, sick, tired and hungry. In the morning, we see one of Ben's friends who has taken the previous ferry. Ben goes to talk with him, and I wave from a distance but don't smile. How can I smile in this hot temperature with little food and poor sleeping conditions?

"My friend just told me to go to the nearest kibbutz. At least we can get a bed there," said Ben.

"That's great, Ben. But how are we going to get there with no money?"

Ben has no choice but to give up smoking, as we end up exchanging his cigarettes for free rides to the kibbutz. It turns out to be a lovely experience as I'm able to look at the beautiful deserted and rocky landscape as we move from place to place and listen to the life story of every driver.

We arrive at the kibbutz in the afternoon and are welcomed by one of the permanent inhabitants. She takes us to our room and explains the procedure of having free lodging and food in return for doing menial tasks for eight hours a day, and there's no salary. There's a diverse population full of locals and volunteers from different parts of the world who work together and socialise. I go outside and look at them, relaxing in deckchairs, playing cards, reading and playing football. Of course, I'm happy that we have a place to stay, nothing could we worse than the camp we've just been in. But there's something about the kibbutz that I don't like, and I think it's the superficial merriness of people being thrown together and forcing themselves to make friends and be content. Maybe I'm being snobbish, but it is how I feel at this moment.

Ben and I are assigned to helping with the preparation of food and washing up in the large dining room, where the entire community comes for breakfast, lunch and dinner. We get up at four-thirty in the morning and are ready to start work at five o'clock and. With so many mouths to feed, we finish work at two o'clock in the afternoon. The kibbutz is self-sufficient, and there are dwellers who look after the growing of carrots, tomatoes, beans, zucchini, potatoes, lettuce, radish, cucumber and various fruits. All of the meals consist of vegetables and salad, which of course are healthy, but it does get boring after a while.

I look forward to the afternoons as Ben and I have a well-deserved and much-needed siesta from two o'clock to four o'clock in the afternoon, then we go for walks, which I enjoy immensely, as I get to see how beautiful Tel Aviv is. We return home, have dinner and then talk with others about their lives and ambitions before having an early night.

The routine makes me restless, so towards the end of the second week, I sneak out of the compound and head towards the city in search of work. It's quite a walk, and I can't remember how long it takes to get to the city centre, but when I finally arrive, I visit various private clinics unannounced and tell the manager that I am looking for work and that I have a diploma. After tirelessly visiting umpteen clinics, a lady generously takes me on and gives me some training so that I can become a proper laboratory technician. This means I'll officially be authorized to analyse blood tests and perform some basic nursing duties. So, every day, I leave the kibbutz at two o'clock in the afternoon, walk to the clinic, attend the training and then head back. I feel guilty leaving Ben on his own, but I keep thinking that if I get a salary, we'll both be able to leave the kibbutz for good. I'm exhausted as I don't get much sleep during these days, but I'm young and determined, and somehow, I manage. A week later, the head of the kibbutz, having noticed my absence, reprimands me for leaving the compound on the grounds of a lack of camaraderie, which he tells me is one of the main principles of the kibbutz. I smile at him and apologise, promising I won't do it again.

Once I pass the exams after the training, I'm offered a job at the same clinic. I can't wait to leave the kibbutz, so I use my first wages to book into a hotel in the city. On the second evening, we meet the owner of the hotel, and Ben embellishes our story and plight in such a lively manner that he takes an immediate liking to us, and gives us a larger room with a fridge in it. It's not long before envious long-term guests hear about the fridge, and they ask us to store food for them, which we do gladly. The owner soon becomes a good friend and he finds a job for Ben as a security guard in a car park during the night. He doesn't particularly like working at night very much, and fortunately, he does it just for a month, as he receives a more lucrative job offer as a private driver one month later. By rights, instead of working, Ben should be doing military service, but he's excused because officially he has to look after me in the absence of our parents.

One afternoon, a young lady and her two children come into the clinic. She has beautiful long black hair, which she keeps brushing out of her face, and she's wearing a stylish light green dress. I look at the similarities between her and her children, who are dressed in a light grey school uniform.

"Hello! I'm Nicole. I've come to get some blood tests for my children. Do I need to make an appointment?"

"Well, actually, I'm free now, so I can take their blood straight away. Why don't you follow me to the testing room, and I will prepare everything?"

Nicole and the children follow me into the testing room, where there is a desk, three chairs and a bed in the right corner. David, the elder of the two children by one year, doesn't mind having blood taken, whereas Robert is so nervous that he looks away when I put the needle into his left arm. I try to distract him by asking him about his school and his favourite subjects, but I can tell he's still nervous. Nicole isn't in a hurry to leave, so we chat for a while, and I tell her all about our lives in Romania and how we ended up here. As she is about to leave, I ask her to come back in three days to get the results. I go back to my desk and realise that she hasn't said much about herself, apart from living in a prestigious part of the city and the school her children go to, and I think it's strange that she hasn't mentioned her husband and family.

Three days later, she comes back without the children, and I give her the blood test results, assuring her that there are no problems.

"Thank you so much for the results. I just need to make sure they're okay."

"It's a pleasure. Anytime."

"Listen, I have to go now. Why don't you and your brother come for dinner at our place on Saturday evening?"

****

I go shopping and purchase a new light purple summer dress with matching shoes, and Ben hires a dinner jacket. Both of us spend hours getting ready and just before we leave, we generously splash cologne on our clothes and I triple-check that my make-up and lipstick look perfect. The private driver, which Nicole has booked, is waiting for us outside the hotel lobby and we ask him to stop by at a shop so we can buy a good bottle of red wine and some flowers. I'm a bit jittery to be honest because I don't know what to expect and I keep fidgeting in the car. It's almost eight o'clock when we reach, what I would call, a palatial house, which was lit up by the surrounding floodlights. When we get out of the car, I can hear the soft, gentle waves in the background and smell the sea air. Ben knocks at the door, and Nicole opens it, and I see that she's linking arms with a tall man dressed in a dinner jacket.

"Good evening!" she exclaims.

She gently kisses me on both cheeks and then turns to Ben and says, "This must be Ben" and offers her hand.

Ben bows and kisses her hand.

"This is Andrew. He's a General in the army!"

Ben and I look at Andrew, and we shake hands with him.

"Please come in! "says Andrew. "We're so pleased to have you. It's always nice to get to know new people, isn't it?"

"Of course, it is!" replied Nicole.

I give them the flowers and bottle of wine and Nicole takes them from us.

"Really, you shouldn't have. That's very kind of you!"

"Let me get you a drink. What would you like?"

I ask for a gin and tonic, and Ben asks for a glass of red wine.

"There are so many people I want you to meet!"

Nicole and Andrew lead us through the hallway into a large sparse and modern room with glass doors opening onto a lit garden. The white walls, which have no pictures on them, contrast with the deep burgundy carpet. I look at the variety of food and drinks on the small round tables which are covered with a white embroidered tablecloth, and the waiters are standing motionless behind them. There's the eloquent sound of soft and relaxing piano music in the background.

I wrongly assume that Nicole must be married to Andrew, or at least courting him, as he introduces me briefly to his wife and colleagues. Nicole introduces me to some doctors who are discussing the latest developments in the medical profession. She tells them that I have a biology diploma and that I'm interested in becoming a doctor one day.

One hour later, I'm still talking with the doctors when I see Nicole and Ben go outside to the garden together, and Ben touches her back as they walk towards the veranda. After a while, they both come up to me, and I can smell alcohol on their breaths.

"I hope you've enjoyed the company of my doctor friends! What do you think? Do you think she has it in her to become a doctor?" asks Nicole.

"Yes, indeed she has. She certainly has the passion and determination. I think she'll make a fine doctor," replies one of them.

At this point, Andrew leaves his wife and colleagues and joins me, Ben, Nicole and the doctors.

"I can see you're having a wonderful time," says Andrew.

"Yes, we are! It's a marvellous evening we're having. By the way, Andrew, I almost forgot to tell you that Ben's a private driver," says Nicole.

"Really? That is most timely, as I've been looking for a new personal driver who can take me, my wife and, of course, my good friend, Nicole, wherever we need to go. Would you be interested?"

I know Ben will say yes because he has taken a liking to Nicole, so he accepts.

On the way back to the hotel, Ben tells me that Nicole's husband left her nine months ago, leaving her with the children, but he doesn't know how she got to know Andrew. Ben is over the moon about his new job, and he spends most of this time with Nicole, going to restaurants, the cinema and having picnics on isolated corners along the coast.

****

Andrew kindly gives us a magnificent place to live, when our parents, Iona, Samuel and their newly born daughter, Ruth, finally arrive in Tel Aviv. And he provides us with plenty of food, which makes me feel guilty, as rationing is prevalent during this time and I know that many others are not as lucky as we are. And it's not as if we're short of money either as my father still has funds in banks in Switzerland and England.

****

Two years later, there is an encounter which eventually turns the page to a new chapter in our lives. Andrew and his wife host another party in the same place, and we arrive in formal attire with a bottle of wine, just as before. I'm less nervous this time. Nicole is talking with some friends, so only Andrew greets us at the door and leads us to a solitary gentleman, who is busy selecting food from the buffet.

"This is Noah," Andrew says.

Noah is a small, well-built man with short, thin black hair and a bald spot on the back of his head and he's wearing a dark grey suit, a white shirt and a maroon tie. He looks up at us with a genuine smile which makes us immediately warm to him.

"Ben and Maria have been here for just over two years. Maria is working in a clinic. She met Nicole there. Ben is my private driver," says Andrew.

"Marvellous!" beams Noah.

Andrew leaves us alone with Noah, who asks us about where we have come from and why we are here, and Ben recounts our story. He laughs at the story about me leaving the kibbutz to seek work and is impressed with Ben's idea about selling cigarettes in exchange for free travel from the camp. He tells us about the time he bought cinema tickets and then resold them at a much higher price outside the cinema, claiming that all tickets have been sold out. Right from when he was a teenager, he washed cars and offered to clean houses to make money, and he helped in his father's grocery.

"Yes, I've heard many stories like yours. It's all about survival," he acknowledges.

Time passes quickly talking with Noha. He looks at his watch and then looks round to make sure no one is listening.

"You know, I've found something that could make me very rich indeed. And I'm looking for a partner."

He quickly drinks half a glass of wine, and then whispers, "Stones!"

"Stones?" Ben looks confused.

"Yes, stones. You know, like sapphire and rubies. They can make a fortune! But I'm looking beyond that. Listen, a good friend of mine works in this trade in India, and he sold me some sapphires and rubies, which I've sold here at a phenomenally higher rate. Then, with that money, I bought some diamonds from the same person and sold them here."

He pauses to let us have some time to take in what he's saying. He asks the waiter for another glass of wine and gulps it down.

"I'm telling you this in confidence, do you understand? Not a word to anybody. This is a risky business, especially if we do well in it."

"Yes, of course. We won't tell anybody," said Ben.

"The reason I need a partner is that I want to take this to the next level. I want to go to India myself and cut out the middleman. If we go directly to India and buy the stones ourselves and then have them refined in Tel Aviv, we could be onto something really big. Listen, I need to go now. You'll have to excuse me."

He reaches into his inner jacket pocket, pulls out a small wallet, takes out a business card and hands it to Ben.

"Think about it. Right now, I've got other business to attend to. If you're interested, give me a call in a couple of weeks."

He shakes our hands and marches across the room, stopping to say goodbye to Andrew before leaving.

****

My parents want me to get married, and they say it's important for someone to look after me, and that I'm not getting younger. Annoyingly, Ben agrees with them, and over dinner, asks my mother who she has in mind.

"Richard."

I put my knife and fork down, and I look at them horrified.

"Why on earth would I marry Richard?"

"He's a good man. He's a hard worker and is now a qualified accountant. He's always been interested in you. Do you remember him sending you all those flowers?" asked my mother.

"Yes, yes, of course," I reply. "But he's cold. I couldn't marry a cold person."

"He'll warm to you. Just give him a chance. He'll be coming to Tel Aviv in a couple of weeks."

"What?" I raised my voice.

When Richard arrives in Tel Aviv, we go out to restaurants and the cinema together, and my parents invite him to family meals. To satisfy my parents, I give in and marry him in Tel Aviv. It's a forced wedding, and I smile at the right time and greet guests as sincerely as I can. The good news is that there's no honeymoon, I don't think I could have managed to go on holiday with him. The bad news is that we have to rent an apartment in the city centre, away from my parents and brother, which bothers me very much. There are many evenings when we just sit quietly in the sitting room with nothing to say to each other. and it's so awkward that I eventually go to my parents' place for dinner. Six months later, he tells me that he's found some work in Paris and he's going to move there and, as his faithful wife, I would follow him there one year later. I'm happy that I can move back to my parents' home, but I'm dreading the day I have to move to France to be with him. He rents a two-roomed apartment near Bois de Boulogne, and when I do move there, I get trained in bookkeeping and work as an accountant, managing the invoices for a company which manufactures men's shirts. As I don't have the right documents to work there legally, I work on the black market and do the night shift, which in a way is a good thing because I don't have to spend much time with Richard. This was short-lived, as one of my colleagues denounces me and I can't work any more so for a while, I don't do much and go out with new friends.

****

Ben starts to trade in diamonds with Noah and becomes a successful businessman, frequently travelling to Amsterdam, Tokyo and India to meet customers and suppliers. He moves to Verona with Nicole and her two children and gets married there. Unlike my wedding, it's such a nice occasion, and we invite guests from different chapters from our lives. It's lovely to see Marcario and Sabella again and learn that they now own a tailor's shop in Bucharest. Stephanie got married a year ago to a gentleman from Lyon, where they are now living, and they're expecting a baby. She tells us that Tomasz is no longer with us as he was executed in one of the concentration camps. In the corner of my eye, I see Noah and his new wife,

Daniella, arrive, and he looks as happy as ever to be with us. My parents, who move to Milan shortly before their wedding, look proud of their son as the ceremony begins.

****

A couple of years later, living with Richard becomes intolerable so we get divorced, and I move into another apartment in Bois de Boulogne. I get a tip from one of my friends that there's a need for men's socks and pullovers from Italy, so I take this opportunity to visit my family and look for suppliers in Modena and Carpi. I find two good manufacturers, and I start to take the items by train to Gard du Nord in Paris, where I would exchange them with my contact person for cash. I accumulate enough money to set up a small shop and acquire documents which allow me to be employed legally at last. I love living in Paris and I've already learned the language well enough to sell garments and make conversation. One day, just over a year later, I go to the shop early in the morning and find the glass door has been shattered. I walk inside, treading carefully between the broken glass and switch on the light, only to see the open till on the floor and five empty coat hangers on one of the rails. I look back on the street and see people walking by as though my ransacked shop is invisible. I collect myself and go to the café where I usually have breakfast, and order a large coffee, a baguette with strawberry preserve and a croissant, and spend this time thinking about what I want to do. I consider reporting the incident to the police, but they'll probably take one look at my Israeli passport and dismiss me. Besides, even if they do take the matter seriously and investigate what has happened, it would take ages to put everything back to normal. On top of that, I don't have the shop insured so there would be lots of additional costs to rebuild and repair the premises. Since most of my family is in Italy, I decide that the best thing is for me to join them. I move to my parents' home in Milan and work as an au pair for a family, performing domestic chores and teaching French to the children.

****

Five months after moving to Italy, my parents become unwell, and both of them die from heart attacks, my mother in July and my father in September. Shortly after the funeral, I stop working as an au pair as I'm much better owning and running my own business so I find a niche in the market and start to buy and sell costume jewellery. Once I have enough money, I rent a small apartment in the Navigli district.

****

Ben and Nicole move to Milan and buy a large apartment there, and invite us all to a housewarming party. Nicole is a fabulous cook and prepares a delicious lasagne accompanied by a fine bottle of red wine, and a tiramisu for dessert.

"I think we're going to need to get some domestic workers in here. You know, some people who can help with the cooking and the cleaning," says Ben.

"Well, it is a large apartment. I agree, we've become so busy with you at work and the children will be at a new school," says Nicole.

"Quite right," he replies. "Who can we employ? It seems that there are not many willing Italians to take on these jobs. Some of my friends have taken on foreign people."

"Where from?" I ask.

"Different countries – Morocco, Albania, and interestingly Cape Verde."

"Are you sure they'll be reliable. I mean, I have heard stories of being robbed by cleaners and housekeepers. In any case, where is Cape Verde? I've never heard of it," says Nicole.

"Neither had I until I looked it up in the atlas. They are tiny islands off the west coast of Africa. Apparently, they are very nice people, and many of them want to emigrate to Europe and America because of the poor conditions out there."

"Poor things. Well, I'm sure they deserve a better life. So, they're African, right?"

"Well, here's the thing. Cape Verde was colonized by the Portuguese for many years, so the Cape Verdean is a person of mixed race: African and Portuguese."

"How do you know all of this?"

"I was intrigued, sweetheart. So, as I was passing the library on the way home, I went in and checked it out."

"Okay. How do we go about recruiting them?"

"There's an advert in the newspaper. Basically, you need to contact an agency which is run by the church, and they take care of selecting people to come and work for you."

The next day, Ben calls the agency and says that we're looking for domestic workers who can do the cleaning, cooking and other chores. A week later, a representative visits Ben and Nicole at their apartment and asks them questions about their background as well as their specific needs. She's satisfied with their responses and tells them that it takes some time to make the right arrangements and that there's a lot of bureaucracy. After two months, she calls Ben and lets him know that three people from the island of São Nicolau are on their way.

And that, my dear Adam, is how it all started. Their arrival changes everything, especially for me. Anyway, you already know that, don't you?

Part Three

One

"In preparation for landing, please ensure that your safety belts are fastened, that your seat is in its upright position and that your tables are folded away."

The air hostess' announcement interrupted Miguel's deep sleep. He yawned and looked out of the window at the deep blue sky and the dotted lights, glowing like candles, coming from the miniature city below.

Just before lunch on the previous day, Miguel was playing with his grandmother and aunt, when his mother arrived out of the blue and said that she was taking him back to Italy with her. They knew how abrupt Ana could be so they hardly said a word over lunch. Miguel tried his best not to cry, as the thought of leaving his grandmother and aunt was daunting, and he didn't like the way that his mother barged into their house without even looking at him. After he finished eating, he stood up and saw his grandmother silently weeping as she collected the plates and took them to the kitchen area. She picked him up and held him close to her chest and then Ana marched in, extruded him from his grandmother's arms, and took him to the airport.

As they got closer to the aeroplane, Miguel put his hands over his ears to mute the tremendous roaring sound coming from the engine. Half-way up the steps to the plane, he let go of his mother's hand and ran back down towards the terminal building, and shouted, "I want to go home!" The security guard caught him and lifted him up. Miguel wriggled with all his might, trying to release himself, but the guard was too strong, and he brought him back to his mother. The plane ascended into the sky, and the lush green landscape below disappeared forever.

In the terminal building in Milan, Ana briskly made her way between the other passengers, dragging Miguel behind her. He had never seen so many people before and he looked at the long neat trousers, shiny black shoes, colourful pullovers, thick coats and different shaped hats as the passengers swerved around him.

Outside the airport, Miguel saw a different world where there were no mules, mountains and sea; instead, there was a car park, a bus terminal and tall buildings in the background. Before he had time to take any of it in, Ana ushered him onto the bus, and they left for the city centre. He looked out of the window at the cars, the colourful buildings with their neat rectangular windows and shutters and the shops with neon signs. When the bus made its first stop, he glanced at a man and a woman sat around a small round table outside a café, the man popped a piece of cake into his mouth, and the woman laughed. Miguel closed his eyes, overwhelmed by the chaos around him, and thought about his home, his lovely grandmother and aunt who were no longer with him.

He fell asleep until his mother nudged him when they reached their destination.

When they descended, he winced at the overpowering smell of traffic and garbage and wondered how anyone living here could bear the stench. His mother got her bearings, and they walked for ten minutes before arriving at a six-storey block of apartments. Ana rang the bell next to a name, which was imprinted in black on a small rectangular gold plaque on the right of a large arched wooden door.

"Who is it?"

"It's Ana," replied his mother.

There was a buzzing sound, and the door automatically unlocked. Ana pushed it open and led Miguel into a dark hallway where some wide charcoal stairs led up to the different apartments. On the third floor, Leticia, who was wearing a white apron over a green dress, was there to greet them.

"Hello, little one! Welcome to Italy!"

She bent down and ruffled Miguel's black curly hair and gave him a hug and a kiss. Miguel smiled at her and smelt the food coming from inside.

"What is that smell?" he asked.

"It's beef, my dear. We're preparing a meal for our employers and their guests tonight!"

"I see," he said.

"Don't worry, there will be some for us after they've finished!" she said.

"Anyway, let's get both of you inside, shall we?"

"How was the journey?" asked Leticia.

"It was fine," replied Ana.

"And Miguel?"

"He'll get used to it. He'll have to."

When Ana went into the bathroom, Miguel decided to have a look round this strange apartment, and he started in one of the two bedrooms, where there were two single beds with blankets, curtains at each side of a tall window and a wardrobe in the corner. After Ana came out of the bathroom, he took a look in there as well and found a white toilet, a bidet next to it, a basin, a bath with a bottle of shampoo and a bar of soap, which smelled of flowers. He tipped some of the thick orange-coloured shampoo onto his left hand and turned on the cold water tap and washed it off, and then ran his fingers along the smooth ceramic curves of the basin. After feeling the soft towels on the rack, he went into the other bedroom and touched the mattress and doughy pillow. He saw a switch near the entrance of the room, so he found a chair, climbed onto it and pressed it, and suddenly, much to his amazement, a shot of white light lit up the room. He kept switching it on and off until his mother found him.

"Stupid boy!" she said, "You'll ruin the lights if you keep doing that!"

She yanked him off the chair and dragged him towards the kitchen, where Angelo and Leticia were busy chopping up vegetables.

At that moment, Nicole came in. She had a tall stature, her black hair was combed back, and she was wearing a smart light grey dress. She walked towards Ana and Miguel, who were standing next to each other, and moved her head up and down, inspecting their differences in height and cast her stern eyes on Ana.

"So, Ana, this is your brother, right?"

"Well, yes, kind of…"

"What do you mean, 'well, yes, kind of'? Is he your brother, or not?"

There was an awkward pause.

"Is Miguel capable of cutting vegetables, roasting a chicken, ironing shirts and blouses, and cleaning the apartment?"

Miguel looked up at her and knew that she was talking about him, but she was speaking in a strange language. Ana looked downwards to avoid Nicole's glare.

"He will be," she said quietly.

"He will be!" replied Nicole, mocking her.

"Yes, he will be one day," said Ana.

"Please don't lie to me, dear. I know very well he's not your brother. He's your son," she hissed, getting closer to Ana.

Ana's heart was beating, and she hoped that Nicole would go away. She coughed, and just as she was about to speak, Nicole shushed her.

"Please don't say any more. You'll just make things worse. This is the last time you lie to me. Is that clear?"

Ana murmured that it was clear.

"And dinner had better not be late," she said on her way out.

"You must be very hungry and tired. I've got some beef and rice for both of you. You can eat it and then get some rest. We have a busy day tomorrow," said Angelo.

Ana and Miguel sat down opposite each other around a large round table whilst Angelo took two plates out of the cupboard above the stove and placed some beef and rice onto them. Miguel picked at the rice and put it in his mouth and then tried a piece of beef, and spat it out.

"It's horrible!" he said, "I want fish!"

"Just eat it! It's food! How dare you spit it out!" yelled Ana.

"Come on, Ana, he's never eaten beef before. Give him a break!"

"He's not your child! Don't tell me what to do!"

"I'm just saying that he's nearly five years' old and he's not used to it."

Miguel finished the rice as quickly as he could and then Angelo took him to the second bedroom, and helped him to get changed into his pyjamas and get into bed. Shortly afterwards, Ana also went to bed. It took one hour to prepare the rest of the meal, and then Angelo and Leticia took the food and wine carefully to Ben and Nicole's luxury apartment on the next floor. It would be a long night as they had to wait for them to finish and then there was the washing up, so they ate some of the beef and rice and chatted.

The following morning, Miguel awoke to the sound and smell of sizzling meat, so he got out of bed and went into the kitchen and saw Angelo and Leticia preparing food. A lady with silver hair and a bronze-coloured face was talking with Ana in the corner of the room. When she glanced at Miguel, she interrupted her conversation with Ana and went towards him. Miguel liked her open, genuine smile, which led to a fountain of green light coming from her eyes, so he smiled back at her.

When Angelo, Leticia and Ana had arrived in Italy, none of them had an idea of how to cook so Nicole had given them lessons in baking, grilling, roasting and frying as well as hygiene and appearance. Ana had been reluctant to learn any of the recipes Nicole had given them, so she was asked to clean, wash and iron, which she didn't like doing either.

On that morning, Ana took Miguel to the upper apartment, carrying a bucket, brush and some dusters. Miguel was impressed with the vast living room, where the light from the large windows exposed the rich and vibrant colours from the antique furniture and framed oil paintings. There was a large embroidered burgundy rug on which stood a small rectangular glass coffee table surrounded by leather sofas, and next to each one, was a small side table with a coaster and an ashtray. Miguel pressed the palm of his hand on the sofa and watched how the texture resumed its normal position after he released it. His attention turned to the loud ticking of an old oak grandfather clock which was next to one of the windows. The wall on the right was covered in shelves, stacked with books of different sizes and colours. He pulled one out and touched the light cream paper and looked at the peculiar markings on each page. On the opposite side, there were glass cupboards full of wine glasses and above them were two paintings, one was a portrait of a bald man against a jet-black background, and the other was a bowl of fruit on an off-white table, again with a jet-black background. He looked back at the windows and watched the lavish apricot curtains on each side shiver as a slight breeze entered the room. With nothing to do, he sat down on one of the sofas and watched his mother meticulously clean every inch of the room with a duster and brush.

It was not long before Nicole came into the room, followed by Ben.

"This is Ana's son, Miguel," she said, pointing at him. "I think Maria has already taken a shine to him!"

Ben was as tall as Nicole, and his spectacles made his brown eyes seem much bigger than they really were. He was wearing brownish-green trousers, a cream shirt with small transparent buttons and a tweed jacket. They both spoke to Miguel with varied cadence and elongated the vowels, but he didn't take any notice of what they were trying to say, as he was trying to understand why these people, and the others he had seen at the airport, had such a contrast in appearance compared to his mother, aunt and uncle, and of course, himself. This was indeed another world, and maybe the aeroplane had taken him to another planet.

Ben pinched his cheek.

"Ciao piccolino!" exclaimed Ben.

They repeated this exclamation three times, before omitting 'piccolino' and just saying 'ciao'. Miguel managed to utter 'ciao' and waved back at them with a big smile, showing a perfect set of bright white teeth.

"Isn't he adorable?" said Nicole.

She turned to look at Ben, who had the same glazed expression as her.

"You have a beautiful son!" Nicole said to Ana, who was busy cleaning the inside of the cupboards.

But Ana chose not to listen to the compliments about Miguel and muttered something under her breath.

Miguel was bewildered when Nicole took his hand and led him to the kitchen and sat him down next to the table. Nicole disappeared for a few minutes, so he looked around the kitchen and marvelled at the black and white marble surfaces and thought it odd to have designated rooms for sleeping, cooking and eating. Nicole reappeared with some pieces of paper and crayons, and for some reason unbeknown to Miguel, she placed her hand on the white paper and drew around it with a black crayon. He watched her attentively, and then she placed another piece of paper and a black crayon in front of him and so he thought he ought to copy what she had just done. He put his hand on the paper, and Nicole stood behind him. She held his right hand, holding the crayon, and helped him to draw around his hand. When they had finished, she cossetted him by repeating 'Bravo' and clapping her hands, so Miguel, still a bit confused, decided to copy her by clapping his hands as well.

"Ben!" she called. "Vieni qui!"

Ben hurriedly entered the kitchen and saw Nicole standing near the table holding the picture of the hand so that Ben could see it.

"L'hai fatto tu?" he beamed.

Miguel shrugged his shoulders.

"He's such a good artist. Aren't you a good artist?" said Nicole.

"Oh, he is. That is a beautifully drawn hand," said Ben.

"Let's draw some more hands and this time we can colour them in? What do you think?"

The next day, Miguel woke up early, and after eating rice for breakfast, he ran upstairs to Ben and Nicole's apartment. Ben was holding a white ball with hexagonal shapes around it. Miguel liked the look of it, so he jumped up to try and take it for himself, but Ben playfully moved the ball behind his back using his right hand and then moved it back in front of him again. Miguel laughed and laughed and ran around Ben again and again until Ben let him have it.

"Honey, we're going to the park!" Ben said.

When Ben and Miguel went down onto the busy street below, Miguel looked at two young couples walking hand in hand amongst the bustle, occasionally looking at shop windows. The traffic was moving slowly, and one pedestrian took advantage of this by crossing the road in front of a slowly moving car, which induced an angry driver to shout some obscenity accompanied by a hand gesture outside the window. Miguel thought this was funny, so he tugged on Ben's shirt and pointed to the driver. Many Vespas were navigating themselves between the cars, and when the traffic lights turned green, they raced with such a loud ripping noise that Miguel had to put his hands over his ears. Ben took Miguel's hand, and they crossed two busy main roads before arriving at the Giardini Montanelli.

There was a narrow runnel in a trench on the left of the entrance and ahead of them were many differently shaped areas of grass surrounded by pebbled pathways. Ben found a space near a tree and squatted to face Miguel and showed him the ball.

"Palla!" said Ben, pointing at the ball. Miguel didn't know what to say so Ben repeated the word, "Paaalllllllaa."

Miguel repeated the word with flawless pronunciation.

"Bravo!" exclaimed Ben, and patted his head.

Ben moved a few metres away from Miguel and gently passed the ball to him with the side of his right foot and then Miguel bent down, took the ball with both hands, and passed the ball back. Half an hour later, Miguel was able to pass the ball towards Ben at varied distances. A passing couple with a pram and two children, who were of the same age as Miguel, stopped in their tracks and called out to Ben.

"Would you mind if they join in?"

"Not at all! Come along, boys!"

The two boys ran up to Ben and Miguel, and they passed the ball to each other in a clockwise direction, and whenever one of them kicked the ball too far or in the wrong direction, Miguel was the one who ran after the ball.

When they returned to the apartment, Ben gave the ball to Miguel.

"È un regalo per te!" said Ben.

Miguel proudly took the ball and went straight into the sitting room, whilst Ben went into his office to attend to some urgent business. Nicole was sitting on one of the sofas and stood up to speak to him.

"Miguel, my darling, have you been playing football with Uncle Ben?"

Miguel looked at her, trying to fathom out what she had said.

"We're having some guests for dinner tonight. One of them is Maria, who you met yesterday! Do you remember her?"

Nicole went downstairs to speak with Ana, Angelo and Leticia, leaving Miguel alone in the sitting room with the ball. Miguel kicked the ball towards the back of the sofa, and it boomeranged back to him. This got boring after a few minutes so he figured that if he ran up to the ball and kicked it with the tip of his foot, the ball would move with more speed and strength, so he placed the ball a couple of metres from where he was standing and about six metres away from the sofa. When he kicked the ball, it had the desired effect, but instead of going back to him, it sprang off the sofa and onto a trolley, toppling over a crystal jug onto the floor. Miguel cusped his hands around his mouth as the glass fractured into a thousand pieces. He heard quick footsteps coming towards him and stood by the sofa, looking guilty.

"What have you done?" asked Ben, looking at the broken glass. "That's very naughty. You shouldn't be playing with the ball in the sitting room. Stay still. We don't want you getting cut glass in your feet."

He lifted Miguel into his arms and carried him downstairs.

In the downstairs kitchen, Nicole was giving instructions about the dinner.

"Ben is going to pick up Noha and Daniella from the airport a bit later. They're staying with us for a few days. Noha is a very important business partner and a close friend, so they both need to be treated with the utmost respect, so I don't want anything to go wrong. And of course, Maria will be coming, so that makes five of us. And just to let you know, I'm going out with friends this afternoon."

Ben put Miguel down next to his mother. Realising he had done something wrong, Miguel, who was still holding tightly onto the ball, looked tearfully at the ground.

"What happened?" asked Nicole.

"He was playing with the ball in the sitting room and accidentally broke a crystal jug."

Ana was furious, and she knelt down next to him and shook him forcefully with her hands.

"What the hell did you do that for?" she shouted.

Miguel didn't have any time to reply as she grabbed him by the arm, took him to his bedroom and pushed him inside and he fell on the floor.

"No lunch for you! Stay where you are until I come and get you. Don't you dare come out!"

She slammed the door and returned to the kitchen.

"I'm sorry about the jug," she said insincerely.

"That was a bit harsh, wasn't it? It's only a jug. And it's partly my fault because I didn't explicitly tell him not to play in the sitting room," said Ben.

"That may well be. But he has to learn," replied Ana.

Ben was dumbfounded at Ana's reaction and left the apartment, and Nicole resumed her cooking instructions.

"Is everything understood?"

"Yes, everything is clear, Signora Nicole."

Nicole started to leave and, without looking round as she approached the door, she said, "And have Miguel come up later to meet our family. I'm sure they would like to meet him."

The dining room was marginally smaller than the sitting room, and there were no portraits on the walls. Framed black and white photographs of Ben and Nicole's family stood on top of the sideboards, inside which there were wine glasses, ornate plates, cups and saucers. The large rectangular table wore a white linen tablecloth with light gold embroidered edges. In the middle, there were two beautiful decanters, each holding a decorative bottle of wine, and next to them were bowls of salad with lettuce, tomatoes, radish, cucumber, carrots and walnuts. Ben and Nicole sat at the heads of the table.

It was half-past eight in the evening, and Angelo, looking smart in his plain blue apron over a white shirt, was in the middle of serving the main course. He served Nicole first, he took a chicken breast with a pair of tweezers from the ceramic container he was holding with his left hand and placed it gently on her plate and scooped some sauce on top of it. Nicole was talking with Noha about her children's education.

Later in the evening, Angelo brought Miguel to the dining room. Michele stared at the family eating sitting on identical padded oak chairs with curved tops. He momentarily cast his mind back to his recollections of eating with his grandmother when she propped him on the bed or her knee and fed him with rice and some fish, using her fingers. When Nicole spotted Miguel, her conversation with Noha came to an abrupt end. She wiped her mouth with a napkin and turned her head to look at him.

"Don't be shy! Come here!" she said, beckoning him with her middle finger.

"I've heard you've been a bit naughty today," said Daniella, with a beaming grin on her face.

"Enough of that." Ben laughed. "He's going to be a professional!"

"Of course, you are!" said Daniella, and Maria and Noha nodded and widened their eyes to confirm this was true.

Miguel smiled back at them.

"Look at that winsome smile!" said Daniella.

"He's got a gorgeous face!" said Maria.

"He's so good at drawing!" added Nicole.

"Well, what a clever boy we have here!" said Maria, who could not take her eyes off him.

Nicole went into the kitchen and brought back the hand he had drawn the previous day.

"A contemporary Van Gogh, I would say," exaggerated Daniella.

"I think he needs to go to bed. He's looking tired," said Nicole to Angelo.

"Yes, of course," said Angelo. "I'll return with the desserts."

Everyone said goodbye to Miguel, blowing him kisses and looked forward to seeing him soon.

The following morning, Ana took Miguel to the upper apartment, just like the previous day. She proceeded to open the windows in the sitting room to remove the odour of stale cigars, and then she polished the furniture with a wet cloth. Nicole was delighted to see Miguel and took him immediately into the kitchen where she took out a packet of cards from her right pocket and spread them face down on the table. She showed him how to play 'pairs' and explained that the object of the game was to collect as many pairs of animals as possible. Each time a card was turned over, Nicole told him how to say each animal in Italian, which didn't interest him at all, until he came across two donkeys. Then he excitedly told Nicole, in crioulo, about how he had seen these animals before. Nicole gave him a puzzled look and presumed that he liked donkeys.

At that moment, the doorbell rang, and Nicole went to let Maria in.

"Thank you for coming," said Nicole. "Ben's gone out for the day with Noah and Daniella. I'm meeting a friend for a coffee in about twenty minutes. I won't be too long. Miguel's in the kitchen. He has just beaten me at pairs. And for some reason, he likes donkeys!"

"That's fine," said Maria. "By the way, it's pouring with rain outside."

"I won't be long, Miguel. Maria will play with you," said Nicole.

She put her long beige coat on, glanced at herself in the mirror near the front door, adjusted her hair, and left with an umbrella.

Miguel smiled at Maria and indicated with his chin that she should sit opposite him so they could play the pairs game. He put his fingers and thumbs spread out in front of her face to show her that they were to play ten games. After losing the first two rounds, Maria prized a banana from the fruit basket, peeled it and broke a small piece off and gave it to him. He looked at her and put it in his mouth and began coughing and spluttering, and the banana piece propelled out of his mouth. Maria went to get a glass of water and patted his back. There was something about Maria that he liked, she looked kind and gentle, and he trusted her, so he took another piece of banana and this time he chewed and swallowed it, and then they returned to the card game.

****

The next two months passed quickly. Miguel was having the time of his life, painting, playing cards, watching and playing football with his new friends. He gradually started to eat more Italian food and speak some of the language. He looked forward to Sunday afternoons when they would watch the football on the television in the sitting room, Ben supported AC Milan, and Miguel supported Juventus. Even more thrilling were the five-a-side football matches which Ben had arranged in the park on Saturday afternoons, and Miguel was happy to see Maria come and watch him. He discovered a passion for football, and he quickly learned how to tackle boys who were older than him and score goals.

On one Saturday morning in January, he opened the curtains to find sugar floating from the sky, so they all went outside. Miguel reached up to catch one of the snowflakes but looked disappointed when it dissolved into water in his hand.

"It's snow!" bellowed Angelo. "Very cold rain!"

"Let's get him back inside, otherwise he will freeze to death," said Leticia.

Miguel could not stop thinking about the snow, and he wanted to spend more time outside. Later in the morning, Ben and Nicole took him to the park, and they built a snowman together, and Miguel observed that the snow was now thicker and it compressed in his hand, unlike the snowflake from earlier. Ben gave him two pieces of coal and a carrot so he could create a face for the snowman, and Miguel laughed at it.

"It looks like you, Uncle Ben," said Miguel.

"That's very cheeky, Miguel!"

Miguel bent down, made a snowball and hurled it at Ben when he wasn't looking, and so, Ben retaliated by throwing an even larger snowball at Miguel. Nicole joined in, and so a snowball fight began, which Miguel enjoyed immensely.

****

On the twenty-third of March, it was Miguel's birthday, so Ben and Nicole organized a spectacular party for him. They had contacted a prestigious catering company, which specialized in children's parties. Balloons adorned the walls, an array of savoury snacks, ice-cream and fizzy drinks surrounded the huge chocolate cake which had five orange candles and the words, 'Tanti Auguri Miguel' written on the top.

"I hope you like the cake," said Maria.

"You made it for me?" asked Miguel.
"Of course, I did!" said Maria.

When Miguel's football friends arrived, he was so happy to see them and loved being the centre of attention. After they had eaten and sung 'tanti auguri', Miguel opened his gifts, which were mainly books and clothes, which he disregarded after receiving the pièce de résistance. He ripped the shiny gold wrapping paper into pieces and took out a black and white top, shorts and football shoes. He couldn't believe it. It was the best gift he had ever been given, and he rushed into the bathroom and changed into his new Juventus top. When he came out, he ignored the mixture of cheers and boos from the other children and went straight to Maria and hugged her legs, as he knew that this was from her.

Ana, Angelo and Leticia were sat together at one end of the table.

"Mamãe! Mamãe! Look at this!" said Miguel, showing her his football outfit.

Ana shook her head.

"Mamãe, I saved you some cake." He presented her with a piece of cake on a paper plate with a paper napkin and put it on the table in front of her.

"Who gave you this?" she asked him, tugging at his top.

He pointed to Maria.

****

At the end of March, Nicole asked Ana if she could do the cleaning at Maria's apartment as well as her

own. Miguel just couldn't wait to see where she lived.
They went through a side gate, passed the porter's
cabin on the left, and saw three adjunct blocks of
apartments, each one having six storeys and those
above the second floor had balconies decorated with
plants and flowers. They went to the last door on the
left block, and Ana pressed a button next to the door.
After hearing the buzzing sound, they went inside, took
the elevator to the fourth floor, and saw Maria waiting
for them. They removed their shoes at the entrance and
walked into the spacious sitting room, which was
smaller than Ben and Nicole's, but much cosier. There
was a long glass dining table on the right, and in front
of the windows and behind the television, there were
various tall plants with large leaves which reached the
ceiling. Whilst Ana was talking with Maria, Miguel
explored the rest of the apartment. There was a roomy
carpeted bathroom and next to it was Maria's bedroom
with a double bed and two wardrobes. He opened the
door of the opposite bedroom and saw a single bed,
empty shelves and a slim table near the window.

When he returned to the sitting room, Maria was
still giving his mother instructions on how to clean the
apartment, pointing in different directions. He looked
at Maria who was wearing different clothes to the ones
he had seen her in at Ben and Nicole's apartment. She
was wearing a light grey blouse with matching
trousers, a gold necklace, several bracelets on her left
wrist, and a small golden watch with a delicate chain
around her right wrist. Her dark red nail varnish,
subtle eyeliners, pencilled eyebrows, various
foundations, powders and highlighters made her look

sharper and determined and more like a businesswoman. Her non-onsense look changed into one of adoration when she saw Miguel standing in the doorway, and she went up to him, bent down and kissed him on his forehead.

"Hello, little one! I'm going to work now, and I'll see you later," she said.

She took a small bronze-coloured leather bag from the sofa and a fur coat from a hanger next to the kitchen and, as she opened the main door, she turned back and saw Miguel still looking at her, so she gave him a friendly wave and left.

Miguel was bored, so he went to the tiny kitchen on the left of the sitting room and glanced at the oven with hobs next to the sink, a small pull-out table and a tall fridge. He went back to the sitting room and took out a colouring book and some crayons from his mother's bag and returned to the kitchen and started to colour in a picture of a garden. It was not the same as having Nicole next to him, complimenting him for everything he did. There was a balcony in the kitchen, which looked out onto other apartments, so after an hour of colouring, he went there and looked down at the people coming and going. He thought about his grandmother and his aunt and wondered if he would ever see them again after his mother had taken him away from them so suddenly.

****

Miguel didn't want to go to school even though he didn't know what school was, and didn't like the idea of being parted from his new family. Nicole took him to his first day at nursery school and spoke with the headmistress, who was an elderly lady with grey hair and a greyish blue dress, and then left.

When he saw toys scattered everywhere, he thought that school couldn't be that bad, but this changed when he was asked to join a group of younger children, who were sat cross-legged on the floor facing a blackboard and a teacher. It soon became apparent that he couldn't speak Italian properly and couldn't add or subtract either, and this made the other children laugh at him, and the teacher didn't help by asking him the most questions. He hated every minute of his first lesson, but he won the admiration of the other children as soon as he got to the playground and played football with them, and he proved to be the strongest and quickest boy in the class. With the help of his new friends, he learned how to speak and write Italian, but dreaded the arithmetic lessons, which were always scheduled before lunch.

A couple of weeks later, Maria left work early to pick Miguel up and take him to a lunch, hosted by Sabrina, one of her customers. She told Ana that she could go back to Ben and Nicole's apartment. She took Miguel downstairs to an underground car park, and they got into her white Toyota and sped off. As they walked towards Sabrina's apartment, Miguel was proud to be next to such a sophisticated and elegant lady. When they arrived, Sabrina opened the door, and Miguel saw a little girl with wavy blonde hair and beautiful blue eyes standing next to her.

"This is Manuela!" Sabrina introduced them to her daughter.

Maria handed her an exquisitely packaged box of chocolates before they moved to the kitchen-diner. Miguel felt privileged to be a guest at a dinner where there were placemats, napkins, glasses and shiny cutlery.

After serving the lasagne, Maria and Sabrina gossiped and laughed about some of Sabrina's customers, whilst Miguel and Manuela got to know each other. Miguel didn't like it when Manuela touched his face and hair and squeezed his cheeks as he thought that she was treating him like one of her dolls. Sabrina and Maria went into the sitting room after lunch, and Miguel followed Sabrina into her bedroom to play with her toys. They built a tower made of lego and Miguel pushed it over, and the pieces went flying everywhere, this amused Manuela so much that they reconstructed it and pushed it over again. When it was time to leave, Miguel unashamedly made a bold move to kiss Manuela on her cheek, and she grinned. Sabrina and Maria looked at each other and rolled their eyes. Then Maria told Miguel to thank Sabrina for the wonderful lunch, and they left.

****

It had been agreed that on Saturday mornings, Maria would look after Miguel, so she decided to take him around Milan and show him the sights, which he found intriguing. He was moved by the enormity and symmetry of the Duomo, so she took him to the top so he could have a view of the square and a closer look at the intricate pinnacles. He marvelled at the dark gothic interior where the only glimmer of light came from the small arched stained-glass windows, and looking up to the ceiling, he was taken aback by the sheer size of the arches. Maria took him to see the religious frescos high on the walls, and he listened attentively to her telling the stories behind them.

On one Saturday, four months after visiting Sabrina, Maria took Miguel to see the Castello Sforzesco and the high fashion shops on Via Montenapoleone. They then had a long walk along the canal in Navigli before stopping at a pizzeria for lunch. When they arrived back at Ben and Nicole's apartment, Miguel saw his mother in the doorway with two small suitcases. Ben and Nicole were standing next to her, looking heartbroken.

"What's going on?" asked Miguel.

"We are leaving," said Ana drily.

Miguel looked at Maria, then at Ben and Nicole, confused about what his mother was suggesting, and hoping that it wasn't true, but they didn't say anything.

"Where are we going?" asked Miguel.

"We're going to stay with our family and friends in Portugal."

"Where is Portugal?"

"It's another country. Haven't they taught you anything at that school?"

"Why?' he asked, weeping.

"Your mother thinks it's better if you're with your own family and friends," said Maria, struggling to contain herself.

Nicole brought her car to the front of the apartment, and Ana and Miguel got in. Miguel tried to fight back the tears and glanced at Maria as the car started to leave, praying that she would contradict what his mother had said. He looked out of the window, desperately wanting his mother to change her mind.

Two

Miguel tried to work out why his mother would do such a cruel thing. Maybe she was jealous of his happiness and how they showered him with adoration and love, or maybe she missed her family and was fed up of cleaning. In any case, it was too late to return now, and as the plane ascended into the sky, he was saddened when he saw Milan covered in fluffy clouds. He couldn't stop thinking about Maria, who unlike his mother, had shown nothing but kindness and warmth, especially on those Saturday mornings. His thoughts were soon interrupted when the plane went through some heavy turbulence, and looking out of the window, he saw a tumultuous storm with spurts of lightning cracking through the charcoal clouds, and wondered whether the climate in their destination would always be like this.

Elena was waiting for them in the arrivals' hall, and she looked pleased when she saw Ana and embraced her. She had recently moved to Vialonga, a suburb of Lisbon.

"Welcome to Portugal! We've all been looking forward to seeing you again! How have you been?" asked Elena.

"We've been fine, but I'm so glad to be here," said Ana.

"And how is Miguel? He's grown, but he still has that cheeky look!" said Elena.

"He's been spoilt rotten by that family in Milan. He was getting too used to their ways. It's better for him to be like us."

"Their ways?" questioned Elena.

"Yes, they're very different from us. They've got loads of money and, well, they're just too different from us."

"Let's go and get the bus, and you can tell me all about it!"

So, she was jealous, thought Miguel. He followed Ana and Elena towards the bus stop, just outside the terminal building and after paying for the tickets, they boarded a raggedy old bus. He knew that they didn't want to sit next to him, so he sat next to a gentleman two rows behind them and closed his eyes, having no inclination to see what was outside.

"They adored him!" said Ana.

"Well, he's got an adorable face, hasn't he?"

"Don't be fooled by that! He's a troublemaker. He'll end up just like his father. Mark my words. You know I can already see José in him. Anyway, they gave him everything he wanted: expensive gifts, rides in expensive cars, nice food, trips around Milan, football in the park. And I'm treated like shit. They give me instructions about how clean everything should be and hardly even look at me! I tell you, it was hard work!"

"You're not jealous, are you?"

"Jealous! Not for a minute. They were giving him far too much. I don't want him to become greedy. And in any case, he doesn't deserve it."

"You don't love him, do you?"

"He's useless, just like his father. He's a leech. I tolerate him, and that's that. Anyway, let's change the subject. What about you?"

"Well, you remember Mateus? He came here with some of his family and built a large house so he could accommodate more family and friends. Then shortly after our mother passed away, he invited Afonso and me to come and stay, and Olivia stayed at home."

Miguel wished he had not overheard them talking, as it hurt him a lot, and he was even more saddened to learn that his grandmother had died. The bus ride was a long, painful journey in the dark, and after an hour, they got off and walked for fifteen minutes until they came to an area full of dwellings of different shapes, sizes and colours squeezed next to each other. Extensions had been added upwards and sideways to accommodate the growing number of residents, and there were cables loosely connected from building to building. Many of the houses had balconies from which hung clothes and bed linen. Miguel regarded the street vendors, barbecuing meat and vegetables, and the stray cats fighting each other as they piled onto the overflowing garbage containers, searching for food. He was curious to see children with the same skin colour and hair as him, running around and laughing. It was a graffiti artist's paradise as every building was decorated with political statements and cartoon-like characters. As they ventured further, the miasma of sewage, food and poor sanitation became overwhelming and made Miguel choke and retch. Ana bent down and shook him.

"Stop that! You think you're too good for this, do you?"

When they finally reached their new home, Afonso came to the door and welcomed them, took Ana's bags and hauled them upstairs. Mateus was so excited to see Ana again, that he ran up to her and gave her a long warm hug, and asked her to follow him into the kitchen, leaving Miguel in the hallway. Miguel turned his attention to a cat, which darted through the front door and swiftly caught a large rat from the inside the cupboard at the far end of the kitchen and raced back outside with it hanging from its mouth. He looked down at the stained pinkish-red carpet with threads teeming from the edges and compared it with the beautiful, spotless floors in Nicole and Ben's apartment. The stench of smoke coming from the kitchen was unbearably unpleasant, and he deduced that there were many people in there from their never-ending animated chatter. He didn't have much choice but to sit on one of the wooden stairs and wait for someone to notice him, it was better for him to stay out of the way.

One hour later, Elena and Ana emerged from the kitchen intoxicated, and wobbled towards the stairs and looked surprised to see Miguel sitting there. Elena invited him to join them as she wanted to give them a guided tour of the first floor, which Miguel thought couldn't be worse than what he had seen in the hallway.

Elena fumbled for the key for Ana's room in her pocket.

"Crime is rife here. We have attempted burglary nearly every day, and sometimes they're successful. That's why we have padlocks," said Elena.

"Can't you report it to the police?" asked Ana.

"Police?" Elena laughed. "There's no police here! The whole place is lawless."

Elena finally found the key and opened the dilapidated door to their bedroom, which stank of horrible stale smoke. The window was wide open, welcoming flies and mosquitoes to freely enter and buzz around the room. The wooden floor was covered with an ill-fitting red carpet, similar to the one Miguel had seen in the hallway, and the walls had cracks on them. There were two dusty mattresses, one single and one double, which looked as though they had already been slept on by thousands of people. Miguel bent down to touch the single one and lifted it up to find three large cockroaches crawling towards the other side of the room. With the dogs barking, people shouting and loud music outside, Miguel doubted he would ever be able to sleep here.

"Let me show you where the bathroom is. Mind you, there's always a queue to get in first thing in the morning!"

The conditions in the tiny bathroom matched the rest of the house. Inside, there was a small broken basin with cold light-brown water continually dripping out from the tap. Next to it, there was a small tub with a couple of old damp brown towels draped over the side. Elena explained that the overpowering odour of urine and excrement was due to the electricity and water being erratic, so they couldn't always flush the chain or have a wash. As she was closing the door, she reassured them that they would get used to it, which Miguel didn't believe. He was determined never to get used to it.

When it was time to go to bed, the humidity made Miguel slumberous, so he slept soundly in spite of the disturbances outside. The following morning, he woke up to the sound of clanging coming from the kitchen as Mateus, Afonso, Elena, Ana and some other friends were making breakfast, so he went downstairs as he was hungry. Mateus grabbed one of the unwashed pans which were untidily heaped up on the surface next to the fridge, and lit one of the hobs with a match and prepared some pancakes.

****

Luckily, Maria had provided Ana with some money for Miguel's education, which she had taken gladly as it would keep Miguel away from her. They had several bureaucratic hurdles to overcome, which meant that Miguel would need to wait at least three weeks before he could start school. Miguel abhorred being inside the house so he made friends with other children and played football with them outside and he would sometimes have lunch in another home.

On his sixth birthday, Miguel knew that his mother would never lay on a party similar to the one he had had in Milan, so he decided to go exploring with Pablo, one of his neighbours. Pablo was a skinny boy and under a mop of greasy black hair was a mischievous look, which made him an ideal companion. He was wearing a large green t-shirt which dropped over his body and shorts. Miguel looked at Pablo's broken sandals and thought for a moment that he wouldn't be able to go exploring wearing them, but there again, in this community, nothing really mattered.

They were sitting cross-legged on an uneven makeshift pavement, and Miguel was rubbing a couple of stones together.

"I'm bored of hanging out here. Let's go and have a look what's outside this place. I think there are some woods over there," said Miguel.

"I'm supposed to be at school today," Pablo said.

"Don't worry about school!" Miguel said. "Anyway, you hardly ever go. Come on, it will be fun."

"Okay. Let's go!" said Pablo

Full of vim, Miguel put his arm around Pablo, and they walked in the same direction that Miguel had entered the favela. He wished that he had the means to get on a bus and plane and return to Milan.

"Where are you from?" asked Pablo.

"I'm from São Nicolau. I don't remember much about being there. I moved to Milan in Italy for about a year and then came here. Mamãe wanted to leave Milan and come here, not me."

"I'm from Boa Vista," said Pablo. "Anyway, it's not so bad here."

"Anyway, better not to think about it. See that tree over there? I'll race you!" challenged Miguel. "Whoever gets there first is the best runner in the world!"

They ran as fast as they could, dodging some of the people sauntering in the opposite direction.

"I won! I won!" said Miguel.

"That wasn't fair!" said Pablo slightly out of breath. "You set off before me."

"This proves I'm the best runner in the world!"

On leaving the favela, there was a marked difference in the surrounding architecture and infrastructure, as the roads became more even and interspersed with neater blocks of apartments. It was a hot and humid day, and Miguel and Pablo were sweating. They were hungry and thirsty, so when Pablo spotted some bottles of water outside a grocer's shop, he ran across the road, snatched two of them and returned to Miguel. They sat down next to a wall and gulped the water down and then looked at each other and burst out laughing.

On their way to the woods, they came across an old and abandoned zoological garden. They went inside and came across a huge tank, which had accumulated water from the rain. Unaware of the millions of diseases they could catch from going into the water, they dived in without another thought and swam and splashed each other, pretending to be sea monsters. Miguel was exhilarated by the coolness of the water, and even though he knew he would eventually need to go back to his mother, he was pleased that he was having some fun with Pablo on his birthday.

When Miguel and Pablo eventually arrived at the woods, they played hide and seek, and when they got bored of that, they used twisted twigs to have sword fights. Three hours later, they returned to the edge of the woods on the hillside and watched the magical and iridescent event on the horizon, as the colossal sun disappeared and was replaced by a bloody sky, blackening all the buildings in the foreground.

"I think we need to go back now," said Pablo.

"Yeah, I guess so."

They had never been away for such a long time, and Miguel wondered whether his mother would realise he was not at home. Reluctantly, they set off, and it took them a long time to find the entrance to the favela as they kept taking the wrong turn and it was difficult to recognise familiar buildings in the dark.

Pablo stopped by Miguel's house.

"See you tomorrow! Maybe we can do this again," said Pablo.

"I hope so."

Miguel opened the door with trepidation and attempted to go upstairs unnoticed when he heard his mother coming out of the kitchen. He turned around and saw his mother's venomous eyes glaring at him.

"Where have you been?" she shrilled.

Terrorised by his mother's loud voice, he stood still and said nothing.

"Are you deaf and dumb? Have you lost your voice as well as your mind? Where have you been?" Ana slurred her words, and she took a drag from her cigarette.

"In the woods," Miguel stuttered, as he looked down.

"The woods! The woods!" she screamed.

Miguel wanted to avoid his mother's anger, so he started to go upstairs, but when he reached the fourth stair, she yanked him down, causing him to fall and bang his head on the floor. She picked him up by his ear and slapped his face repeatedly and then excoriated him further by burning the back of his right hand with the cigarette end. Miguel screamed.

"That's what you get for misbehaving! And don't even think about sleeping in the same room as me tonight!"

She tripped as she went upstairs and closed the bedroom door behind her with a bang.

Miguel put his left hand over the cigarette burn, hoping that the pain would go away if he didn't see it. He looked at the single light bulb hanging loosely from the ceiling covered with flies and tried to make himself as comfortable as possible on one of the stairs.

The following morning, he woke up and went into the kitchen and sat down on one of the chairs next to the table. His mother came in and saw him but didn't say anything.

"Mamãe, how should I behave?"

"Not like you did yesterday," she said.

She was looking for something. She opened each of the cupboards above the sink until she came across her pack of cigarettes.

"I've got a terrible headache," she said,

"How can I behave well if you don't tell me how?"

Ana sighed irritably and sat down opposite him. She lit a cigarette and inhaled deeply.

"Okay. Firstly, don't just disappear like you did yesterday otherwise the others will think I'm a bad mother. Secondly, don't talk unless we talk to you. Do as you're told. What else? Don't get in the way."

****

Two weeks later, Mateus and Elena took Miguel by bus to his first day at school. It took about thirty minutes to reach the building, which had a red façade and lots of windows and shutters on all four storeys. Mateus and Elena waved him goodbye, and one of the teachers accompanied him to a bright open room where twenty children were sitting behind different coloured round tables. Miguel sat behind his table and looked at the teacher, a slim lady with grey hair pushed back, an oblong face, large protruding eyes, and she was wearing a shabby blue dress. She tapped a piece of chalk on the desk in front of her, and the children immediately stopped talking, then she sat down and called every pupil's surname, and they responded 'yes' to confirm their attendance. She stood up and read out the timetable, which had been written on the blackboard behind her. Miguel didn't understand everything she said, but he did grasp the subjects: Portuguese, science, history, religion, geography, music, art, physical education and his least favourite, mathematics. Just before the break, the teacher explained the school rules and distributed a copy to each pupil.

During the break, he wasted no time and introduced himself to his classmates and asked them if he could play football with them at lunchtime. It was the only thing he looked forward to as he found it incredibly difficult to sit still and pay attention during the lessons, so he would often look for distractions. On one day during this first week, he started a ruler fight with one of his new-found friends, and the teacher sent them into a corner for one hour.

Miguel soon became known as a troublemaker, and no doubt, he was the subject of many staff meetings as practical jokes became a regular pastime. His favourite was balancing two large polystyrene cups of water on top of a door so that the person entering the room would be taken by surprise and soaked. When one of the teachers became the victim of his tomfoolery, he was dragged by his ear to the front of the classroom, bent over and caned ten times. He didn't like the humiliation at the beginning, but this soon wore off as he thought the jokes were worth the risk of being punished.

It was Friday, five weeks later, that Miguel plucked up enough courage to speak to the most beautiful girl in his class. He loved her light brown eyes and chestnut brown hair, so when he told her how good-looking she was, he was stunned when she slapped him on his face. It was not a nice way to end the week, and he felt despondent, so to cheer himself up, he decided to return to the woods on Saturday, but this time he would go alone and make sure he didn't return late.

Once he reached the edge of the woods, he sat and watched the captivating sunset and lay down to look at the sky as it transformed from light blue to a mixture of brown, orange and red. As it started to get dark, he closed his eyes and fell into a deep sleep. He was not aware of what time he woke up, but realised that he had to return home as soon as he could to avoid his mother's wrath. Without Pablo, it was even harder to reach home, and when he finally arrived at the doorstep, he knew it was too late and was nervous about what his mother would do to him.

As soon as he entered the hallway, he saw his mother and immediately went back outside and started running, but his mother was too quick, and she caught him in the middle of the street, and repeatedly slapped and punched his face until his mouth and nose were bleeding. She pulled him inside, up the stairs, pushed him into the bedroom and locked the door behind her. Miguel felt his face and tried to rub the blood off with his hand, and exasperated, he lay down and went to sleep.

The following morning, he woke up and tried to open the door but it was still locked, so he tried knocking on it and shouting, "let me out", but no one came. He sat down on the mattress, bewildered about his mother's temperament. Had he done something so bad to deserve being imprisoned in his room with no food and water? Surely, Maria, Ben and Nicole would never have burned or hit him if he had done something wrong. He desperately wanted to return to Milan and never see his mother again, and he thought that perhaps someone at school could at least take him to the airport. But that was a ridiculous idea as he didn't know how to let Maria know unless his mother had her telephone number somewhere. And they would never let a six-year-old onto a plane by himself.

At ten o'clock at night, Mateus opened the door and let him out. He looked at the dried blood on his face and took him into the bathroom to wash it off.

"I think you need a bath," he said. "Here, let me help you."

Mateus ran a cold bath for Miguel and then took him downstairs to the kitchen where he saw his mother with some unfamiliar faces sitting around the table and sniffing some powder.

"Ignore them," said Mateus. "Let me make you some spaghetti."

Whilst Mateus was cooking, Miguel could not stop himself from glancing at his mother and her friends. She was wearing a flimsy, red bright dress, and she had splashed over an overpowering fragrance which masked the smells of stale food and cigarettes. Her hair was neatly combed back, and she had prominent make-up on her eyebrows, eyelids, lips and cheeks. She took out a small rectangular mirror from her new shiny black handbag and checked her appearance before confidently standing up with her friends and striding out of the kitchen. As she left, Miguel looked at her short pink skirt, black tights and shiny pink high-heeled shoes.

"Mateus, why has Mamãe changed her clothes?" asked Miguel.

"She wants to look good! Like most women. Don't worry about it!"

"But she looks so different."

"Yeah, I suppose she does."

"Who are those people, Mateus?"

"They're your mother's new friends."

"And where are they going?"

"They're going to a party."

"And what was that powder they were sniffing?"

"All these questions, Miguel! Listen, I have to go and get ready. I'm going out with some friends tonight. Enjoy the spaghetti!"

Mateus left Miguel alone in the kitchen and went upstairs. Miguel was still hungry, so he went inside the fridge and saw a large chicken breast on the third shelf, so he plucked a piece from the top and discovered a maggot den underneath. He dropped the chicken piece on the floor, closed the fridge door and went outside to see if any of the other children were about but there was no one.

****

At school, Miguel proved to be an outstanding footballer and sprinter. He was disappointed when he was rejected from the school cross-country running team because of a lack of resistance skills. He built a good rapport with the trainer and thanks to him, he became more resilient and competitive and eventually won several races. His glory came to an end when he sprained his ankle, so he took up catch wrestling, which was short-lived because it didn't give him as much pleasure and satisfaction as football and running. He loved the challenge of playing football with boys who were older than him, but he was often turned down from joining the Vialonga team because he was too young.

****

In the following three months, Miguel seldom saw his mother, which was a blessing. He became accustomed to seeing her in the evenings with her friends, dressed up and sniffing powder which he presumed was some form of medication.

Then things changed. One Saturday afternoon, Miguel was playing football in the street with Pablo and some other friends, when he heard the sound of shouting from his house. He signalled to his friends that he was going to see what was happening, and crept into his house and sat on one of the stairs in the hallway and listened.

"Do you think I wanted this?" asked Ana furiously.

"Actually, I think you do want it. There are loads of jobs in the favela and even outside. There are shops and restaurants which all need cleaners and people to cook, manage the till and…" replied Elena.

"And sell groceries like you do!"

"At least it's honourable work."

"At least it's honourable work," mimicked Ana. "Honourable! We haven't got a choice to be honourable. Who do you think brings the money in?"

"Yes, and I'm grateful but what I'm trying to say is…"

"What you're trying to say is stupid!"

Miguel decided to have a peek to see what was happening, so he crept towards the kitchen door and looked through the gap and saw Ana sitting opposite Elena at the table. His mother took a cigarette out of her nearly-empty packet and lit it.

"So, you're not ashamed of being a whore and a drug addict?" asked Elena defiantly. Ana threw a mug of lukewarm coffee into her face and stood up to leave just as Elena hurled the mug towards Ana, narrowly missing her head and it shattered to bits on the ground. Miguel ran back to his stair, knowing that his mother was about to come out. Now he knew more about his mother's debauched lifestyle and was saddened by her icy heart.

"At least I'm having a bit of fun in this hellhole, like everyone else, which is more than you are having. I'm out of here. Give me two days to find a new house. Don't worry. I'll make sure I pay rent for the two days. Then you're on your own, sweetheart!" said Ana.

****

Ana kept her promise and found a larger and even shabbier new house, which was not so far away, Miguel had his own bedroom. The size allowed her to accommodate new acquaintances, so it soon became full of permanent guests and short-term visitors. Miguel didn't know who lived there and who didn't, all he knew is that his mother went out late at night and returned home between two and three o'clock in the morning with a different man. The first time this happened was two days after they moved in. He awoke at two o'clock in the morning to go to the bathroom, and when he came out, he saw his mother with another man, who was the same height as her, clean-shaven, with gelled black hair pushed back, wearing a bright turquoise t-shirt, tight jeans and sandals. He laughed at everything she said. The man waved at Miguel as he entered his mother's bedroom. Miguel lay on his back with his eyes wide open, and was forced to listen to their brief conversations, the sound of the rushed undressing, his mother begging for sex, the groaning, the muffled sound of relief, the voice of the man leaving her some money before leaving, and then his mother's loud snoring. Miguel was, for several weeks, distressed by these sounds, and he found it hard to sleep and work out what his mother was actually doing.

****

On one Saturday morning four months after they moved in, he spilt some milk on the floor in the kitchen and this aggravated his mother so much, that she sent him away for hours.

"Don't you dare show your face here! You can return at five o'clock and not before. And don't even think about going to the woods again or there will be real trouble."

When he came back, he went to his bedroom and was disgusted to see that other people had been using his bed, as the covers and sheets were more ruffled than how he had left them. He went downstairs and heard his mother call him from the kitchen.

"Miguel! Can you come here for a minute," she said.

Miguel was surprised to hear her call him by his name and hoped that she was not going to punish him again. He went into the kitchen and saw his mother looking terrible, she had not removed her make-up, she was dressed in some off-white pyjamas, her hair was all in disarray, and she stank of cigarettes.

"Sit down," she said. She lit a cigarette.

"Listen, I've had enough of staying here. I've been in touch with Maria, and we're going back to Milan in two days. The flight is booked."

She coughed and drank some coffee.

"I'll be working with another family as Leticia and Angelo were thrown out of Ben and Nicole's apartment. They accused them of stealing. Bastards! Anyway, they've gone back home for the time being."

Miguel didn't know what to say. His prayers had been answered.

"Thank you for letting me know," he said politely.

He wanted to kiss and embrace her, but he knew better. She would probably push him away.

"Off you go!" she said impatiently.

Miguel was now the happiest boy in the world, and he couldn't wait to tell his school friends and Pablo that he was leaving. He wouldn't miss school at all, but he would miss playing football with Pablo, and he would always remember their adventure in the woods and looking at the stunning sunset.

Three

When they arrived at the tram stop, Ana hurriedly walked towards Maria's apartment, pulling Miguel behind her. Miguel was thrilled with the prospect of seeing Maria again so much that the previous evening he had mentioned her name in nearly every sentence, and by doing so, Ana flipped and threw a glass at him which landed forcefully on the right side of his head, leaving a trail of blood. His wailing had infuriated his mother even more, so she shouted at him to be quiet, or she would throw another glass at him.

When they reached Maria's apartment, Ana warned Miguel not to say anything about his injury. As the door opened, Miguel slid through the gap and held onto Maria's legs so tightly that she nearly lost balance with the strength of his grip. He released her, and she opened the door fully to let Ana in. Maria, dressed in a beautiful grey business suit and wearing a silver necklace, greeted Ana and looked at Miguel and saw a streak of dark red clotted blood on the right side of his head and a black eye.

"What's happened?" she asked him.

"Nothing," he murmured. If he told Maria what had really happened, she might have reprimanded his mother, and this meant that her temperament would have been aroused again, and goodness knows what she would have done to him.

Maria glanced at Ana, and thought that it would make matters worse if she accused her of hurting her son, so she asked her to take a seat whilst she took Miguel into the bathroom. After closing the door behind her, she asked Miguel to sit on a small stool, and she washed her hands. Miguel looked into the mirror in front of the basin and saw what the black eye looked like and turned away.

"Does it hurt?"

"Yes, very much."

She went into a drawer and pulled out a flannel, a packet of plasters, a tube of antiseptic cream and some cotton wool. She doused the flannel in cold water and gently placed it on his head, and he flinched in pain. She then massaged some damp cotton wool around the wound to remove the dried blood and applied the antiseptic cream onto the cut itself and then placed a plaster on top.

"Does that feel better?"

"Yes, thank you, Signora."

"Hang on, we haven't finished yet. We need that eye sorting out as well."

Maria took another soft flannel and soaked it in cold water and held it onto his eye to reduce the swelling.

They went back to the sitting room, where Ana was sitting impatiently.

"I don't know why you fuss about him so much."

Maria offered her some tea, which she accepted, and Miguel accompanied Maria into the kitchen.

"Can I help you, Signora?"

Maria made a cup of tea for Ana and asked Miguel to take it to her, and then they sat down on one of the sofas.

"So, you decided to come back to Milan."

"Yeah. Some of my relatives and I didn't see eye to eye," she replied.

"I see," replied Maria. "Where are you working and living now?"

"In a house near Porta Venezia. A Lebanese family owns it. I do the cleaning."

Ana sighed and took out a packet of cigarettes.

"Sorry Ana, you can't smoke here."

Ana put the cigarette packet away and rolled her eyes.

"We couldn't go back to your family, could we? They didn't steal anything! Bastards! You already know about this, of course, but you didn't do anything. Angelo and Leticia are not thieves! Do you really think they would take jewellery from your brother's wife?"

"Where are they now?" asked Maria.

"After they were arrested, they went back to Cape Verde. I warned them against this, but they didn't have any choice, did they? And this is thanks to you and your rich family."

There was an uneasy silence. Ana took a few sips of tea.

"So why have you come to visit me?" asked Maria.

"I want to talk about the child."

Maria asked Miguel, who had been sitting still, to follow her to the guest bedroom, which was not as empty as the last time. There were some fashion magazines and a table lamp on the desk, the bed had a chequered blue and black cover and pillow, and the shelves in the cupboard were full of books and photograph albums.

"Why don't you get some rest? We won't be long," said Maria.

"Of course, Signora," said Miguel.

Maria gave him a comforting smile, closed the door and went back to the sitting room. Miguel looked around the room and felt at home here. It could be his room, he thought, but that was just a dream. He was now living with Bilal and Malak, and their six children, who were friendly enough even though he didn't understand what they were saying, but they never had time for him, not like Ben, Nicole and Maria. He shared a dark, windowless room with his mother, which was terrible because he was scared about what she might do to him if she woke up in the middle of the night when he was sleeping. It was bad enough having nightmares about her chasing him with a knife or trying to attack him with a hammer. He skimmed through one of the fashion magazines, but they didn't interest him, so he went inside one of the cupboards and took out a photograph album, sat on the bed and looked at the old black and white photographs of Maria and her family. Then he stood up and opened the door just a little so he could hear what his mother and Maria were saying about him.

"So, what do you want to talk about?" asked Maria.

"I'll get to the point. I've had enough of him. He's always with me, like a leech, trailing behind me wherever I go, slowing me down. He doesn't do what I tell him to do, causes trouble and gets in the way of what I want to do. I don't have the energy to look after him anymore. But Signora, he's taken a liking to you, hasn't he? So maybe you could look after him."

"You mean permanently?" asked Maria.

"Yes, of course, I mean permanently," said Ana.

Maria had never imagined taking care of a child and wondered if she could give Miguel a future, a good future, the right future. She knew it would change her life completely and she didn't know whether she could be a good mother or not, and here was Ana asking for an answer right away. She needed time.

"Well, this is the first time I've ever seen you without words, Signora," said Ana, patronizingly.

"Well, I have to say that it has come as a bit of a shock."

"What's there to think about? You like him, and he likes you. It can't be simpler. It's a win-win for all of us."

"Let's do this. Let him stay with me for a few days and see how we fit in with each other. I would also like to ask my brother and sister-in-law to get their opinion."

"That suits me fine. I'll leave you to figure it all out with your family," said Ana sarcastically, wearied by Maria's business-like manner. She stood up, made her way to the door and left.

Miguel was over the moon when he heard he could stay at Maria's and sleep in his dream bedroom. In the morning, he went into the kitchen and saw Maria talking about food with a small plumpish lady.

"Good morning, sweetheart! This is Signora Elisa. She'll be looking after you today. I'm going to work, and then I'll go and see Uncle Ben and Aunty Nicole."

Miguel's eyes lit up.

"Can I come with you?" he asked

Maria smiled.

"Not this time. But we will go another time, for sure. I promise you."

Miguel looked disappointed, so she patted him on his head and left.

After work in the late afternoon, Maria went to see Ben and Nicole to talk about Ana's proposal.

"I think it's preposterous!" exclaimed Ben. "How on earth will you have the time to look after him?"

"We could look after him. We could get him a nanny and send him to a boarding school," said Nicole.

"No, that's not the point. We can't manage him either. I know he looks sweet and there is a likeable mischievousness about him. But think about the huge responsibility. And ask yourself if you can realistically give him the attention he needs to adapt and live here."

"I see what you mean, Ben. I feel so sorry for him. I just feel we are his only chance," said Maria.

Ben lit a cigar, took a sip of gin and tonic, and looked into the air, thinking about the choice they had to make.

"Listen. Consider the red tape and all the approvals. We have passports from Israel, and he has a passport from Cape Verde. The authorities will never allow it," said Ben.

"We can always check. I have some friends who work for the Comune di Milano. They will be able to advise us," said Maria.

"Even if they approve, remember he is African or from African descent. They're different from us, and he could be exposed to all kinds of trouble, such as racist attacks and bullying at school. He's already behind with school so he'll probably be teased for that as well. Maria, there is an alternative. He could go back to Cape Verde and stay with one of the many relatives he no doubt has out there. Honey, what do you think?" asked Ben.

"Ben's right. He's very sweet, but he's very sweet now. What about when he reaches fifteen or sixteen. What will he be like then? You know, when they left for Portugal, it did cross my mind to persuade Ana to leave him with us, but I was afraid of the commitment we would have, and I wasn't sure that we could offer him the right life," said Nicole.

Maria could not bear to think of Miguel alone and imagined his look of despair if he had to leave her again. He trusted her, and her heart told her that she should probably take the risk and take him into her custody as she was the only one who could give him a life.

"Maria." Ben placed his hand on her shoulder. "We all want the best for you. You know that. It's up to you whether you take him or not. We just wanted you to be aware of the many hurdles."

Maria smiled and thanked them. On her way home, she thought about how guilty she would feel if she didn't take him in. Yet there was a nagging thought that she should follow what seemed the most reasonable thing to do, given the circumstances, and let him go.

When she arrived home, Miguel ran up to her and talked excitedly about all the things he had done with Elisa. They had been for a walk in Navigli, had lunch at home and played cards but Maria wasn't listening, and Elisa could see that something was bothering her.

"Are you alright, Signora?"

"Yes, I'm fine, thank you. Just a little tired."

Maria woke up several times during the night, playing different futures in her mind. The sleeplessness became intolerable so she left her room on tiptoes and went onto the balcony to look up at the stars and full moon, hoping that the answer would come from them. She heard light footsteps coming towards her. Miguel had woken up.

"Please Signora, could I have some water?"

Interrupting her trance, Maria looked back at him and poured some cold water from the bottle in the fridge into a glass. He drank it all at once and placed it on the small pull-out table.

"Please Signora. I don't want to leave again. I'm happy here, and I don't want to stay with my mother. I want to stay with you."

The following day on her way to work, she paid another visit to Ben and Nicole to let them know her decision. Nicole thought she was deluded and had not properly thought it through, whereas Ben was more understanding. On her way home, she repeatedly played back Nicole's words, "On your head be it!" and Ben's words, "It'll be all right. We'll help you."

She went shopping with Miguel to buy some summer clothes and swimming gear. In each shop, she asked him to go into a small changing room and threw clothes over the door for him to try on. Eventually, he became impatient and said that he had had enough, but she persisted because she wanted him to look good. On the way home, she could hardly see outside the back window, as she had put all the bags full of clothes on the back seats, with Miguel sandwiched between them. When they got back to the apartment, Miguel looked at Maria in astonishment as she unpacked the bags full of pyjamas, swimming trunks, sport shoes, sandals, t-shirts, short trousers, long trousers, sunglasses, hats, caps and light pullovers. Never had he seen so many clothes in his life.

Miguel was startled when he saw the blurred image of Maria becoming sharper when she woke him at five o'clock in the morning the next day. He sat up and saw her dressed in sporty summer clothes. There was not a moment to lose, as Maria had prepared his clothes neatly on the desk, ran him a bath, made him a cup of milk and placed some biscuits on a plate.

"Where are we going, Signora?"

"It's a surprise. You'll love it!"

Three hours later, Maria was driving around some windy roads on a hillside with views of the sea, and Miguel wound down the window to feel the sea breeze as they passed the many bays with stony beaches.

They ascended and parked next to a small sandy coloured building, then Maria opened the car door, and Miguel leapt out and looked out onto the offing. He hadn't seen the sea for a long time, and his memories of his grandmother taking him to the coast on São Nicolau were sketchy. He remembered being petrified by the violent black and choppy waves crashing onto the coastal rocks, yet here the sea was much calmer, and the water near the beach had a lucid, turquoise colour.

Maria opened the door to the apartment, and they entered a dark living room with a kitchenette. She opened the shutters and blinds and went outside and brought the suitcases inside.

"You must be hungry! Would you like some pasta?"

"Yes, please, Signora. Where are we?"

"We're in Camogli. It's a small town in Liguria. We're going to stay here for the summer. Would you like that?"

"Yes! Can we go to the sea?"

"Of course, we can! After lunch, we'll go to the sea and have a walk. I'll introduce you to some friends as well!"

Maria parked the car close to a hotel, which was on the left side of the bay. She took Miguel by the hand and they went up some wooden steps, which led to a long decking overlooking the sea where there were ten small cabins, impregnated into the rocks. Striped brown and yellow shades covered the wooden tables and benches, and at the end of the decking, there was a restaurant. Miguel went to the edge and looked down at the shore at the sunbathers lying on inflatable boats, and at others who were snorkelling, splashing each other or playing water polo. At the end of the bay, a tall pink campanile rose above the surrounding buildings. Below the cross, there was a belfry and four clock faces. Pastel coloured buildings were adjoined to both sides of the church, and in the background stood three momentous mountains. Maria unlocked the door to the cabin and Miguel went inside to put his swimming trunks on. When he came out, he sat on one of the benches and whilst Maria was smothering sun cream on his back, he saw two grown-ups and a child coming out of the restaurant towards them. Maria stood up and greeted them.

"This must be Miguel," said the slim woman with dark brown hair. "Now I understand what you were saying about him."

"Yes, he's a good boy," said Maria.

"Is he here for good? Are you looking after him now?" asked the man with long blonde hair and oval brown eyes.

"I think so. We just have to manage the paperwork," replied Maria.

"That's wonderful news! I'm so happy for you. Let's celebrate this evening. You must come for dinner at our place," said the woman.

"Okay. That would be very nice. Thank you."

"Miguel. Let me introduce you to Sara, Alessandro and Mario," said Maria.

"Can we go to the beach now?" said Mario impatiently. Mario resembled his father, but Alessandro was considerably portlier.

"Yes, we're going right now. Miguel, would you like to come with us?" asked Alessandro.

Miguel nodded shyly.

"I'll take Miguel with us. You two ladies can stay here if you want. I'm sure you have lots to catch up on, right?"

Alessandro took some towels and a ball from their cabin and took the children onto the beach.

At dinner, Alessandro opened up a bottle of champagne, but he didn't notice Maria's uneasiness at the presumptuous celebration, and he toasted Maria and Miguel's future and good health, and Sara served the gnocchi and pesto sauce.

"So, what did you two get up to at the beach?" Sara asked.

"We played water polo, and I won!" exclaimed Miguel.

"No. That's not right! It was a draw!" replied Mario.

"Come on boys! Don't start arguing," said Sara.

"I was teaching Miguel how to swim!" said Alessandro.

"Oh. Thank you. I was going to send him to swimming lessons," said Maria

"He's a natural. Within a week, he'll be winning races," exaggerated Alessandro.

Over the next four weeks, Alessandro took Mario and Miguel to the beach every day. In the evenings after dinner, they would go for walks to see the magnificent boats in the harbour, then would wander along the seafront and would stop by a gelateria.

Miguel and Mario became inseparable friends. During dinner one evening, Miguel heard that Mario and his parents lived in the north of Milan and that Alessandro worked in a bank and Sara was a primary school teacher.

Maria brought her red motorboat and some snorkelling equipment on a day trip to the Cinque Terre, and Miguel and Mario looked in awe at the figure of Christ below the water. On their last day, they went to Portofino, and Maria treated them all to dinner at one of the finest restaurants.

Miguel didn't want to return to Milan, he loved the sea and being with his new best friend, but Maria promised him that they would see each other again and they will go back to Camogli soon. When they got home, Maria opened her post box, which was located in the hallway and sifted through all the letters to see if any of them looked more urgent than others. She stopped when she saw a letter with her address written in Ana's handwriting, and immediately opened it.

Maria – I tried to call and visit you, but I don't know where you and my son are. Please call me as soon as you get back. I have some news for you. Ana

Maria looked worried.

"What's wrong?" asked Miguel.

"Nothing, sweetheart! Are you going to help me to bring in all the bags?"

Four

Maria was unsettled about Ana's message and chose not to tell Miguel about it. Ana was unpredictable enough to change her mind about her taking custody of Miguel, and after all, no official documents had been signed or approved. She hoped she wasn't going to tell her that she wanted to return to Vialonga with him. Maria arranged for Miguel to visit Mario and his parents on the same day that she had made an appointment to see Ana, and she postponed two customer meetings so she could see her as soon as possible.

Maria kept looking at her watch, as Ana was already twenty minutes late. When she did arrive, she was accompanied by a large muscular man who was almost twice her height, and he had a much darker skin tone and a permanent inane grin on his face. Maria looked up at him and raised her voice so that he could hear her.

"Good afternoon. I'm Maria. Pleased to meet you!"

"Pleased to meet you too. I'm Antonio. I've heard all about you," he replied.

Maria asked them to come into the sitting room and sit down. "Can I get you anything to drink or eat?"

"Just some water," replied Ana.

Maria went into the kitchen and poured cold water

into two glasses and went back to the sitting room, where she found Ana snugly sat next to Antonio with her minuscule hand on his knee. It appeared as though they had given a great deal of thought about having matching coloured clothes. Ana was wearing a revealing yellow blouse, miniskirt and black high-heeled shoes, and Antonio was wearing a tight-fitting bright yellow t-shirt with yellow shorts and flip flops. Maria wanted to tell him that he was in the middle of Milan and not on the beach, but she didn't, and she had to restrain herself from laughing at the comical incongruity of seeing them together.

"Antonio's my fiancé," Ana proclaimed, looking provocatively at Maria.

"Well, that is wonderful news! I'm very happy for you."

"He's also from São Nicolau, and we're going to live together in Veneto. We're going to do the cooking and cleaning for an Italian family."

"Good for you! That family must be very lucky to have you!" said Maria.

Antonio was staring at Maria, as though he was expecting her to contradict what Ana was saying. They finished drinking the water, and then Ana opened her small brown handbag and took out a document.

"Here!"

Ana stood up, stretched out her arm and handed it to Maria.

"I've been to the local government. They're all bastards, making us wait hours and hours. I explained the situation to them. I explained you are from

Romania and you have residency here. I explained that my son is from Cape Verde. They say it is possible for you to take custody of the child, but we need to go together to the local government with passports and other papers. On the piece of paper, it tells you what you must bring with you. We have an appointment at eleven o'clock next Thursday. You will be free?"

"Of course. I will make myself available."

Maria took out her spectacles from a small case and started to read the document.

"You don't need to read it all now. It gives you a headache. Believe me. I also have one. In any case, don't make any meetings with your customers on that day, as we will probably be there for hours. Then we have to wait weeks and weeks for approval. You see what the Italian system is like!"

Maria lifted her head.

"Very well. We'll meet next week."

****

The following Thursday, Ana and Maria were interviewed in separate rooms, and it reminded Maria of the time she had been interrogated by a Russian soldier years ago. Two representatives from the local government asked her questions about her background, her family, her residency, marital status and employment. And they went on to question her on how she would educate a young child from a different culture, and how she would integrate him into Italian society. When Maria told them that she was divorced, one of the representatives frowned and scribbled some notes on his pad. Once the interview came to an end, the representative took some documents from Maria and informed her that the duration of the approval process would be approximately three months. In the meantime, someone would visit her to check if her home was adequate for the boy to live there.

****

Maria thought that the best way for Miguel to become more accustomed to Italian culture would be to attend a boarding school during the day and come home for the weekends. She realised that she could not look after him all the time as she had started to go to Paris on business trips more frequently. She knew that this detachment during the week would upset him and, as he was so behind with schoolwork, he would need to get used to being in a class where his fellow pupils were two years younger than him.

"Would you like some more?"

Miguel eyed the spaghetti with seafood.

"Yes please, Signora."

"Next week, you're going to start a new school!"

"No! I don't like school. It's boring."

"Well, all the other children are going to school. Mario is also going to school. You don't want to be left out, do you? And you'll get to meet other friends, and play football with them!"

Miguel lightened up at the thought of playing football with other children.

"During the week, you're going to stay in a dormitory with other children, and I'll pick you up on

Friday after school, so you'll spend the weekends with me," she continued.

Miguel didn't want to be separated from Maria again, and maybe she wouldn't return for him, and he would be left alone.

"No, that's not fair! You're leaving me again."

He threw his fork across the kitchen and burst into tears. Maria stood up and held him in her arms.

"Why are you leaving me? I don't want you to leave me!"

She looked at him and held his shoulders.

"Listen, sweetheart. I will never leave you. I love you so much. Trust me. It will be good for you. And I will come to get you every weekend. What about some ice-cream?" asked Maria.

She leapt off her chair and went into the freezer, and Miguel wiped his tears away with his arm and looked forward to the dessert.

Five

A week before Christmas, the approved documents arrived, and Maria held them close to her chest as if letting go of them would forfeit their validity. She was almost certain that Ana's disdain for Miguel and lack of financial stability would have made the decision to entrust him to her an easy one.

On the last day of term, Maria went to pick Miguel up from school. She stood by the car and smiled as she watched him appear from the school entrance, surrounded by friends all wishing him a merry Christmas.

"We'll beat you next term! You'll see!" shouted one of the boys.

"No, you won't. You'll never beat us!" said Miguel.

Miguel knew that Maria was waiting for him, but he had something important to do before he went home, otherwise he would regret it. The slim, blonde girl, who he had relentlessly tried to get to notice him, was standing alone waiting for her parents to arrive, so he ran up to her.

"Merry Christmas, Antonella!"

"Merry Christmas to you, Miguel!" she said and gave him a kiss on his cheek, the best Christmas present of all time.

When they arrived home, a monumental Christmas tree adorned with homemade baubles and different coloured lights with presents around the base was waiting for him.

"Can I open them now?"

"It's not Christmas yet! Why don't you go and have a wash? I'll make dinner."

Miguel headed towards the bathroom.

"Hang on a minute! Can you give me your school report?" Maria called out to him.

Miguel went back into the sitting room, and plucked a sealed envelope from the clothes and books in his bag, and gave it to her. Whilst he was in the bath, Maria sat on the sofa and opened the envelope with her silver letter-opener, and put on her spectacles. Once she had finished reading the grades and the teachers' comments for each subject, she sighed, folded the report in half, placed it on the coffee table, and wondered what she would say to him.

She had prepared some risotto, and they sat opposite each other on the small pull-out table in the kitchen. Miguel was happy to be back home with Maria, but he missed the comradery at school.

"How were the last days of term?"

"They were great! We had our final match, and we won!"

Miguel's eyes lit up as he relived how he scored three consecutive goals, the speed and the manoeuvres, and the icing on the cake was winning the medal after the final match. Somehow, he had been coerced into being one of the kings in the nativity play, which was not as electrifying as the football by any means, but he had made the rehearsals more fun by having water fights between the three kings, dressed in golden robes, and Joseph and Mary. The headteacher had reprimanded him for slowing down the rehearsals and asked him if he really wanted to play the part of one of the kings or not.

"Listen, sweetheart. I've just read your school report. I'm so pleased that you've made new friends and that you're good at football. But you need to take the other subjects more seriously. Your teacher told me that you mess around a lot, and your grades are below average, except for English."

"They're all boring. And I don't like the maths teacher because he keeps shouting at me."

"Yes, but why is he shouting at you? It's because you're misbehaving and he's there to teach you. And the headteacher told me that you haven't been to many of the maths lessons. The art teacher sent you to see the headteacher after you were caught flicking paint at one of the other pupils."

Miguel laughed, "That was hilarious!"

Maria put her fork down on her plate and looked at him earnestly.

"It's not funny, sweetheart. You need to study these subjects so that one day you'll be able to get a job and earn money. And I understand most of the other children have better marks. So, will you try harder next term, for me?"

"Okay, I'll try. Can I go and watch television?"

He slid off his stool and went to the sitting room whilst Maria remained at the table with her head in her hands, asking herself what she could do to encourage him to study more.

On Christmas Eve, they loaded the presents into the car and drove to Ben and Nicole's apartment. Inside the sitting room, glitter hung above every window and there was an even bigger Christmas tree in the corner. When Miguel went into the dining room, he sat down next to Maria and saw two young men opposite him, who he had never seen before.

"These are our two sons, David and Robert! They're both studying medicine in London, and they've come home for the holidays," said Nicole.

The two waitresses hurriedly entered the dining room with a trolley and placed bowls of vegetables and pasta on the table and returned with a large oblong plate with a huge salmon on it.

"Hmm. That smells good! Do you like fish, Miguel?" asked David.

"Yes!"

"You must be so proud of your boys," said Maria.

"Yes, we are. David's now in his fourth year, and Robert will finish his second year in June," said Nicole.

"I'm sure you are having a lot of fun! Best time of your life!" exclaimed Ben.

"It's intense. It's not easy at all. No matter how many hours of research we do, the professors always find ways to criticise our essays and dissertations. And the worst part is when we have practice sessions in the hospital, and they pick on one of us when they ask us to diagnose a patient's symptoms. And when we get it wrong, the professors and doctors take pleasure in humiliating us in front of the others. It's not fun at all," said Robert.

"Come on, Robert! It never bothered David. Think about it. You have five years of study. You don't have to think about earning money and making a living. You attend lectures, write essays, take exams and party at the weekend. What could be better?"

"You never went to university, so how do you know?" retorted Robert.

"Help yourselves everybody!" interrupted Nicole.

David lightened up the conversation with a story about having made an arrangement to meet a French girl at a party.

"I had been playing indoor soccer with some friends, then we went for drinks, and I got so drunk that I mistakenly took an American girl for the French girl I planned to meet. I got chatting with her, and we went dancing all night, and I gave her my number. The morning after, I woke up with a terrible hangover and she called me to go for coffee, and it was then I realised from her American accent that I had not been dancing with the French girl at all, so I made an excuse not to meet her, saying I had to study. Anyway, on the way to the library, I bumped into the French girl walking in the opposite direction, but she didn't even look at me."

"You see!" said Ben. "That's what I call having fun!" he laughed, and so did Nicole and Maria.

Once they had finished eating, Miguel asked, "Signora Maria, please could I have some more fish?"

"Of course! What an appetite you have!" said Maria, and took the tweezers and pulled off a piece of soft, flaky salmon and put it on Miguel's plate.

"He's such a polite boy!" said Nicole.

Maria glanced at Ben and then looked at Miguel.

"Listen, sweetheart. You don't have to call me Signora Maria. You can call me Mamma." "Okay, Mamma!"

"And why don't we call him Michele, instead of Miguel? It's better for him if he is to make Italy his home. It will help him fit in," suggested Ben.

"What do you think?" asked Maria gently.

Miguel nodded his head.

"So, let's go and open some presents, Michele!"

They went into the sitting room, and Michele opened his presents: toy cars, a new football, more swimming gear, action men, and writing paper. He played with the cars whilst the others opened their presents.

At half-past eleven, Maria got ready to leave and gave Michele his coat.

"What do you say to Uncle Ben and Aunty Nicole?" asked Maria.

"Thank you for dinner. It was delicious. And thank you for the presents."

"I'll help you put the presents in the car," said Robert.

"Thank you. That's a huge help. We're going to midnight mass now."

"I see. You better hurry up, as you don't have much time. And it will be hard to park at this time of night."

Six

"Michele! Michele! Wake up! We have to leave in half an hour!"

"Can't we go later, Mamma? I'm still sleepy."

"No, darling. We need to avoid the traffic. Come on, I've prepared breakfast for you!"

"Okay. Give me a few more minutes."

"I know you. You'll go back to sleep. We're going to Uncle Ben and Aunty Nicole's villa in Lake Garda. Remember?"

"Can't we go skiing? You promised me we would go to the mountains."

"Yes, yes. We will go to the mountains. Just not now. Your uncle and aunt have invited us to stay. And if we arrive on time, Uncle Ben will take you for a drive in his new car."

Michele had become obsessed with cars since he received some toy ones for Christmas, so the thought of getting into a new car with Uncle Ben made him get out of bed. With blurry eyes, he went into the kitchen, drank a glass of cold milk and ate some chocolate biscuits, whilst Maria packed a small suitcase for him.

"Who will be there, Mamma?"

"The whole family will be there. And you will get to meet my sister, Aunty Iona, and her husband and daughter."

"What about David and Robert?"

"They will be there as well. We're going to be celebrating Passover, which is a Jewish holiday."

"What's Passover?"

"You'll see. "

Michele occupied himself in the back of the car, playing with the toy cars and make crashing noises as they collided. The automatic gridiron opened slowly, then Maria drove down a narrow road with neatly cut hedges on either side. She peeped her horn at the two gardeners who were busy trimming the leaves and opened the car window to greet them and let them know that she would be staying for a week. Further down the road, there was an opening which led to the villa. The car crunched over the pebbles and Maria parked her car between a mountain blue Lamborghini and a black Porsche.

Michele was in awe of the size of the villa, and its fantastical semblance reminded him of the castles and palaces in fairy tales and adventure books that he had read at school. Ben, who was dressed in short beige trousers and a white t-shirt, came down the steps from the front door and embraced Maria.

"It's a lovely day!" he remarked. "We're planning to go to the lake after lunch."

Maria opened the back door to let Michele out.

"Hello, Uncle Ben!"

"Welcome to Lake Garda, Michele!"

He rustled Michele's hair affectionately, took the suitcases from Maria, and they went inside.

Michele looked at, what seemed to be, a labyrinth of corridors and he never imagined he would ever see a place grander than Ben and Nicole's apartment in Milan. Inside the sitting room, Michele went to the French windows and looked at the immense orchard with apple, lemon and orange trees. Noticing Michele's fascination, David took him outside and showed him where potatoes, zucchini and green beans were being grown. They then went into the greenhouse to look at the tomatoes.

"You're growing your own vegetables?"

"Yes! They're much tastier and fresher. Here, look at this!"

David took a small packet of seeds from one of the shelves and poured a few of them onto Michele's hand.

"We plant these in the ground, and they become zucchini. We have to put some pesticides on the soil so that the bugs don't get to them."

"Do you do this all by yourself?"

"No, not at all! We have gardeners to help us."

"How many gardeners do you have?"

"Ten. It's a big place. They have to attend to different lawns, the trees, bushes, hedges, and plants. And you know Aunty Nicole, she's a perfectionist, so she likes everything in place."

"I see. Can I help next time you plant the seeds?"

"Yes, of course."

The others had made themselves comfortable in the sitting room. There were glasses of white wine and nuts on the side tables.

"We have a new gardener, Mamma!" said David, putting his hand on Michele's shoulder.

"Well, in that case, we can fire Eduardo. He's not doing such a good job, and Michele can take his place!"

"Mamma, look what David has given me!" Michele showed Maria the seeds, which he had clenched in his hands.

"A gardener and a football player!" exclaimed Ben.

"Well, it's better than doing nothing. If he becomes a professional footballer, he'll make a lot of money!" said Samuel.

"Let's not get carried away. He's only eight years old," said Nicole.

"This is Aunty Iona, Uncle Samuel and Ruth," Maria said.

Iona had wavy black hair, large brown eyes and pale skin, and she was wearing a loose-fitting light green dress. Samuel, who was smaller, had brown hair and was wearing sky blue trousers and a white short-sleeved shirt. Ruth looked like her mother, having the same stature and hairstyle but slightly more tanned and she was wearing tight jeans and a light pink blouse.

Michele went up to them and gave each one a hug and two kisses on their cheeks.

"He's already Italian. Welcome sweetheart! We've heard so much about you. We couldn't wait to see you. How are you doing at school?" asked Iona.

"I like football, running and the girls. But I don't like any of the other subjects, especially maths. Maths is boring. And I don't like the teachers very much either. They keep shouting at me."

"A lady's boy!" exclaimed Ben. "That is funny. He will fit in as a professional footballer."

"That's enough," replied Nicole, glaring at Ben.

"Come here, sweetheart," Nicole said softly. "Listen, I know you are good at football. But you need to pay attention to the other subjects as well."

"Okay, I'll try," he said.

"Have you spoken to the teachers?" Nicole asked Maria.

"Yes, I have. They say the same. No problems with settling in and making friends. But he can't seem to sit still in the classroom and keeps messing around and playing jokes on his classmates and the teachers."

Ben burst out laughing.

"Shut up, Ben. This is no laughing matter. You're just making it worse!" shouted Nicole.

Robert was looking serious. Next to his glass of wine was a thick hardback medical book with a bookmark protruding from the middle.

"Robert, why are you so quiet?" asked Iona.

"He's got exams next term, and he can't think about anything else. He's probably going through all the parts of the body as we speak," said David flippantly.

"Well, you've got exams as well, David," said Nicole.

"Yes, I have. I'm taking this week to rest and from next week, I'll be back in London."

"When are you going back to London, Robert?" asked Iona.

"Straight after Passover."

"So soon?"

"Yes, I have to revise. The exams are extremely hard. This afternoon, I'm going to study after lunch when you go to the lake."

"I'm sure you can afford to come to the lake with us."

"Sorry, aunty, but I have to study."

"You should take it easy!" suggested David.

"Take it easy!" Roberto said aggressively. "What is easy about a degree in medicine?"

"Let's go and have some lunch!" said Nicole.

Everyone stood up and went into the bright, rustic dining room, which had white walls with no pictures, and there was a high ceiling. The four cooks brought in bruschetta, matzo and insalata caprese.

After lunch, they made preparations to go to the lake.

"Are you coming with me?" asked Ben.

"Yes, of course! Which car are we going in?" asked Michele.

"Either the Porsche or the Lamborghini. It's up to you. Would you like to see them first?"

"Yes, definitely."

"You're spoiling him too much!" said Maria, smiling.

"Not at all. He needs to get used to this when he becomes a professional footballer."

Maria rolled her eyes, and Michele followed Ben outside.

"If we go in the Porsche today, can we go in the Lamborghini tomorrow?"

"Of course!"

"Is Mamma coming to the lake as well?"

"Yes, they're all coming. But we'll be the first to arrive," said Ben.

Michele liked the idea of coming first.

"You know, Mamma and Aunty Nicole have a point. You need to study other subjects to be successful. I know it's hard, but keep trying," said Ben as he was driving.

"But the teachers hate me!"

"No, they don't hate you. It's okay to joke sometimes, but if you show them you are taking the subjects seriously, they'll be impressed. They're there to help you. Just don't make their life difficult by fooling around the whole time. I was a bit like you at school. I liked playing football. I had loads of friends, and I dated girls, but I knew I had to take school seriously."

"Yes. I suppose you're right, Uncle Ben. I'll give it a shot."

"It's better for you. You'll be fine."

They stepped out of the car, took the bags and deck chairs out of the boot. As they were making their way to the beach, Michele saw three teenagers staring at them.

"Don't take any notice of them! They're jealous of the fine car we have."

When they found a good place to sit, Michele looked at the still water in front of him. "It's like the sea but with no waves,"

"Well, it's not always like that. There are waves, but they tend to be gentler than the ones you find in the sea. There are loads of windsurfers who come here, but I'm afraid there's not much wind today."

When the others arrived, they lay down on the deckchairs and sunbathed whilst David and Michele played volleyball. It was not long before two boys went up to them and asked if they could play too, so Gianni joined Michele, and Tommaso joined David. They played a set of ten, and Michele was riled when David and Tommaso won, so he kicked the ball into the lake. David shook his head, and walked back to his family whilst Michele and Gianni ran into the water to collect the ball. Michele was determined to get the ball before Gianni so he could at least win something, so he swam with all his might, then dipped his head under the water and reappeared with the ball in his hand.

"I won! I won!" said Michele proudly.

They returned to the shore and sat on the beach with Tommaso.

"So where are you from?" asked Gianni.

Michele felt uneasy in the way Gianni asked him the question, somehow it felt like more than a curiosity, so he didn't reply.

"Is that your family over there?" Gianni persisted.

"Yes, it is. "

"You must be very rich. I saw you coming out of the Porsche with someone."

"He's my uncle. My mother is the one sleeping over there. She's the one on the blue deck chair."

"What are you doing here?" asked Tommaso.

"My uncle owns a villa nearby, so we're staying with him and my aunt for a week."

"A villa!" exclaimed Tommaso. "You must be filthy rich. Only film stars and football players can afford villas."

"Who told you that?"

"My mum said that all these posh houses and villas belong to film stars and professional football players."

Michele laughed. "Well, my uncle is not a football player or a film star."

"Then what does he do?"

"I don't know. He's a businessman."

"So is my Pappa. But he can't afford a villa."

"Where do you live?" asked Gianni.

"In an apartment with my mother in Milan," replied Michele.

"I bet it's huge."

"It's not that big."

"We also live in Milan."

"So why are you here?

"We came for the weekend. Tommaso and I go to the same school. We're staying in a hotel nearby."

"I see."

"You still haven't answered where you are from. Are you from Africa?" asked Tommaso.

Gianni sensed Michele's uneasiness, so he gave Tommaso a light push on his shoulder and threw the ball into the water again, and challenged Michele to another race. Michele leapt into the water, and even though Gianni had a head start, he managed to catch the ball again, and they trod water.

"Tommaso thinks too much. It's okay. You don't have to answer him. Listen, when we get back to the beach, I'll get Mamma to get your phone number from your Mamma, if that's okay. Then we can meet in Milan. There's an amazing swimming pool near my house so we can go there at the weekends if you're free."

"Will Tommaso be there as well?"

"Sometimes he comes with us. Once you get to know him, he's all right."

"Okay, let's do that!"

Tommaso went back to his parents, and Gianni dragged his mother towards Maria, who was engrossed in a thick novel. Maria looked up, and saw a skinny boy with a dark bronze complexion and blue swimming trunks, holding his mother's hand, urging her to move more quickly towards her.

"Good afternoon. Pleased to meet you. I'm Sandra. Gianni has been playing with Michele today and would love to see him again. I understand you also live in Milan," Gianni's mother said.

"Good afternoon, Sandra. I'm Maria. It's wonderful that Michele is making new friends. I'd love to spend more time with you, but we have to move back to our villa in a few minutes."

Maria reached for her mauve leather handbag and pulled out a pen and notebook, scribbled down her name and telephone number, and handed it to her.

"Call me any time you want. I'm sure Michele would like to see Gianni again."

Once they arrived back at the villa, the kitchen was full of chefs, preparing for the Seder. Ben took Michele into the kitchen and sat him on a stool.

"It's like this. Do you remember when Mamma took you to mass at Christmas?" asked Ben. Michele nodded.

"And you've been having lessons at school on religious education."

"Yes, I know what religion is."

"Well, I think Mamma already told you that we are Jewish. We pray to the same God, but we have different traditions and celebrations. So today, we are celebrating Passover with Seder. There is a certain order to the foods we eat, and it represents the Jewish people moving from slavery to freedom, according to the Book of Exodus."

Michele was perplexed, but he decided it best not to ask more questions.

"And if you're really good, I'll let you read from the Haggadah!"

"What's that?"

"It's a mixture of things. It contains prayers and songs, and includes the meaning of the food that we eat."

Later that evening, they took it in turns to read parts of the Haggadah and congratulated Michele after he had flawlessly recited a prayer.

****

Over the next five days, they went to the lake every afternoon, so that Michele could play football and volleyball with Tommaso and Gianni. He was reluctant to leave the villa and his new friends, but he was happy that Maria had reassured him that he would meet them again in Milan.

On the way back, there was a traffic accident on the road, so Maria entertained Michele with some word games to pass the time. They arrived home late, so

Maria left the luggage unpacked in the entrance hall, and they went straight to bed.

Whilst they were having breakfast the following morning, the telephone rang. Maria ran to the living room.

"Good morning, Signora," said Ana.

"Ana. Good morning. How are you?" asked Maria.

"I'm not so good."

"What's wrong? Have you finished with your boyfriend? Did you lose your job?"

"I'm not very well. I've got flu and cramps. I've also been sick many times, and I think I might be pregnant. Antonio suggested I contact you to get your help. And I'd like to see my son."

Seven

Ana had taken the intercity train from Veneto to Milan, and when she arrived at Maria's apartment, she was hardly recognizable. She was wearing a shabby, green dress. Her greasy hair was awry, and she had tired eyes. It was obvious that she hadn't had a wash as her overpowering body odour smothered the pleasant smell of coffee coming from the kitchen.

"Michele! Your mother's here."

Maria beckoned Ana to have a seat in the sitting room. Michele didn't want to be in the same room as her as he didn't feel safe. He remembered every word she had said about him on that bus going from Lisbon to Vialonga, and he remembered how afraid he was of her, especially when she was about to punish him. He nervously came inside and saw his mother giving him a faint smile, something he had always longed for.

"You've grown, haven't you?" said Ana.

Michele didn't say anything. He sat down next to Maria and looked into his mother's drained eyes and felt sorry for her. He told her about his visit to the villa, his time at school, and Christmas, but she wasn't listening. She put her head in her hands and sobbed.

"Go and get her a tissue, Michele. There's one over there on the table," said Maria.

"I'm so sorry," said Ana.

"Michele, why don't you go and get your things from your room? I'm going to drop you off at Uncle Ben's, whilst I take your mother to the hospital," said Maria.

"I'd like to take Miguel to Veneto for the weekend," said Ana.

"You know that's not possible, Ana. You may remember that the agreement states that he cannot be left alone with you."

"But I've changed!" Ana insisted, sniffling with tears in her eyes.

"That may be. But I'm afraid that it's not possible."

Ana looked away and up to the ceiling, wondering what had become of her life.

"Miguel, please write to me when you get a minute, I just want to know how you are. I don't want to lose you," said Ana, when they reached Ben and Nicole's apartment.

"Okay. I will."

He had never seen his mother looking so fragile, so he smiled at her as he left the car.

In the hospital, they had to wait for two hours before a gynaecologist was available to examine Ana. The waiting time was rather awkward as Maria didn't wish to talk to her, so she immersed herself in a newspaper whilst Ana looked into space or slept. Finally, a slim lady with a white overcoat called Ana's name, and she stood up and followed her into the surgery. Half an hour later, the gynaecologist called for Maria, as Ana had named her as the next of kin.

"We've taken some blood tests, so the results should be ready next week or the week after. She's suffering from fatigue, and she's told me that she regularly consumes a lot of alcohol and smokes around fifty cigarettes a day. I understand her son is now under your responsibility. We conducted a pregnancy test, which showed positive. I'm concerned that due to Ana's poor health, the new baby may not make it. She would need to stop smoking and drinking, start eating sensibly and get some rest. The blood tests will show if there is anything else."

"Thank you, doctor," said Maria. "Is there any medication she needs to take?"

"We'll let you know once the blood test results come through."

When they left the doctor's surgery, Ana started crying uncontrollably, so Maria embraced her and patted her back.

"So, what will you do?" asked Maria.

"I'll go back to Veneto and come back in two weeks."

"You need to look after yourself, Ana. Please take note of what the doctor has said. Are you living in a nice place?"

"Oh yes. It's very comfortable."

"Then why are you so tired?"

"We usually go out after we've finished work and get back in the early hours of the morning."

"I see. But if you want this new baby, it would be a good idea to get some rest, and maybe not go out so often."

"Yeah. I suppose you're right. Can you drop me off at the train station?"

Once they reached Milano Centrale, Ana got out of the car and Maria wound down the window.

"Ana, please look after yourself. Call me if you need anything. And see you in two weeks. Let me know what time you arrive, and I'll pick you up from the station."

****

Ana came back two weeks later, and Maria picked her up from the station and was dismayed to see her in the same state as before. She hadn't given up smoking, drinking and going out late, but Maria didn't express her disapproval, she thought it was tragic to see such a determined person deteriorate.

The doctor told them that she had cirrhosis of the liver and prescribed some medication for her. He repeated the need to cut out cigarettes and alcohol if she wanted to get better and that there was a high risk of losing the baby. They left the hospital and Maria went to the pharmacy to get the medication, whilst Ana remained in the car. She then took her to the train station, parked the car, and accompanied her to the platform.

"I'm really worried about you, Ana," said Maria.

"Why should you be worried?"

"Well, it's clear to me that you're not looking after yourself and I don't want you to lose your baby."

"You don't care at all."

"Actually, I do care. You need to cut down on cigarettes and alcohol."

"It's my life. I'll do what I want."

The train arrived, and after the passengers got off, Ana went inside the carriage and didn't look back.

****

One day in July, a few days before they left for Camogli, Maria received a telephone call, which would seal Ana's fate. Maria was in the bathroom when the telephone rang, so she called out to Michele to answer it, as there was a telephone in his bedroom.

"Mamma. It's the police!"

Maria rushed to the telephone in the sitting room and picked up the receiver, unaware that Michele was also listening.

"Yes, Signore. How can I help?"

"We've been given this number regarding the boy, Miguel."

"Yes, so? What's happened?"

"His mother, Ana, has been arrested for stealing jewellery from the family she's been working for. She's been found guilty, and she'll be deported to Portugal. We thought it was right to let you know so that you can inform her son."

Michele was devastated. How could his mother do such a thing? He didn't know whether to be ashamed or sorry for her. He knew that he didn't hate her anymore and didn't know why he felt such a sense of loss with her leaving for Portugal.

Maria sighed and put the receiver down, and Michele came into the sitting room, looking miserable.

"You were listening, weren't you?"

Eight

One week after his thirteenth birthday, Michele went to Puglia with Gianni and his mother, whose sister lived there. He had never been to the south of Italy before, and when he accepted the invitation, he did not realise how long it would take to get there.

"Nine hours! Nine hours!" exclaimed Michele.

"Yes, nine hours! Now hurry up and get into the car, Michele!" said Sandra.

"Can't we go by plane?"

"Stop complaining Michele. You can look at the views from the window."

They left at three o'clock in the afternoon on Friday and fortunately for Sandra, Gianni and Michele went to sleep, so she turned the radio on to listen to the news and music. One hour later, she looked at the mirror and saw Gianni waking up with a yawn.

"Are we nearly there?"

"No, we've still got hours to go," she said impatiently.

"I'm hungry."

"If you look inside the rucksack on the floor, there are some salami, cheese, grapes, chocolate and bottles of water and there are some hand wipes, so make sure you clean your fingers. I don't want grease all over my car seats."

Michele also woke up, ate some of the food, and then reached into the rucksack in search of the chocolate.

"Signora, the chocolate has melted. I don't like chocolate like this."

"Well, don't eat it then!"

"I don't like it like this either, Mamma," said Gianni.

"Will both of you shut up! I'm trying to drive," she shouted.

Gianni and Michele passed the next couple of hours playing cards and listening to the radio.

"Mamma, I'm bored," said Gianni. Sandra ignored him.

"I know, let's have an arm wrestle," suggested Michele. "The best out of ten."

Michele won the first two rounds, but the third round ended up to be more than an arm wrestle and developed into a friendly fight as Gianni wrapped his arm tightly around Michele's neck and tried to make him swear that he was the strongest. But Michele released himself quickly and did the same to Gianni.

"Oww, you're hurting me," said Gianni.

"Do you surrender? Do you surrender?" asked Michele.

At that moment, the car screeched and came to a halt on the hard shoulder. Sandra, who was at the end of her tether and probably regretting the whole trip, leapt out of the car, opened the rear passenger door and pulled Michele and Gianni out.

"If I get any more nonsense from either of you, I will leave you here! Do you understand me?" she shouted in their faces.

They arrived at a hotel in Bari at midnight, and out of exhaustion they fell asleep. This was indeed the longest journey Michele had ever taken, and he could not believe they had to continue driving the following day.

****

After breakfast, they set off towards Locorotondo, and it took an hour to get there, and on their way to Selva di Fasano, Michele looked at the beautiful panorama of fields and woods. Ten minutes later, they passed vineyards and a myriad of olive groves and just before they arrived at Valle d'Itria, their destination, Michele was amazed when he saw the strange white cylindrical dwellings with conical roofs lined up on each side of the narrow streets.

"Signora, what are these buildings for?"

"You meet the 'trulli'. In the past, they were used by farmers and shepherds. Now they are used as homes, churches and museums. Do you like them?"

"Yes, they look incredible."

Sandra's sister's holiday home was an isolated modern white villa with broad arches and huge windows, situated on an incline. Michele got out of the car and looked at the spectacular view of the woods, trees and fields with the magnificent blue ocean in the background.

Sandra and her sister greeted each other and Gianni took their bags inside. Michele was still looking at the view, deep in thought. In the corner of his eye, he saw a bench and a table, so he went and sat down.

"Are you coming inside, Michele? My sister would love to meet you."

"Yes, give me a few minutes. Signora, do you have a piece of paper and a pen?"

Sandra went back inside and came out and gave him a note pad and a ballpoint pen.

"Are you okay, Michele? You're very quiet," said Sandra.

"Yes, I am okay, thank you. I just need a bit of time alone."

Sandra put her hand gently on his shoulder and left him.

Michele felt the warm breeze on his face and looked thoughtfully at the view, conjuring up the words he would use in a letter to his mother.

Dear Mamãe,

Thank you for all your letters. I did read them but didn't know what to write. When I heard that you were caught for stealing jewellery, I was angry with you, and I didn't want to have anything to do with you anymore.

At the moment, I'm with Gianni, who is a good friend. I met him in Lake Garda. We're in a beautiful place in the south of Italy, and I just felt that this is the right time to write to you. I'm happy that you got married to Antonio, and I hope you are happy with him. I'm so sorry to hear that you lost your child shortly after you went back to Vialonga.

Maria has taken good care of me. In the summer after you left, she took me to Israel for the first time, and we spent three weeks there. It was hard to get through passport control because the authorities had never heard of Cape Verde, so Maria had to draw a map to show them where I'm from. Tel Aviv is a huge city with the best beaches in the world, and I spent days playing beach ball with friends and surfing on the waves. In the evening, we went out with family and friends to restaurants and had hummus, pita bread, salad, barbecued chicken, beef and lamb kebabs. Maria took us to her favourite fish restaurant, and you should have seen the size of the fish! In the last week, Maria thought it was a good idea for me to have an experience in a kibbutz to show how important it is to help the community. This meant getting up early, setting the table in the canteen and then helping to wash and dry plates for lots of people. I made a few friends there, but I was pleased when I left, as I longed to go back to the beach.

At Easter, we go skiing in Courmayeur. It only takes two hours to get there by car. Maria has a small apartment there. The mountains are breathtaking, especially when they are covered in thick snow. I attended some skiing lessons, and within two weeks, I became a competent skier and managed to descend some of the most challenging slopes, much to the surprise of the instructor. Gianni comes with us sometimes – we're always competing with each other. He's also a good skier but not as good as me! He took much longer to learn as he kept falling over. In the evenings, Maria cooks dinner, and we play card games until late.

Two years ago, Maria and I went to New York for a week to visit her customers. I was so excited as I never thought I would get the chance to go there. We travelled business class, so we were first in the queue at the airport. The seats were much more comfortable and the food much nicer. I didn't understand why Maria dressed up for the journey, as she wasn't seeing any customers on the plane. Maybe she thought she had to wear business clothes to be in business class. When we got to the airport, there was a long queue at immigration, and the security guard at passport control asked my mother a lot of questions and took a long time to look at our passports, one from Israel and one from Cape Verde. It was quite funny because Maria already had a map of Cape Verde in her handbag, which she got out to teach the passport inspector about the geography of Africa.

After security, a man with a uniform was waiting for us in the arrivals' hall, and he had a placard with Maria's name on it. He greeted us and took our suitcases and directed us towards a shiny black limousine. We arrived at a boutique hotel near Times Square, and Maria unpacked. Then we had a light dinner in the hotel before going to bed.

The following day, Maria had two meetings with customers in the morning, so I stayed in my room and watched television. I tried to watch a film, but the English was too difficult, so I switched channels so I could watch cartoons. We spent the rest of the week visiting the sights in Manhattan. My favourite was the Empire State Building: we went right to the top and could see the whole of New York below. We went to a couple of art museums, but honestly, they were boring, and Maria got annoyed at my lack of interest. Sometimes, she takes me to the opera or theatre in Milan, but I don't like them at all.

I still often think about where I come from and all the things that have happened. Even though I haven't written to you, I've never forgotten you, and I always say a special prayer for you when Maria takes me to mass. I pray that God guides you to do the right thing and protects you. I hope that one day we can meet again.

I look forward to receiving your letter.
With affection,
Miguel

Nine

Maria was worried about Michele's future because, despite all her encouragement and sending him to one of the best schools in Milan, his grades were well below average, except for languages. One of her clients had told her that being able to speak different languages could open doors, so she had sent Michele to short intensive language courses in France and England during the summer holidays. Recently she had read an article about the booming economy in Germany in the business section of Corriere della Sera, so she arranged for Michele to attend a three-week language and sports course in Altensteig, a small town in the south.

When Maria had first sent Michele to a language school near London, he had defiantly resisted because he firmly believed that he should not study during the summer holidays. He soon discovered that the language schools were not proper schools at all, not like the normal ones where he had to take exams. These were schools where he could have fun, play football and meet new friends. And on top of that, Maria always bought him new fashionable clothes, sunglasses and cologne, which made it easier for him to date girls.

At Stuttgart airport, there was a meeting area where Michele introduced himself to other students, and then two school representatives arrived and directed them to the bus. When they arrived at their destination, the driver said, "Welcome to Altensteig" and everyone got off and proceeded towards the main entrance. Inside there was a poster pinned onto the notice board with information about where the students would be sleeping, and there was a banner with 'PLEASE MEET IN THE HALL AT SIX O'CLOCK' written in large letters at the bottom.

Michele burst into his bedroom and threw his new red sports bag onto his bed. His roommate didn't turn around to greet him. Instead, he continued looking out of the window.

"Hello. I'm Michele."

The boy turned around and looked startled.

"Hello. I'm Adam," he replied quietly.

In front of Michele stood the skinniest person he had ever met, he had curly blonde hair and blue eyes, and he was wearing a white shirt, which was far too big for him, drooped over loose light blue trousers.

"Where are you from?" asked Michele.

"England," replied Adam.

"I'm from Italy," said Michele.

"Excuse me, I have to make a call," said Adam courteously and left the bedroom.

Michele shook his head, confounded by such a stilted introduction. He looked at his watch. There was still an hour before they needed to be at the main hall, so he went outside to look at the tennis courts and bumped into one of the students he had met on the bus.

"I didn't catch your name."

"Massimiliano."

"I'm Michele." They shook hands. "Which house are you staying in?"

"I can't remember the name, but it's the one next to the main hall. What about you?"

"It's just down there by the trees. What about your roommate. Have you met him yet?"

"Yes, he's from Lugano. He seems okay. I haven't spoken with him very much."

"My roommate is English, and he's very shy. When I came in, he looked as though he'd seen a ghost."

"That's funny! So, do you play tennis?"

"Not much. I played a bit at school. Do you know if they have any racquets?"

"Let's ask."

At six o'clock precisely, the head of the school, a bald and stocky man with a dark pea green suit, began to address the one hundred and twenty students, half were from Italy, and the other half from other European countries. Michele was restless, and he only heard a few of the rules that the headteacher was saying, as he was busy eyeing up girls and chatting with Massimiliano.

"Rule Number Five: Male students are not permitted to visit the female students' accommodation. And likewise, female students are not permitted to visit the male students' accommodation. Any student found breaking this rule will be asked to leave the school, and a letter will be sent home to his or her parents."

"It wasn't like this in France or England," whispered Michele to Massimiliano.

"I'm definitely breaking that rule!"

"Me too!"

"Rule Number Nine: All students should be present in all lessons and arrive punctually at eight o'clock. Rule Number Ten: Students are not permitted to leave the premises without the approval and supervision of a staff member."

There were other tedious rules about homework, respect for the teachers and general conduct, and finally, the head of the school pointed to the lists at the back of the hall, which showed the classes the students were in.

"If you have any questions, you can ask a member of staff. In the meantime, I wish you a very pleasant stay in Altensteig."

When the head of the school finally concluded his speech, the students went to the back of the hall and clambered over each other to see which groups they were in, the top group, level six was for those who were more advanced. Michele found his name under level five and then caught sight of Adam, who looked alone and anxious, probably distressed by all the chaos around him. The announcement of dinner being ready in the canteen was almost inaudible.

By the time they reached the canteen, the Italian students had magnetised themselves to each other and made sure they were sat next to each other by reserving seats around the rectangular wooden tables. It was a shame that there was only room for six people, so

Michele and Massimiliano started to put four tables together, then the head chef intervened and told them that this was strictly forbidden and that the tables should remain where they were. After dinner, the Italian students congregated outside, and spent hours getting to know each other, until the security guard ordered them to return to their rooms as it was ten o'clock.

Massimiliano had told Michele a funny story about a schoolfriend who had dated three girls at the same time. This had made Michele laugh so much that he had hiccups and he thought that he would tell this to Adam to cheer him up. When he got to his bedroom, the curtains were drawn, and Adam was already sound asleep, so Michele crept out of the room with his soap, towel, toothbrush and toothpaste, and went down the corridor to the bathroom.

The following morning, Michele went into the classroom early and noticed that there was a beautiful slim girl with short dark brown hair and brown eyes, so he boldly went up to her and sat down next to her.

"That blouse suits you!" said Michele.

"Thank you," she replied without looking at him. She took out her dictionary, and a pad of paper from her bag, and the other students came in and filled up the other seats. Then entered the teacher, wearing a white t-shirt with beige trousers, and he distributed the books, which were sitting on the front desk.

"Guten Morgen. Mein Name is Herr Becker," he said. "In the first part of the morning, we will study conversational German. After the break, we will study German literature."

Michele liked him. He had a relaxed and friendly demeanour, but the thought of studying literature was daunting, to say the least.

"We are going to read a short article from 'Die Zeit', which is a national newspaper. And then we will discuss it."

Herr Becker gave each student a photocopy of a recent article on the challenges of university life in Germany. As Michele was reading, he pretended not to understand one of the words, so that he could talk to the girl next to him.

"What does 'Vorrichtung' mean?" he asked the girl on his left.

"Did you not bring a dictionary with you?"

"I forgot it. I left it at home."

"It means 'device'," she said coldly.

"So, what do you think? Will university be useful for us in the future or not?" asked Herr Becker.

"It won't be. I won't be going to university. I'm going to be a professional footballer and play for Juventus!" exclaimed Michele.

The other students sniggered, and the Italians booed his choice of football team.

"You're supporting the wrong team, my friend! Anyway, you've got three weeks with us. That's enough time to convince you to change allegiances. You should come to Florence and see how real football is played!" shouted Massimiliano in Italian.

At that moment, Michele discovered that there were many Italians from Florence in the class, as they were all agreeing with Massimiliano and they started talking loudly in unison about the latest football results. Michele stood on his chair, so he could make himself seen and heard.

"You'll never convince me. It will be me who convinces you! You have no idea! No idea!" said Michele.

Herr Becker looked bemused and, in an effort to return to the subject, he yelled "Auf Deutsch! Auf Deutsch!"

"Okay, Herr Becker," said Massimiliano.

"Thank you, Michele. I'm sure you will become a mighty football player," he said once the students had calmed down.

When Herr Becker announced that it was break-time, the girl next to Michele took her bag and walked briskly out of the room, with Michele in pursuit, and he caught up with her.

"Hey, what's the matter? Are you trying to get away from me?"

"No. I just want to talk with my friend. She's also from France but in a different group."

"Okay."

Michele somehow didn't believe her, so he went back to the main hall and took a banana from the fruit bowl and went to talk to his classmates.

****

At lunchtime on the third day, Michele was about to sit down at a table with Massimiliano and four new friends, when he caught a glimpse of Adam who was at the back of the canteen, eating alone.

"Hang on. Listen, I'm going to skip lunch with you today. I'm going to sit with Adam."

Michele surmised that there was something wrong with Adam, so he wanted to find out why he was always alone, even if there weren't any other English students. He placed the tray on the table and sat down opposite him.

"Tell me, Adam, why are you sitting all by yourself?"

"I'm okay!"

"No, you're not okay. I can see you're not okay. You're not talking with anyone, and you're always alone."

Adam looked up and over Michele's shoulder to glance at the French girl, who had just walked by them. Michele turned around.

"You like her?" he laughed.

Adam blushed and looked down at his plate.

"There's nothing to be shy about! Have you spoken to her yet?" asked Michele.

"No."

Michele paused, desperately thinking about what he could ask or say next.

"What are you doing here? You obviously don't want to be here."

"I'm here to study German so I can pass my exams. Next year is my last year in school. Why else would I be here? Why are you here?"

"To have fun, of course! I've already been to two other schools like this one, and they were much less strict. Come on! Lighten up! You don't need to take the German too seriously. There's sport in the afternoon and discos in the evening. At the weekend,

we're going to the water park and then a barbecue!
Are you good at football?"

"No, I'm not good at sport."

"It doesn't matter. Why don't you come and play
football with us this afternoon?"

"Really. I'm no good."

"I'll teach you!"

"No, no. Thank you anyway."

"Well, at least come and watch."

"Okay."

That was something, Michele thought, at least he
was talking.

"You're from Italy, right?" asked Adam.

"Well, as you can see, I'm not originally from Italy.
I come from a small group of islands called Cape
Verde. I've been brought up in Milan, and I'm lucky
because my mother has taken me so many places and
I've had the chance to see a bit of the world. We're
going to Brazil next year."

"That sounds good."

"What about you? Which part of England are you
from?"

"Manchester. I've still got one more year to go at
school. I'm studying life sciences, English and German
at school. I don't know what to do next. I've always
dreamed of becoming a journalist, so maybe I'll study
media studies at university."

"That's a weird combination! Anyway, you know,
I'd also like to be a journalist. I'm also interested in
tourism. I'd like to work at a travel agency. That's if
I don't become a professional footballer!"

Adam smiled.

After lunch, Michele and Adam went to the football pitch and whilst Adam sat on the side, Michele joined the others as they picked sides. After twenty minutes, Michele ran up to Adam, took his hand and pulled him onto the pitch and told the others that he was part of his team. Adam reticently accepted, and every time Michele passed him the ball, Adam passed it onto another player and received a brief applause from the team players. After the match, Michele congratulated him on how well he had played and invited him to play volleyball the following day.

On their way to the barbecue on Saturday, Michele was happy to see Adam chatting with other students on the bus. When they arrived at a massive field in the middle of nowhere, Michele organised a game of 'pass the rugby ball', whilst the staff were preparing the cooking equipment and food for the barbecue. There were Thomas, Christian, Sacha, Adam and himself. Adam kept dropping the ball, so Michele took him aside for two minutes to show him how to catch and throw, then they went back to the circle.

A girl with a mass of blonde curly hair came up to Michele and asked him if she could speak with him in private, so he left the game, took her hand and they sat down on the grass a few metres away.

"You're Valeria, right?" asked Michele.

"Yes, I'm in the same class as you," she replied sheepishly.

"Yes, I know," he said. "So, do you like barbecues?"

"Sure, I like barbecues. But that's not what I wanted to talk to you about."

"Oh, I see," he replied.

"It's just that, how can I put it, I really like you, even from the moment I saw you on the first day but you never kind of noticed me."

"I like you too," he said.

She was quite attractive, definitely not stunningly attractive, and definitely not his type, but he couldn't tell her that. He didn't want to hurt her.

"I know this is going to sound presumptuous, but would you mind if I kissed you,"

"Not at all, let's kiss,"

At that very moment, the rugby ball came to his rescue as it landed on his lap, Adam had thrown the ball too far once again, so Michele felt obliged to pick it up and go back to the game, and he told Valeria, who was looking mortified, that he would see her later.

At approximately five o'clock in the morning, Michele heard retching sounds, Adam had been sick.

"Are you okay?"

"No, I've been sick," said Adam.

"Yes, I know. I can smell it. Let me go and tell the housekeeping staff,"

A large lady came in and started cleaning the sick with a bucket and mop as Michele was writing a note to Herr Becker stating that he would not be able to make it to school that morning, as he needed to take care of Adam, who was not to be left alone. After dropping it off in the classroom, he picked up some bananas from the dining room, and went back to his room, lay on his bed and listened to Def Leppard on his Walkman.

When Adam awoke, Michele went to sit next to him and gave him a banana.

"How are you feeling now?"

"A bit better, thank you. Shouldn't you be at school?"

"No, not at all. I'm here to look after you. But I will need to play football this afternoon."

"I must have eaten something bad yesterday,"

"Well, maybe it was that steak that you covered in tomato sauce. Is that what English people normally eat?"

"Maybe it was. No, it was just that the steak didn't taste that good, so I covered it with sauce. Anyway, who was that girl who came to you yesterday?"

"That was Valeria. She likes me."

"I see. You're lucky. Loads of girls like you."

"Well, girls would like you if…"

"If what…"

"Okay, don't be offended, Adam. But you seriously need to do something about your clothes, and you're just too skinny. You mustn't eat very much at home."

"I eat loads."

"You need to work out then."

"And what do you mean about my clothes?"

"Have you not noticed? They're too big for you. And look at those multi-coloured short trousers you've been wearing! And those mirror sunglasses don't suit you. You need to come shopping with my mother and me. We'll sort you out!"

****

One night after dinner during the third and last week, Michele proposed to Adam that they visit one of the girls' houses.

192

"Come on! They'll be waiting for us. I told them we'd be coming."

"What? We'll get caught. Then they'll send letters back to our parents, and we'll be sent home. Did you not hear the head of the school on the first day?"

"We won't get caught. I know you like the French girl. I've seen you staring at her. Don't deny it! And I want to see Monica."

Adam looked uneasy.

"If we wear black, we won't be seen. Where's that black pullover you've been wearing all week? Hurry up! Put it on!"

"But people will hear us! The guards will be at the front door!"

"For crying out loud! There are no guards! And we're not going via the front door. We're going through the window."

"Well, I don't know about that. The window isn't big enough to let us out."

Michele opened the window to show how far it would open. He was becoming impatient, so he asked Adam to find the black pullover, helped him to put it on, switched off the light, and they went outside.

Michele led Adam to some bushes close to the girls' house.

"Okay, it's safe to move. We need to run to the front door. Can you manage to do that?" Michele asked despairingly.

They hurried to the front door and went into the building.

"How will we get back?" asked Adam.

"Shh. We'll think about that later."

They went up the stairs and knocked on the door marked '209'. Ariane, the French girl, and Monica were waiting for them.

"I thought you weren't coming," said Monica.

"We got a little held up. Anyway, we're here now!"

"So, this is Adam?" asked Ariane.

"Yes, don't judge him by his clothes!"

Ariane was sitting on one of the beds, and she patted the place next to her, indicating that Adam should sit next to her. Michele sat on a chair, and Monica sat on his knees with her arm around him. Ariane caressed Adam's hair.

"He could do with a haircut as well," said Ariane.

"So, what type of girls do you like, Adam?" asked Monica.

"I haven't given it much thought," replied Adam politely.

"Come on, there must be a type of girl you like," said Michele

"Well, I like dark-skinned, slim and a nice smile."

"Exactly like Ariane," teased Monica.

Adam's face turned red, and he looked down.

Monica started to massage Michele's back. Ariane laid the palm of her hand on Adam's right leg, and Adam touched her face gently with his thumb. After thirty minutes, Monica decided that it was time for the boys to return to their bedroom.

"It's late," declared Monica.

Michele looked at his watch. "It's only eleven-thirty!"

"We can see each other another time. Ariane and I need our rest, and so do you!"

"Okay"

Michele gave Monica a kiss on her left cheek. Adam closed his eyes and did the same to Ariane.

"I can't believe they turfed us out so early," said Michele once they returned to their room.

"Well, it is rather late," said Adam.

"No, they're playing hard to get. You better get used to it."

****

On the last day, the teachers performed a cringy dance with umbrellas to 'It's Raining Men', and then the head of the school gave a monotonous end-of-school speech with the same dampened enthusiasm as his introduction. The highlight of the last day was the disco and the beer. All those acquaintances turned into romances with promises of keeping in touch forever.

Michele liked Adam. He had changed so much, and they were now friends, so at the airport, they exchanged addresses and telephone numbers.

"Just a second, let's get someone to take a photo of us," said Michele.

He took out his camera from his hand luggage and asked a lady sat next to him to take a photograph.

"I'm waiting for you in Milan," said Michele.

"Please keep in touch."

They shook hands and Michele walked to his gate.

Ten

Maria had written to the head of Michele's school, requesting ten days' absence in early March, just before Lent, so they could visit Brazil and experience the carnival in Rio de Janeiro. The head sent a letter back, saying that he didn't have a choice, and reminded her that Miguel was behind in his schoolwork and being absent for such a long time would have huge consequences. He added that his new friends had a bad influence on him as they often played truant and any deterrent or punishment had not worked. This letter made Maria consider finding another private school, which was managed by nuns, and instead of sleeping at the school during the week, he could stay at home where she could keep an eye on him.

Michele hated the stultifying routine at school, so missing two weeks of lessons was a blessing, and having watched numerous gangster films with Brazil as the backdrop, he was excited about visiting Rio de Janeiro. Maria had told him that many people from Cape Verde had migrated to Brazil and he wondered if he would meet any of them. David, who was now a general practitioner in London and recently engaged to an English lady, had been invited and would look after Michele whilst Maria was visiting potential customers.

They arrived at a five-star hotel on Copacabana beach at nine o'clock in the evening. Michele opened the door to his bedroom, which had a king-size bed, an enormous bathroom and a separate living room with a television.

Maria had organised a private driver to take them to the statue of Cristo and the Sugar Loaf Mountain in the morning, and in the afternoon, they went to the beach. Michele wanted to surf on the long waves, they reminded him of his time in Israel, so David bought a surfboard for him from a nearby sports shop.

In the evening, they went to the carnival at the Sambodromo where choreographed and erotic dancers, most of whom were wearing white masks and playing tambourines or drums, surrounded the variegated floats. On their way to the beach to see the balls, they jumped into a bandas on one of the nearby streets, and two dancers took David and Michele's hands and danced with them. One African girl sensually twirled around Michele and moved her hands over the contours of his body. He soon became so captivated by the aphrodisiac dancing and the accompanying rhythms from the percussion instruments that he completely lost track of time until he spotted David watching him. He had been dancing with so many girls for so many hours, and he wanted it to last forever, but he didn't want David to keep waiting for him, so he forced himself to step away from the parade, and wiped his forehead with his right arm. His bright red t-shirt was glued onto him with sweat.

"Where's Mamma?" Michele shouted into David's ear.

"She went back to the hotel a few hours ago. She got a bit tired."

"What time is it?"

"It's nearly four o'clock in the morning!"

"Wow. I had no idea."

"You were enjoying yourself." David laughed. "Shall we go back to the hotel?"

"Yes, all right."

Michele woke up bleary-eyed at two o'clock in the afternoon, he had a shower, got dressed and on his way out, he noticed a 'Do Not Disturb' sign hanging on the handle, which David must have left. He found David reading a newspaper and drinking coffee in a café overlooking the beach.

"David!"

David looked up from his newspaper. "Would you like some coffee?"

"Yes, please. Is there something to eat?

"I'll call the waitress."

The waitress arrived, and he ordered a pancake.

"What time did you get up?"

"About eleven o'clock."

"I see. And where's Mamma?"

"She's out with customers today, and she has dinner with them this evening. So, you're stuck with me!"

Michele and David spent the afternoon surfing and went to a marvellous steak restaurant for dinner in the evening.

"David, why don't we go to a nightclub?" asked Michele.

"I'm not sure about that, Michele, and besides, Maria would never trust me again," said David.

"It's okay. We don't need to tell her. So, what's stopping us?"

After having another shower, Michele took out a light purple shirt, a pair of dark grey trousers and his black shoes from his wardrobe and got changed. He sprayed some cologne on his shirt and went to the lobby where David was waiting for him. The traffic was heavy, and it took them almost one hour to reach the club, and then they had to wait half an hour in a queue before the bouncers scrutinized them and ushered them inside.

It was a typical nightclub with red and green lasers shooting in different directions, and there was a deejay playing modern international and Brazilian music. It was crowded with mostly Brazilian people in their late teens and early twenties. David pointed at an empty table with two chairs. Michele sat down and David went to the bar to buy two tequilas. When he came back, Michele was staring at a young woman, dressed in a black miniskirt and top, sitting on a stool at the bar and drinking a cocktail through a straw. She turned around, so Michele was able to see her straight black hair and prominent make-up. She caught Michele looking at her. Now was the right moment, Michele drank the tequila in one shot, and walked casually over to her, and asked her if she wanted another drink. She accepted, and said she would be back momentarily as she needed to use the bathroom. He panicked as he had no money, so he went back to David.

"David! I've just met this really hot girl at the bar, and I offered her a drink. And I don't have any money!"

David reached for his pocket and took out a wad of Brazilian Real notes from his wallet.

"Don't spend it all at once. That's all I'm giving you. Make sure you are back here in two hours."

"Okay."

Michele rushed off with the money, and asked the barman for the same cocktail for the girl and another tequila for him, and Michele sat on the stool next to hers. When she returned, they sat opposite each other, their legs touching, and she took out a packet of cigarettes from her black handbag.

"You didn't tell me your name," she said.

"Michele"

"I'm Isabella. So, Michele, do you smoke?"

"No, I don't smoke."

"Is that 'you don't want to smoke' or 'you've never tried'?"

"Of course, I've tried," he lied.

"Well, try another."

She gave him a smirky smile, knowing that he hadn't smoked before, popped a cigarette between her lips, lit it, inhaled deeply and handed it to him, and prepared one for herself. Michele looked intently on how she went about smoking a cigarette and tried to copy her but ended up coughing and spluttering. This was going to ruin everything, he thought, she would laugh at him. And indeed, she did laugh at him, and she could see how awkward Michele was feeling.

"Tell me about yourself," Isabella said.

"What do you want to know?"

"Anything. Start with where you're from."

"I'm from Cape Verde, but I live in Milan, Italy."

"Are you Italian?"

"Yes, I suppose I am."

"An immigrant from Cape Verde living in Italy. Interesting. I love interesting people."

"I'm on holiday here with my mother and cousin."

"Ah, that's sweet. Did you go to the carnival?"

"Yes, it was amazing. I danced all night! Did you go?"

"Yes, of course! I go every year. I'm an awesome dancer."

"I don't believe you. Show me."

Isabella put her cigarette on the ashtray and took Michele by the hand and they performed a sensual samba dance, so sensual that other dancers stopped to watch them. Hopefully, his dancing would compensate for his failed attempt to smoke, he desperately wanted to impress her. When they returned to their stools, Michele ordered two more drinks and they chatted, smoked and drank cocktails for the next two hours.

"So, what now?" she asked.

"Well, you could come with me back to my hotel."

"That's a bit presumptuous, isn't it?"

Michele shrugged his shoulders. "It's up to you."

Michele went up to David, who was talking with one of the bartenders, and introduced him to Isabella and told him that she would be coming back to the hotel with them.

"Pleased to meet you," stuttered Isabella.

Isabella tripped over the stair by the exit, so Michele held on to her as she left the nightclub and got inside the taxi. David sat in the passenger seat next to the driver, and Isabella and Michele sat in the back. There was not so much traffic, so it didn't take much time to return to the hotel.

The elevator stopped on the third floor, and David said, "Good night!" and left, leaving them alone. As soon as the doors closed, Isabella held Michele's head with both hands, and they kissed passionately until they heard the sound of the elevator's doors opening on the sixth floor. In the bedroom, Isabella went straight into the bathroom and came out wearing skimpy black underwear, and she lay down on the bed and dimmed the lights. Then Michele went into the bathroom and looked at himself in the mirror and took some deep breaths. He went into the shower and scrubbed himself, and then put on some fresh boxer shorts, his heart beating at a phenomenal rate, and he went to sit next to her on the bed. Michele was nervous, and she could tell, so she took control by moving him gently so he was on top of her and they were facing each other. She removed her underwear, took off his boxer shorts and reached out for a preservative on the bedside table.

When Michele woke up at half-past eleven in the morning, Isabella was already sitting up watching television. He could not stop thinking about what had happened and was hoping that Isabella would do the same thing again.

"Good morning, Isabella!"

"Good morning, sweetheart! You slept well."

"Yes, I did, I did. Listen, about last night…"

"I know. You want to do it again, right? I can tell. But last night, I started it. Now, it's your turn."

Michele was a tad baffled, but he thought that maybe she was trying to teach inexperienced him how to be sexually intimate with a girl. In any case, he was less nervous now so he playfully took her in his arms and they had sex again. Afterwards, they lay in bed for another hour before getting changed, and they went to the ground floor where they found Maria and David in the lobby.

"You must be Isabella," said Maria, who was dressed in casual clothes.

"Yes."

"I am Michele's mother."

Michele hoped that David had given an abridged version of what had happened at the nightclub. The good news for Michele was that she was in good spirits as she had won some new customers the day before, so even if she had instinctively figured out what had really happened, she was not in the mood to show any signs of disapproval.

"We're about to have a light lunch and then head off to Buzios. We'd love you to come," said Maria to Isabella.

"Yes, that would be great. I don't have anything to do today."

"That's settled then. We've hired a yacht," said Maria.

"I don't have my swimming gear with me."

"Very well. We can drop you at your place, you can pick up your swimming gear, and we can go to Buzios. I'm looking forward to getting to know you better!"

Michele, Isabella and David slept for most of the journey, whilst Maria admired the views and changing landscape. The driver parked near one of the beaches, and Michele got out and looked at the smaragdine sea with thick, rich green vegetation smothering the rocky hills in the background. They looked at the pristine white yachts, which were swaying calmly on the surface of the sea.

Like two excited children, Michele and Isabella, hand in hand, hurried onto the beach. Michele let go of her hand, ran into the sea and dived under the water, a few seconds later he arose and called out to Isabella. Not knowing what to do with her bag, she looked behind her, thrust it into David's hands and ran into the sea and swam up to Michele and put her arms around him.

"Have a look under the water. You'll see the most amazing coral," said Michele.

Under the water, Michele took her hand and pointed to the greenish-brown spikes and pink tubes. They went back to the surface and crawled towards a crevice on the left on the bay, and Michele placed his left hand around her waist, and his right hand behind her back and they kissed. Michele wasn't too happy when David appeared all of a sudden, interrupting their lovemaking. How on earth did he find them in this crevice?

"Sorry to interrupt but Maria asked me to fetch you as we are going for a late lunch."

Michele could see that Maria was irritated with their leisurely stroll from the sea to where she was sitting. She had been sunbathing with David under a small green sun umbrella, and she gave both of them a towel.

"Dry yourselves quickly because we need to go and have lunch and we have a yacht booked for four-thirty this afternoon."

Maria randomly selected a small restaurant on a quaint, enchanting cobbled street lined with trees and cafés, and ordered seafood dishes and a bottle of wine. Michele was rightly worried that Maria's impending interrogation of Isabella was about to begin. She had recently started to measure the eligibility of Michele's friends on their grades at school and how serious they were.

"So, Isabella!" Maria smiled at her patronisingly. "What do you do for a living?"

"I'm a waitress at a fish restaurant, not so far from Copacabana beach. I've been doing this for a couple of years now. I want to be a cook or a chef, and hopefully one day, I'll have my own restaurant. In my spare time, I experiment with new recipes at home, and I invite friends to try them. I like to cook fried and grilled fish with different vegetables, rice and sauces. Being a waitress helps me to understand different tastes, what customers like the most and how we can increase the number of dishes on the menu. I have a good relationship with the manager and the chef, and they listen to my suggestions. They recommended that I go to a cooking school to learn more, so I'm currently saving up to go there."

"That's very commendable," said Maria. "And what about your family? Do you live with your parents? Have you got any siblings?"

"Yes, I live with my parents and younger sister. My father works in a bank, and my mother works part-time in a nursery school. My sister is still at school. She's a really good artist, so we're hoping that she will go to an art school. I wasn't as good as my sister at school. I passed most of my exams but then left school at sixteen."

Michele was relieved that Isabella had shown herself to be a worthy friend, or girlfriend, even though she had left school at sixteen. The waiter arrived with the seafood platters and wine, and they continued to make small talk about the weather, the scenery and the food.

They took a dinghy to the boat, and one of the crew helped them to get on board, Maria and David settled at the front and Michele and Isabella at the rear. There was just the right amount of wind for the yacht to sail round the spidery coastline gracefully. Whilst the crew talked with Maria and David, Isabella and Michele sat next to each other with their hands locked. A couple of hours later, the sun set on the horizon, spreading a deep red glow across the sky, Michele's favourite event. Questions about seeing each other again were left unspoken, as Michele would be leaving soon, so he held her tightly to create a memory he would treasure forever.

Eleven

Maria helped Michele to some more pasta with seafood.

"Listen, I've got some news for you, and I've been meaning to tell you for some time now. And I hope you'll like it. I've managed to get you into a new school for your last two years. It's not so far from here, and you're going to stay at home instead of at the school during the week."

"Why are you taking me away from the other school? All my friends are there. I don't want to go to a new school," he shouted.

"But it'll help you to get into university."

"I don't want to go to university! Have you ever thought about that? Just when I'm happy, you take everything away from me, just like my mother did."

"I just want the best for you. I think …"

"You think? You don't know what is best for me!"

"It's as simple as this. All your friends will be studying to pass their final exams. And I mean, studying hard. That includes Mario, Gianni and Tommaso. Then they'll most likely go to university and get a degree, which will help them to get a job and earn money."

"I don't want to study hard. I hate school!"

"Then what will you do when you leave school?"

Michele could take no more. He slid off his stool, grabbed his coat and went towards the door.

"I should have stayed in Brazil with Isabella," he shouted, slamming the door behind him.

He walked and walked and walked, and after twenty minutes, he arrived at an Irish pub not far from Cadorna. Why did Maria keep nagging him about school? He didn't like studying, but at least he had friends at the school he was going to, and now she wanted to take him away from them. What for? Did it matter that much that he played truant and got lower grades? Surely, he could find a decent job without going to university. He needed alcohol to help him forget the unpleasant confrontation he had had with Maria, so he ordered a large glass of draft beer and sat at one of the tables and looked at the people around him: young couples, students, colleagues meeting for an aperativo. They all seemed lively, and there was him, all alone. He wished he could be as happy as they were. He gulped the beer down, and ordered another. In the back of his mind, he knew that Maria was right, and that he shouldn't have spoken to her like that, but at the same time, he just could not achieve what she wanted. He moved to another table to watch the football on the television, this would be a good distraction. After a few more beers, he left the pub when the match finished and staggered through Castello Sforzesco towards Parco Sempione, where he found a bench, lay down on it and went to sleep. Half an hour later, a trickle of light rain on his forehead woke him up, so he continued to walk through the park and through the exit.

"Negro!"

Michele had never heard someone hurl an insult at him because of his colour. He ignored it and concentrated on flagging a taxi, but there wasn't a single one in sight, and the roads were almost empty. He wondered what time it was.

"Are they all deaf where you come from?" he shouted pugnaciously.

Michele looked around briefly and saw two intoxicated boys, probably teenagers, one of them was holding a bottle of beer and wearing a cap with the brim on the back of his head.

"Did you know it's very rude to ignore someone? But there again, you apes are all rude. And dumb."

Michele heard the other boy with the cap laughing maniacally. His fear and adrenaline made him sober and more attentive as he heard their footsteps getting closer, so he increased his pace.

"You don't belong here! Why don't you go home to the jungle or wherever you live?"

It had never crossed his mind that he did not belong here because of where he came from. He was angry but also ashamed. Before he had time to think what to say back to them, he felt a piercing blow at the back of his head. The boy with the cap had thrown the empty beer bottle at him, like a dart. He felt the trickle of blood on the back of his head and turned around to face them. Rage got the better of him, so he punched both of them hard in the stomach until they were on the floor, retching and he walked away. Luckily, a taxi arrived ten minutes later, so he hopped in and went home. He opened the door and went inside quietly so he wouldn't wake up Maria, and as he was walking through the sitting room, he saw that she was sitting dressed in her pyjamas on a sofa in the dark, waiting for him.

"Where the hell have you been?" she cried. "I've been so worried about you!"

"I've been out."

Maria switched the light on and saw the state of him.

"You stink of alcohol. What on earth have you been doing?" she demanded.

"I just went for a walk," he replied.

"I don't know what to say. I've given you everything you wanted. What is wrong with you?"

The last question deeply struck him. It was similar in vein to the abusive comment that came from the intoxicated teenager. What is wrong with him? He doesn't belong here. He didn't listen to Maria's unpleasant stream of words, and after she went into her bedroom, he went into the bathroom, doused his head in cold water and collapsed on his bed.

Michele awoke at ten o'clock the following morning, and made a bath for himself, the warm water helped him to relax. After he got changed, he went into the sitting room and sat next to Maria, who was skim reading a fashion magazine.

"I'm sorry about yesterday," he said. "I shouldn't have said those things, and I shouldn't have gone out. I know you want the best for me."

He touched the back of his head. The blood had clotted but it still hurt.

"Michele, sweetheart. I know how difficult things can be. But trust me, things will be all right. What have you done to your head?"

She stood up and looked at the back of his head.

"How did you do that?"

"I fell."

"That looks nasty. We should go to the nurse and check it out, and have it bandaged properly. Why don't you have breakfast? I've prepared a mug of tea and some of your favourite biscuits. We can then go to the clinic."

****

Just after lunch on the Thursday before Easter, Maria, Michele and Gianni left for Linate airport to pick up Adam. Michele had written to Adam after they had returned from Brazil and invited him to stay during the Easter holidays. He had put that he and his mother would be waiting for him in the arrivals' hall. When Adam appeared with his enormous blue suitcase, Michele went up to kiss him on his cheeks, but he stepped back and stretched out his hand. Adam still had a lot to learn, Michele thought. He introduced him to Gianni and Maria.

"We're going to Courmayeur. We have an apartment there. You know how to ski, don't you?" asked Michele.

"I've never skied. Well, actually, I did have a go on the dry slopes not far from my home, but I kept falling over, and I burned myself badly."

Michele should have known.

"Don't worry. We'll teach you!"

The white exterior of the apartment block was surrounded by a sloping landscape, which was covered in trees, vegetation and snow. Maria reversed the car so that the boot was close to the main door and they unloaded the luggage and took the elevator to the second floor. Adam looked at the wooden floor and columns which gave the apartment a warm and cosy feel to it. In the sitting room, there were two large sofas and a round dining table, and on the right, there was a small kitchen. There were two bedrooms: one for Maria, and one for Michele and Adam, Gianni would sleep on the sofa bed in the sitting room.

Maria cooked some penne pasta and tomato sauce, and they sat down at the table and watched Adam struggling to eat it.

"Do you like the pasta, Adam?" asked Maria.

"Yes, thank you."

"Have you had pasta before?" asked Gianni.

"No, we don't eat pasta at home. We had spaghetti at school, but it wasn't very nice."

"You don't eat pasta in England? What do you eat?" asked Michele.

"Usually meat, like lamb or chicken, casseroles, vegetables."

"Unbelievable. I can't imagine life without pasta," said Michele.

Adam managed to eat all of the pasta by sipping red wine between each mouthful to hide the taste and texture.

"So, tell us what you are doing," said Maria.

"I'm in my first year at Kent University. It's a beautiful university in the south-east of England, and I'm reading life sciences and Italian."

"That sounds very good. I also enjoyed life sciences and biology at school. But why Italian?"

"I've always been interested in languages, and I suppose meeting so many Italians in Altensteig made me want to learn it."

"Are you enjoying it?"

"Yes, very much. In the first term, the professor taught us about the grammar, and we learned some basic vocabulary. We're now studying 'Il ventaglio' by Goldoni. We have exams in May."

"We'll help you with the Italian, won't we?" said Maria.

"Yes, and I can give you some cassettes with Italian songs," said Michele.

After serving some fruit, Michele and Maria cleared the table, and they played cards for a couple of hours before going to bed.

The following morning, Michele, Gianni and Adam went to the ski slopes, and Maria visited some friends. Michele helped Adam to put his skis on, and they went to a gentle incline so they could teach Adam how to ski. They realised that there was little hope as Adam kept falling over so after half an hour, Michele asked Adam to sit on a deckchair and they would come back to him later.

Two hours later, Michele and Gianni found Adam asleep on the deckchair and looked in horror at the sunburn on his face, so they woke him up and took him straight back to the apartment.

"Go and get the after-sun cream quickly!" said Maria.

Adam sat down whilst Maria put lathers of after-sun cream on his face and Michele used a magazine as a fan to cool him down.

"What is your mother going to think?" Maria asked repeatedly.

When they were satisfied that they had done all they could do to relieve Adam of the sunburn, Maria and Gianni went to the balcony to sunbathe, and Adam and Michele went for a walk in the town.

"You know, my mother likes you very much," said Michele.

"Thank you! I'm pleased."

"She doesn't like everyone."

"Why not?"

"She's very strict. She likes you because you're polite and you're studying. But she nags me when I introduce her to someone who likes to have fun or doesn't take school seriously."

"What are you studying?"

"Everything. I have one more year to go."

"What would you like to do?"

"I think I told you in Altensteig, I'd like to be a journalist or do something with import and export. To be honest, I'm not sure. Mamma is doing everything she can to get me into university. Gianni suggested I study political science. He said that it would be easier and would open doors for me. I hate studying. There are times when I force myself to read and study, but most of the time, I don't feel like it and get distracted."

"By what?"

"By girls!" He laughed.

"Yes, I know what you mean! I only have twelve hours of lectures a week, and I'm not a quick learner, so I have to spend hours studying to pass exams. So, I organize my day as though it's a job, and when I'm not in lectures, I'm in the library. Once you get into a routine, it becomes much easier."

"I like that. Treating it as a job."

"By the way, I was expecting to see an African lady with you at the airport."

"Ah, you mean my mother. Well, as you can see, she's not my biological mother, but I've been entrusted to her ever since I was little. That's why I consider her to be my mother. She's not Italian. She's Jewish and from Romania, and her family is also in Milan. Hopefully, you'll get to meet them one day, they're really nice. Honestly, I couldn't wish for a better person to look after me because she cares about me very much. And she's taken me to so many places, like Tel Aviv, Rio de Janeiro and New York, so I've got to see a bit of the world."

They continued to walk for another hour and returned to the apartment.

"It was very nice talking with you," said Michele.

Two days later, they returned to Milan and Adam slept on a camp bed in Michele's room. Adam woke up at seven o'clock and tiptoed to the bathroom as Michele was still in a deep sleep. After getting changed, he went into the kitchen and had breakfast with Maria. She prepared some freshly squeezed blood orange juice and some biscuits for him and she saw how much he liked the orange juice, so she poured him another glass.

"Do you have blood oranges in England, Adam?"

"I don't think so."

"Well, I can see how much you like them! Anyway, I wanted to thank you for coming to visit us. Michele is still very young for his age, and it's important that he's with the right people. He's easily influenced by others, and he's not good at studying. So, it would be helpful if you could have a word with him about how important it is to study."

"I already did when we went for a walk."

"I see. And what did he say?"

"I think he took it well. He should treat studying like a job."

"That's good. Well, at least he listens to you. More orange?"

She poured him a third glass of orange.

"Does he not listen to you?" asked Adam.

"He does and he doesn't. It depends on the moment and who he is with. He doesn't think about his future, and that's what worries me."

At that moment, Michele walked into the kitchen and sat down next to Maria.

"Did you sleep well, my darling?"

"Yes, thank you." Michele looked at Adam and smiled. "Adam looks like a matchstick!"

"I know. Goodness knows what his mother is going to think."

"What are you doing in the summer?" asked Michele.

"No plans yet."

"Why don't you come with us to Camogli?"

"That's a wonderful idea," said Maria. "We have an apartment there, and it's near the sea."

"Okay, I would love to come."

On the way to the airport, Maria stopped at the market and purchased fifty blood oranges.

"Mamma, what are you doing? They have oranges in England," said Michele.

"Yes, but not blood oranges."

"They won't fit in his luggage."

"Yes, they will."

In the departure hall, Adam opened his bag and put all the oranges inside. Adam was more relaxed, and this time he did not retract from the warm embrace that Michele gave him before he went through security.

****

During the break on Michele's first day at his new school, everyone stood up and chatted with each other in the corridor outside the classroom. One girl, who was chewing gum and reading a magazine, remained seated with her chair leaning against the back wall.

"Chiara, are you coming?"

One of her friends had popped her head back into the classroom to invite her for their usual walk.

"No, thanks. I'm staying here. There's some major gossip in here!" She pointed to her magazine.

Michele glanced at her. She was wearing tight denim jeans and a short-sleeved white blouse. Her hair was stylishly messy, and she looked as though she didn't have a care in the world.

One of his classmates put his hand on Michele's shoulder.

"Forget it, my friend. She's a beautiful rebel. She'll eat you alive!"

Outside the classroom, Michele heard her annoying hysterical loud guffaws, she had clearly found something comical in the magazine. There was something he liked about her, neither of them liked school, so they did have something in common.

When they finished school, Michele followed her out of the building, and he saw her turn left with her rucksack slumped over her right shoulder.

"Hey!" he shouted.

She stopped and turned around.

"What do you want?" she asked impatiently.

"Nothing. Just that I hadn't introduced myself to you."

"Does that matter?"

"It does to me!"

"I'm Chiara. Pleased to meet you." She held her hand out.

"I'm Michele."

"Great. Now I have to go. See you tomorrow."

Things were going well during Michele's first week of school, he was determined to pass exams, so he would study every evening after dinner. He remembered Adam's words about getting into a routine, and that's what Gianni had told him as well.

Michele invited Chiara to go out with him on Friday evening. Maria gave him some money so he could pay for dinner and make a good impression. He had booked a table at a small trattoria in Navigli, and Maria advised him to arrive on time. Chiara arrived half an hour late, and Michele saw her defiantly brush past the waiter, who had asked her if she had made a reservation, and sat down opposite him.

"So how do I look?" she asked.

"Well, you look very beautiful."

"Beautiful! Yuk. I don't want to look beautiful."

"You look like a rebel," said Michele, recalling his classmate's word to describe her.

"I like that. A rebel."

The more wine they drank, the more they talked. Michele placed his hand on top of hers and looked into her eyes, and thought that she could become his girlfriend. After dinner, Chiara took out a packet of cigarettes and a lighter and lit one and passed it to Michele.

"You've got an extraordinary story!" she said, after her first drag of smoke.

"I suppose so."

"I like boys who are different."

"Am I different? In what way?"

"You know, you haven't got the usual mundane story of growing up with parents, going to school, doing sport, listening to music."

"Yes, but I don't know whether that's a good thing or not."

"It doesn't matter. You don't know it any other way. I'd like to meet your mother. She sounds intriguing."

"I'm not sure that's a good idea, Chiara. I mean we've only had one date."

Michele could already see Maria's look of disapproval.

"So now you're trying to slow things down! You were the one almost begging for a date. Arrange it. I'm coming to your apartment next week, and I want to meet your mother."

Michele drank the last bit of wine, thinking he would need something much stronger to cope with them meeting each other.

They left the trattoria and wandered down the bustling street next to the canal, and they went into a bar. Chiara ordered two glasses of limoncello and they sat on two small stools in the corner and chatted. After smoking another cigarette, they left the bar and walked along Viale Cogni Zugna until they reached Chiara's apartment. They stood next to the arched doorway and kissed each other until Chiara pushed him away playfully before disappearing inside.

When Michele reached home, he looked up and saw that the light in their apartment was still on.

"What on earth have you been doing?" Maria asked sternly.

"I told you, I went out with Chiara for dinner."

"Yes, but I didn't expect you to get drunk. You reek of cigarettes. Don't tell me you've been smoking as well."

"I may have had one or two."

Exasperated, Maria looked up to the ceiling.

"One or two! One or two! They're very bad for you. And it becomes a habit. I bet it was Chiara who got you to smoke."

"No, it was my choice. She offered me one."

"Well, I don't want you to smoke again! Do you hear me?"

The following morning, they had breakfast in silence and avoided looking at each other. Maria read the newspaper.

"Chiara wants to meet you," Michele said.

"Good! I want to meet her too!"

Maria gathered her bags, put on her fur coat and left in a huff just as Elisa came in.

Five days later, Chiara arrived at Maria's apartment at four o'clock in the afternoon. Michele could see straight away that Maria didn't like her aloofness. She went into the sitting room, sat down on the sofa and asked Michele to sit next to her and placed her hand on his thigh.

"Would you like some tea, Chiara?" asked Maria.

"No, I don't," she replied. Maria sat down.

"How are you doing at school, Chiara?"

"So so. I mean the classes are utterly boring, and so are the teachers. They're all nuns for crying out loud. How can we take them seriously? But I get through the day. I don't need school as I'm going to be an artist when I finish."

Michele never wanted Chiara to meet Maria, she was saying all the wrong things, and he could see Maria muttering something under her breath.

"What kind of artist?"

"Pop artist. I'm a good singer and I'm in a band with two friends. One of them lives outside Milan and has a garage so we practice there. Then we play at some local bars. We're really good, and we're looking forward to getting our own record label. Would you like to hear some of it?"

In a flash, she pulled her personal stereo out of her rucksack and handed it to Maria.

"I'm sure it's very good. Maybe another time," said Maria, trying her best to compose herself.

"Suit yourself."

"You never told me about this band. Even at dinner," said Michele.

"You never asked me!"

"What was there to ask?"

She touched his chin with her thumb. "I was going to tell you, babe. In fact, I wanted to introduce you to my two friends. I think you would get along with them very well."

"Okay. But when?"

"End of the week. On Friday evening. You can come and see us practice."

"But I've got soccer on Friday."

"Well, come after soccer!"

"Tell me about your family," said Maria.

"My father sells furniture abroad, so he's not often at home. He's always at exhibitions. My mother works part-time at a primary school. She used to work as a teacher for a secondary school, but she had a nervous breakdown because she couldn't control the kids. They offered her an easier job, but she didn't take it. Then there's my younger brother, who's a nerd. He's always in the library studying. He gets bullied at school for being such a nerd. He should chill out a bit more. We don't talk much."

"I see. Do you go away for the holidays?"

"We used to, but now I'm grown up, I go to Rimini with my friends, especially in the summer."

Chiara paused and looked at Michele.

"Babe, you can come with us! You'll love Rimini. I know you will. It's full of clubs, discos and bars. We're planning to go for a weekend just before Christmas. Please tell me you'll come!"

"Yes, all right," said Michele, knowing well that Maria would never let him.

"I've got to go shopping. It's been a busy day. It was nice meeting you," said Maria.

Maria stood up and went to get her coat. Chiara was puzzled, Michele had told her that Maria had wanted to see her, but she imagined that it would have lasted more than ten minutes.

By the door, Maria called out to Michele.

"Yes, what is it?"

"I'll be out for an hour. By the time I come back, please make sure that she's not here."

The door closed.

"What was all that about?" demanded Chiara.

"Nothing. Just leave it. Let's go to my bedroom. We can have some fun there!"

Twelve

Over the last two days, Mario had become restless, so his mother and father were overjoyed to see Maria and Michele arrive on the decking. This time, Adam was with them, and they welcomed him to Camogli. After Michele and Adam came out of the cabin with their swimming trunks on, Maria insisted that Michele put lathers of sun cream on him. She didn't want a repeat of what had happened in Courmayeur. How can someone be so ghostly white, thought Michele.

"You need to get a tan," said Michele. "Let me take a photo of you and Mario together and then you'll see how white you are when we get it developed."

Mario was wearing orange swimming trunks which blended nicely with his heavily tanned skin, and having a photograph of them together would somehow prove to Adam that he needed to do something about his image, and this started with getting a tan. Adam wanted to swim to the church and back, and Michele and Mario went with him. When they came back, Mario and Michele went to play tennis, and Adam put his shorts and t-shirt on and sat on one of the benches and read his book.

After an hour, Maria went up to him.

"Where are Alessandro and Sara?" asked Adam.

"They're sitting on deckchairs below. Listen, can I get you anything to drink?" Maria asked

"I'd love a bottle of water," replied Adam, and Maria went to the restaurant and returned with a bottle of still water and sat opposite him.

"How are you doing at university?"

"It's going well. I'm enjoying it, and I passed all my exams," Adam said, smiling.

"That's good. I'm so pleased. I'm sure you'll do very well. And how is the family?"

"They're also very well, thank you. They were amazed when they saw all the oranges in my suitcase, so my mum bought a fruit squeezer and made some blood orange drinks for all of us."

"She must have thought I'm mad!"

"Not at all," Adam lied. "How is everything with you?"

Maria sighed, she wanted to use this chance alone with Adam to talk about Michele.

"You know, Michele is a good boy, but he still lacks maturity. I recently asked him to come and help me in my office and visit customers. He's good at that because he's confident and gets on with people. After you left at Easter, he took studying more seriously. When I arrived home, he was in his bedroom, reading and doing his homework, and he began to talk more sensibly about his future. It was so reassuring when he told me that he realised how important it was to pass exams and go to university to study politics or media studies. And for the first time, I noticed that he was more mature and less reckless. But the moment he meets someone who is hot-headed, he becomes like them, like a chameleon. For example, he met this girl from school, Chiara, a rebellious, carefree and ill-mannered girl, and started dating her. Then things started to fall apart as he stopped studying and went out nearly every night and smoked and got drunk and came back late. I've been so worried about him. Most of the time, I don't know where he is and who he is with. The headmistress called me one day and asked if everything was okay at home, as Michele was always tired and didn't do his homework. Needless to say, I was disappointed when I saw his poor exam results, that is apart from French and English. And then he's rude and shuns me when I warn him about dating the wrong girls and remind him to study. I even tried to get him interested in art and music by taking him to the Colosseum, the Vatican, Verona and an opera at La Scala but he showed no interest and told me how boring they were."

"That's a shame. I hope things improve."

"I'm sorry to let off steam with you, but he listens to you. Try to talk with him. By the way, don't mention that we've had this conversation."

"No, I won't. I'll find some time to talk to him. I'm sure he'll be all right."

At that moment, Michele and Mario arrived out of breath with their tennis racquets. Michele looked suspiciously at Maria and Adam, they had been talking, and most likely Maria had been venting about him.

"Who won?" asked Maria light-heartedly.

"Michele," said Mario. "But only just."

"Well done, sweetheart!"

Michele ignored her. He didn't like her talking about him to anyone. He imagined her telling Adam about his immaturity and his disdain for studying.

"After you've had a shower, let's take the boat out!" suggested Maria.

"Great idea! Give me half an hour," said Mario.

Mario and Michele lifted the red motorboat from the beach and took it to the shore. As Mario was driving the boat, Maria lay down at the back to catch some sun, and Michele and Adam sat next to each other at the front. Mario stopped the boat and Adam dived into the sea and swam to a nearby crevice. As he was about the climb back on, Michele looked down and frowned at him.

"My mother's been talking to you about me, hasn't she?"

"No, not really. We talked about university and stuff."

Michele didn't know whether to believe him or not, in any case, it didn't matter, Adam was not to blame.

"Come here." Michele reached out his hand and lifted Adam onto the boat.

In the evening, Mario and his parents had been invited for dinner by some other friends, so Maria made some pasta with pesto sauce for the three of them, and opened a bottle of red wine. After dinner, Michele and Adam went for a walk along the bay.

"It's nice to see you again," said Michele. "We'd like you to come and see us more often."

"Thank you. Yes, I'll come again for sure."

"Your Italian is getting much better. Did the cassettes help?"

"Yes, to a certain extent. Take Marco Masini. I understand what he's singing, the words I mean, but

I don't get what he's trying to say, it doesn't translate well. Or maybe it's me. For example, 'Ti vorrei nel chewing gum, mentre vado a lavorare in tram' translates as 'I'd like you in the chewing gum whilst I go by tram to work'."

"Yeah, they are pretty weird. And depressing. To be honest, I don't understand them either! My favourite song at the moment is 'Dieci ragazze', meaning 'ten girls'!" he laughed.

"Yes, that was one of the songs on the cassette!" said Adam.

"Why don't you have a game of tennis with me tomorrow?" asked Michele.

"I don't know how to play tennis."

"You said that about soccer two years ago. Don't underestimate yourself. You can do it. I'll teach you. You have to believe more in yourself. Do you work out at all?"

"No, should I?"

"Well, you're as skinny as a rake. So, if you want to have a nice girlfriend, you need to build yourself up! I'll show you some exercises that you can do."

Adam tried to picture himself with abs and a six-pack and smiled at the image.

"Have you got a girlfriend?" Adam asked.

"Kind of. Chiara. I met her at school. Hang on, let's get an ice cream."

Michele slid through a disorderly queue and brought out two cones with strawberry ice cream, and they walked further along the bay.

"The thing is, my mother doesn't like her at all. She always likes to control who I date and what I do. You know, she even came on the school trip to Hungary, just so she could keep an eye on me and it was so embarrassing. I felt as though I couldn't move and that she was looking at me the whole time. Anyway, back to Chiara. So what if she's a bit rebellious and likes to have fun. But think about it, you're only young once, so you don't always have to be sensible, you can be like that later in your life. My mother keeps going on at me when I don't study or come home late, and the more she nags me, the more I resist. I know it doesn't sound very nice, but I sometimes feel suffocated by all these rules she has for me. I'm an adult now, and I should be able to do what I like."

They finished their ice cream, and Michele led Adam into a small bar, and he ordered two glasses of beer and they found a table outside and sat down. There was a pleasant breeze, and Adam looked at the picturesque enclosure, with lights highlighting the different pastel colours of the buildings.

Michele sipped his beer, and took out a cigarette from his pocket and lit it.

"What do you think?"

"If your mother didn't care about you, she wouldn't keep nagging you about these things, would she? I'm sure she means well, otherwise she wouldn't have sent you to that school. So, I think she wants you to do well. What you're doing now is having fun and not thinking about your future. It's not about doing one or another, it's about doing both. If you show her that you're serious about studying, I'm sure she'll cut loose on you going out."

Michele looked over Adam's shoulder towards the sea.

"Listen, I know my mother is a special person, and I don't like arguing with her. You're right. She does care about me."

"It's better than having someone who doesn't care about you."

"Yes, that's true."

After they finished the beer, they stood up and walked back along the promenade.

****

Maria believed that Adam's visit had had a profound influence on Michele, he was calmer and more settled, and miraculously, he passed most of his exams before Christmas. And he stopped dating Chiara, routinely reviewed the lessons and completed his homework.

After playing football on a Saturday afternoon, Michele volunteered to help Maria with the food shopping. When they arrived home, they had dinner in the kitchen.

"How was the football? Did you win?" asked Maria.

"Of course, you don't need to ask. They have a star player!" said Michele.

"Oh, and who is that?"

Michele laughed.

"I scored two goals."

"Well done!"

"When are you playing again?"

"Tomorrow afternoon."

"Okay. I was planning on going for a walk around Navigli tomorrow morning. Would you like to come?

"Yes!"

"There are some very nice small art galleries, and I'd like to get a gift for one of my manufacturers."

"Okay, I will help you choose!"

Maria's angst about Michele melted away. As she ate her soup, her mind wandered back to when he was eight years old, and she could now see the revival of his younger persona. She was the proud mother of a charming and hard-working young gentleman. She brushed away thoughts of him living on the streets with no education and formed images of him dressed in a smart suit, being a successful journalist or tour operator, going to his apartment, where his beautiful, charming wife and well-mannered children were waiting for him. They would regularly visit her, and she would visit them. And they would live happily ever after.

"I talked with Adam on the phone yesterday. I went over the options I have for university and decided it was better for me to study political science."

"Are you sure?"

"Yes, I'm sure. It's something I'm interested in and he said it would open doors. Gianni said the same thing. You get to articulate points of view, analyse what people have said and explain your opinions. I've got an appointment with one of the professors at the Università Statale at four o'clock in the afternoon on Thursday. You can come if you like."

Thirteen

Mario had advised Michele, albeit patronisingly, that it would be tough to work and study at the same time. Michele was tired of asking Maria for money, and he desperately wanted a job so he could spend his own money on whatever he wanted. He had called Mario and asked him if he could meet him urgently at a bar, and when they met, Michele thought he looked like a tree-cutter with his new beard.

Just as things between Michele and Maria seemed to be getting better, they were at loggerheads with each other during a recent visit to Courmayeur, and this is why he came back to Milan earlier than he had planned. Every single conversation was about studying and work, and she would painstakingly remind him again and again about the need to think about the future. He realised he couldn't concentrate for a long time, but this wasn't a good enough reason for Maria, and her nagging had become so tortuous, that he did everything he could to avoid her. Therefore, he forced himself up at eight o'clock in the morning, showered, went skiing all day, came back home at five o'clock in the evening, and went out again to have an aperativo with some new friends he had been skiing with. The painful part of the day was having dinner with Maria in silence. As soon as he finished, he went out once again to the discos and came back drunk in the early hours of the morning. Maria was at the end of her tether but, for some reason, she tolerated it for four days, and then she decided to draw the line. Enough is enough.

"I hardly see you. I pay for your skiing. I make you dinner. And what do you do? As soon as you finish dinner, you go out, smoke and get drunk! What kind of a life is that? You haven't opened a single book since you've been here," she shouted.

"You can't tell me what to do," he shouted back, and left the apartment forgetting to take his keys with him.

When he got back at half-past one in the morning, he banged on the door and heard footsteps scurrying on the other side.

"How dare you come back at this time! I explicitly told you not to go out. You think that going out and getting drunk is okay? You have no idea what is right and what is wrong. Think of all the things I've done for you, all the sacrifices I've made. And you continue to be rude and disrespectful," she shouted at the top of her voice, no doubt waking all of the neighbours.

She opened the door and looked at him.

"And look at the state of you! What's that scar on your forehead? Have you been in a fight? You stink of smoke. How many times have I told you not to smoke? You never listen!"

He brushed past her in the direction of his room.

"You just do what you like. You're selfish. You don't care about anyone else. You're destroying yourself, and I'm suffering every single day because of you," she ranted.

At that moment, the door from the opposite apartment opened, and a lady with grey hair and pink pyjamas appeared.

"Is everything alright?" she asked.

Maria ignored her and closed the door.

In the morning, Maria asked him if he had been in a fight. Michele knew she would be upset if he told her what had really happened, so he made up a story about separating two boys who were in a scuffle, one boy clenched his hand, aiming to punch the other boy's shoulder, but landed on Michele's forehead, hence the scar. This sounded much better than telling her that after drinking a few Martinis, he started to flirt with a beautiful girl at the bar, not realising that her boyfriend was in the washroom. When he came out, he saw Michele trying to kiss her and threw a punch at Michele's forehead, and just as Michele was about to retaliate, the bartender escorted them outside and told them that they were barred from coming into his bar again.

Michele went to his room and packed his bag. There was only one thing he could do, living with Maria was unbearable.

"I'm going back to Milan," he said.

"Do what you like," Maria said.

Michele took the bus back to Milan and arrived at half-past four in the afternoon. He bought a bottle of Martini from a small supermarket close to home and spent the next two hours watching television and drinking before falling asleep on the sofa. In the morning he awoke with a terrible hangover, so he took a couple of paracetamol tablets and made himself a bath. He wished that Adam had been there to hear him out, but he wasn't, and he needed to talk with someone. That's why he called Mario.

"I need to move out of Maria's apartment," said Michele.

"Are you not getting along with her?"

"That's an understatement! It's a long story. Anyway, I'm going to be starting university soon."

"Okay. That's good news! When do you start?"

"On the fourteenth of October."

The waiter brought two large glasses of draft beer and placed them on their table.

"What are you looking for?" asked Mario.

"Somewhere near the university. Maria has agreed to pay for the rent. I just need to cover the rest, that's why I need a job as well."

"There's a guy called Giuseppe. I don't know him very well, he's a friend of a friend. He's about twenty-seven, so I think he's not got long to go until he graduates. He's already sharing with someone, but that person's moving out after Christmas."

"That's great! Could you look into it?"

"Yes, sure. I'd be happy to."

One week later, Michele started work as a concierge for a hotel in the centre of Milan. His hours of duty were from eleven o'clock in the evening until seven o'clock in the morning, five days a week. Michele thought that this was a job no one wanted, few guests checked in and out between those hours, so he was left with nothing to do. Still, it was a five-star hotel, and he was being paid two million lire per month for doing almost nothing. He broke the monotony by sleeping in a comfortable armchair and chatting with the receptionist.

On his first day at university, Maria went to Paris, her favourite city, for three weeks to visit customers and friends and Michele was glad to have the apartment to himself. He had to substitute daytime sleeping with going to lectures, which, as Mario had said, would be difficult, but he was determined. On the third day, he arrived home from a lecture at five o'clock in the afternoon and ate some tuna salad, which Elisa had prepared for him, then he fell asleep on the sofa. At a quarter to eleven, he awoke with a start, he had fifteen minutes to have a wash, get changed and get to the hotel. The hotel manager reprimanded him for arriving late and told him that if it ever happened again, he would be fired. And that is what happened, a day before Maria returned from Paris two weeks later, he arrived one hour late at the hotel, and the hotel manager dismissed him.

"Certain people don't want to work," said Nicole.

Nicole had come to visit Maria on Saturday morning. Michele stumbled out of bed. When Maria returned home the previous evening, he had told her that it was impossible to study and work at the same time, and Maria had replied that he had no stamina and motivation. She was now telling Nicole about what had happened to Michele at the hotel, and Michele heard them talking about him as he went to the bathroom.

"Yes, he's just bone idle. He doesn't want to do anything. He lacks determination," replied Maria.

Fourteen

Late afternoon on the fourth of January, Michele took the metro to reach Giuseppe's apartment near Corso Buenos Aires. After two stops on the green line, he took the red line towards Corso Venezia. When he arrived, he put his two bulging suitcases on the ground, reached for a large key in his coat pocket and opened the arched door. Inside, he found a light switch and pushed the two suitcases into the tiny elevator and went to the first floor, and then knocked on the apartment door.

Giuseppe let him in.

"You must be Michele. Don't you have a key? Come on in!"

Giuseppe was plump, he had greasy black hair which was parted on the left, and his large brown eyes and broad face gave him an amicable appearance. He was wearing a white t-shirt which hung lazily over his baggy navy-blue jeans.

The entrance of the apartment led to a sparse sitting room, where there were two sofas and a television. Having been interrupted to open the door, Giuseppe returned to his slovenly position on the sofa, took his lit cigarette from the ashtray and turned his eyes back to the television. Michele went into his bedroom, emptied his suitcases and put his clothes neatly in the small wooden wardrobe and the drawers. He was about to go and sit with Giuseppe, but when he glanced at the pile of unwashed dishes and cutlery heaped up near the basin in the kitchen, he decided to go and wash them all. When he finished, he went to the sitting room and asked Giuseppe if he wanted any pasta, which he accepted. This was the best way to get to know him. After all, they were going to be sharing an apartment for the foreseeable future.

They had dinner on their knees and watched a music channel on the television. Giuseppe reached out for a nearly-finished bottle of whisky on the floor, and poured some into a stained glass and passed it to Michele. But Michele declined and handed it back to him.

"Are you studying at the Università Statale?" asked Michele.

"Yeah. I started political science about two years ago. I've only had time to do a few exams."

"What have you been doing?"

"Partying most of the time. You're only young once!"

Giuseppe went to his bedroom and returned with two joints of weed and sat down.

"Do you want some weed?"

"No thanks."

"Come on! It's good stuff. Makes you feel good!"

"In any case, I don't have money for that kind of thing."

"It's okay. Consider it a gift. You look as though you need cheering up!"

"No, it's okay. Anyway, it's dangerous."

"It's not dangerous. If you take a little now and then, it doesn't do any harm. Don't worry, it's okay!"

"Nah, it's okay. I'll leave it. Thanks anyway."

"Listen, why don't we have a spliff together. It won't take more than five minutes. And if you don't like it, you don't need to do it again."

He prepared one joint and lit it. "Here! Take it."

Michele took the joint and inhaled it and lay back on the sofa, feeling sedated.

"That's more like it!" said Giuseppe.

Giuseppe then lit one for himself. "It's good, isn't it?"

Over the next three weeks, Michele spent most of his time studying at the university, trying to make sense of the lectures, whilst Giuseppe stayed at home with a fever. Every evening, Michele prepared dinner for Giuseppe and cleaned the apartment. On Saturday night, Giuseppe was feeling better and invited Michele to a house party.

"Listen, Michele, I'm broke. Could you lend me fifty thousand lire? I'll pay you back. I promise!"

"What do you need it for?"

"Just stuff. Nothing you need to worry about. Come on! Trust me. We're friends, aren't we?"

Michele took out his wallet, withdrew some notes and handed them to him.

"You better pay me back."

"Thanks! I won't be long."

Giuseppe took went to his room, put his coat on, and left in a hurry.

****

The apartment, where the party was being held, was only ten minutes' walk away, so Michele and Giuseppe left at eleven fifteen. Giuseppe banged on the door. A girl, wearing a small white blouse and denim jeans, appeared and welcomed them.

"This is Michele. We share an apartment. You don't mind if he comes, do you? He's at a bit of a loose end."

"Not at all! I'm Simona!"

Giuseppe snaked through the vast number of students and disappeared. Michele guessed that he was going to meet some of his friends. He didn't mind though, as he was left with Simona, a dainty girl with such bold charm. She picked up a bottle of wine and two plastic cups, and led him outside and they sat on the steps for a while.

"It's a bit noisy in there," said Simona

"Yes, it is a bit," replied Michele. "Do you live here?"

"Yes, there are five of us, and we're all students. I'm studying economics. What about you?"

"Political science. One day I want to become a journalist after I graduate."

"I have no idea what I want to do in the future."

She poured some wine into the two plastic cups, and gave one of them to him.

"So, you're living with Giuseppe. How is that working out?"

"It's okay."

"He's quite a character, isn't he?"

"Yes, he is. You can say that again!"

They drank some more wine, and they went back inside. Simona pointed out some of the students and told him their names and where they were from, but Michele wasn't interested. He hadn't kissed or been with a girl for a long time, and even though Simona wasn't his type, he now had a strong desire to kiss her. So, he looked into her eyes and leaned forward and kissed her gently on her lips.

"We should join Giuseppe," she whispered.

She took his hand and pushed her way through the students towards a corridor, and they went into a dimly lit bedroom on the left, where there was a dozen of her friends sitting on the floor with their backs to the wall. They were all chatting and taking turns to take a drag from the same joint.

"Come and join us!" Giuseppe said.

He made room for Michele and Simona next to him. Giuseppe passed the joint to Michele, who inhaled it deeply, before passing it onto Simona, and they spent the next hour smoking, drinking and kissing

Giuseppe nudged Michele. "When you're ready, you can go to the bedroom opposite this one."

Simona and Michele looked at each other, and went into the other bedroom, which was dark, save for the lamp with the red lightbulb in the corner of the room. There were three single mattresses on the floor, two which were already occupied by two couples who had also had a brief encounter that evening. Ignoring them, Simona and Michele knelt opposite each other on the middle mattress and undressed each other.

****

Michele's determination to study started to fade, he spent less time at university and more time enjoying the sedated sensation of smoking hashish with Giuseppe, and this helped him to escape from the incomprehensible, mundane lectures, and his uncertain future.

On Wednesday, he went to two seminars on sociology, as he found his subject mildly interesting. Afterwards, he intended to go for a run around Parco Sempione, so he went home, put his tracksuit and trainers on, opened the drawer to take his personal stereo and earplugs, but they weren't there. It had to be Giuseppe, he deducted. He had never paid back the money he had lent him, and he didn't do anything all day. Maybe he stole it and sold it to get more money.

"Have you seen my personal stereo? I left it in my drawer, and now it is gone!"

"Don't look at me! I haven't taken it."

"Don't lie to me. Who could it have been? You're the only one in this apartment. And it's not as if we have guests."

"Michele. Vaffanculo! I've not taken it."

"And you still owe me. Where's that money?"

"I haven't got it. Just chill, will you? You'll get it."

Michele left.

"Negro!" said Giuseppe under his breath, took a sip of whisky and continued watching television.

Michele took the bus to Parco Sempione and ran around the parameter twice. He stopped outside Castello Sforzesco and decided to visit Mario and tell him about Giuseppe.

"What a nice surprise! How are you, Michele?" said Sara.

"I'm okay, thank you. Well, not so good actually."

"Why don't you come in? Mario's in his room."

Michele found Mario reading at his desk. Mario stood up and embraced him and invited him to sit down on the bed.

"So, what's up?"

"Giuseppe. That's what's up. How on earth did you become friends?"

"We aren't friends as such. I've only met him once. I told you, he's a friend of a friend. I knew he was looking for a new flatmate so I thought you would be interested. I heard he's a bit insane but harmless. What has he done?"

"He's borrowed money from me, and he's stolen my personal stereo."

"I'm sorry to hear that."

"Plus, I do all the cooking and cleaning."

Mario laughed. "That's very good of you."

"It's not funny, Mario."

"I know. Sorry."

"So, what should I do?"

"Only one thing you can do. Get out as soon as you can before he takes anything else. Do you want me to come with you?

"Yes, that would be good. I'm going to see my mother now and see if I can move back into her apartment. Can we meet at seven o'clock at Giuseppe's apartment?"

Michele felt relieved after visiting Mario, but anxious about going back to live with Maria. Surprisingly after all that had happened between them, she was glad to see him and offered him some lunch, and he told her what it was like living with Giuseppe, omitting the party and the hashish. Mario was a good friend. He took care of contacting the landlord and helped Michele pack his suitcases.

Fifteen

It took a few weeks before Michele found another job. He was already in debt, and he had used all the money he had earned from his brief time as a night porter on food, drinks and hashish whilst he was living with Giuseppe. He imagined it would have taken a lot less time had he taken another night porter job, that's the last thing he wanted, so he settled with less money working as a part-time receptionist in a hotel, close to the central station. In this way, he could work in the mornings and attend lectures in the afternoon. His employer told him he could take time off for his exams in sociology and history in June, which were just two months away.

Michele went to the library and picked up the recommended history and sociology books, and put them in his bulky blue rucksack. In his bedroom, he opened the history book and turned to the back page. When he saw that he would need to read nine hundred and seventy-four pages, he closed his eyes and wondered how he would ever manage to read it. He switched on the table light, took a pad of paper and pen from the drawer and started to read the first page. There were too many words he didn't understand, and he was disoriented by the length of the sentences with all their relative clauses. Even after reading the sentences several times, he only partially comprehended the meaning, and he was desponded when he realised that it had taken him one hour to read all of three pages. If that's how long it took him, how many hours, days and weeks would it take him to read the whole book? And who cared what happened in 1870? He stood up, went into the kitchen and poured himself a glass of water and returned to his bedroom, closed the history book and put it back into the rucksack and opened the slimmer book on sociology. He read the first chapter on inequality, diversity and society, and it was indeed much easier than the history book. He set himself a target of reading ten pages a day so he would finish it in three weeks. Failing to understand the history book made him feel inadequate as Mario had made an indefatigable effort to read it and had passed the exam with a high grade. He had told Michele that once you get into it, it becomes easier. That was the problem, he couldn't get into it, it was too long, too hard and he wasn't interested in it.

Maria came into his room and was surprised to see him studying.

"Michele! What a nice surprise! How is it going?"

Michele turned around.

"Not very well, to tell you the truth. It's so hard. I can't seem to understand anything in the history book."

"Don't give up. I know it won't be easy at the beginning. But think of what you will achieve if you pass the exams!"

Maria left his room and went into the kitchen to prepare dinner.

Michele got up at six o'clock in the morning and went to the hotel. Time passed quickly because he got to meet different guests from all over the world, and he liked making small talk with them. He would remember regular guests and ask them about what they had been doing. "How is your son's leg?" "How was your trip to Hong Kong?" "Did you manage to visit your cousin in the end?" "How is your grandmother?"

In the afternoon, he had to face the lectures. Maybe he would be more motivated and inspired if he studied in the library instead of at home. After attending a two-hour lecture on the Franco-Prussian war from 1870 to 1871, he went to the library and sat down at a table and attempted to read the history book again from page one. If Mario could understand it, so could he. But after twenty minutes, he just couldn't concentrate anymore, and he gave the history book back to the librarian, never wanting to see it again, and left. Books, books and more books, how could people possibly read them?

It was chilly outside, and it was getting darker. Instead of taking the tram back home, he walked towards the Giardini della Guastalla. He needed to let off steam. As he got nearer to the entrance to the gardens, he looked up and saw a girl with a denim jacket, spiky bleached hair and pale skin, walking towards him. Their eyes met. After she passed him, she stopped and looked around, and Michele did the same.

"Do I know you?" asked Michele.

"I don't think so," she said. "Would you like to know me?"

"I think so," said Michele, grinning.

"I'm Rachele."

"I'm Michele."

Rachele took a packet of cigarettes from her small black shoulder bag.

"Cigarette?"

"Thank you," he said.

"Where are you going?" he asked.

"To meet some friends. Would you like to come?" she asked.

"Yeah. If you don't mind."

Two boys were waiting for her outside the gardens. One had black hair and was wearing tight black jeans and a black coat, and he was leaning against a wall talking to his friend who had his head tilted upwards, so he could blow the smoke up into the sky. He was lanky and tall and was wearing a leather jacket with black trousers.

"Hey! This is my new friend, Michele," said Rachele.

"Sabrino," said the black-haired one.

"Sandro," said the lanky one.

They shook hands with him.

"You got the stuff?" asked Rachele.

"Sure, let's go to mine," said Sabrino.

They took the tram to Corso Buenos Aires and walked to Via Tadino. Sabrino opened the gate, and after passing through a courtyard, they went upstairs to Sabrino's studio apartment on the first floor. Sabrino switched on the light. Inside there was an empty bottle of vodka and an ashtray overspilling with cigarette butts on the floor next to the sofa bed. On the left, there was a tiny kitchen area, and on the right, there was a small bathroom. They sat on the floor, leaning against Sabrino's bed and Sandro prepared some hashish, whilst Rachele opened a bottle of vodka, which she took from the fridge. She took a swig and handed it to Michele, and Sandro inhaled the hashish and passed it to Rachele.

"This is amazing," said Rachele.

"Yeah. It's quality," said Sabrino.

"Have you done this before, Michele?" asked Sandro.

"Yeah, and it was really good!"

"Why did you take it?" asked Sandro.

"It helps me to escape. You know, forget all my problems."

"Everyone does it for that reason," said Sabrino.

They spent the next hour smoking and drinking and Michele got so high that he kissed Rachele.

"I think I'm in love," he said.

"Steady on!" said Rachele.

At nine o'clock, they finished the hashish and vodka.

"Time to go," said Sabrino.

"Michele, we meet every day at this time. If you want, you can come again. Hashish costs, so you would have to pay for it," said Sandro.

"Okay," said Michele.

Rachele helped Michele to his feet, and they went to the metro station.

"Will you be able to get home by yourself?" she asked.

"Sure, no problem."

"Okay. See you at the metro station, Corso Buenos Aires at seven o'clock tomorrow."

"Okay."

After leaving the station, Michele stopped by a takeaway pizza place and bought a slice of pizza and ate it as he was walking home. When he opened the door, Maria was startled to see him, she thought he would have been studying in his room just like on the previous day, and she had prepared dinner for him.

"Where the hell have you been? I prepared some dinner, and it's gone cold."

Michele didn't have time to reply, he ran straight into the bathroom and vomited in the toilet.

"That'll teach you not to drink and smoke," Maria said.

"Just shut up, will you?" shouted Michele.

His head was throbbing, so he went to his bedroom and closed the door behind him.

Now Michele had a new routine: hotel in the morning, failed attempts to understand lectures in the afternoon, then hashish with Rachele, Sabrino and Sandro in the evening. At nine o'clock, he would take Rachele into the park and make love to her on a secluded bench, and then go home. Maria didn't talk to him, and he didn't talk to her.

Three weeks later, Michele received his first paycheque, so he put it into his bank account and withdrew cash and used most of it to buy hashish from Sabrino. He went less frequently to Sabrino's apartment, and he lost interest in Rachele. He ascertained that he didn't need people around him, he was in good company with a bottle of vodka and some hashish.

****

On the evening before Michele was supposed to take the history exam, he went to Parco Sempione and sat on a bench with his most trusted friends, and spent two hours smoking and drinking until these friends were no longer with him. He hobbled towards Castello Sforzesco and found an empty bar on Via Dante.

"Please Signora. I have a terrible headache," he said to the lady behind the cashier.

"Have a seat," she said sympathetically.

She asked one of the bartenders to fetch a plastic bag full of ice cubes from the kitchen, and she then rubbed it on his head.

"You've had too much to drink, haven't you?" she said.

"Please, where am I?"

"You don't know where you are? Where do you live?"

Michele told her where he lived, and she called for a taxi to pick him up and take him home.

The following day, he called in sick at work and didn't take the history exam. Feeling a bit better, he got up at two o'clock in the afternoon, had a bath, put his suit on and went to the bank. He asked the bank manager for a loan and produced the contract he had with the hotel and was pleased that his request was accepted. Right now, he wanted to do something that made him happy, so he went to a car showroom and purchased a CTI Peugeot.

As he was driving back home, he was in two minds, whether to call Rachele or Chiara. He hadn't seen Chiara for ages. He had explained to her, irrationally, that it would be harder for them to meet so regularly as he would be working and studying. And when they did occasionally meet, he didn't appreciate her not wanting to make love with him anymore. If he showed her the spanking new car, she would surely change her mind. He parked the car and went to a phone box.

"Long time!" Chiara said when she picked up the telephone.

"Yes, too long," said Michele. "I've missed you."

"Have you?"

"Yes."

"What have you been up to?"

"Not much. Hotel and university. Same old boring life. And you?"

"We went to Rimini many times without you. You were too busy. We've made some new songs."

"Oh, nice! Listen, Chiara. You're going to love this. I bought a new CTI Peugeot today. Would you like to go for a spin?"

"Now that's what I call cool! Definitely. Can you pick me up on Friday? Let's say at seven o'clock?"

On Friday evening, Michele put his best clothes on and proceeded to Chiara's apartment. She got in, and they sped off.

"So where would you like to go?" Michele asked.

"I don't know. Let's just go for a ride."

"Okay, and then we can go for a pizza together in Brera."

"I'm sorry. I need to be back at nine."

"Why?"

"I was going to tell you earlier. I'm seeing someone else. Andrea. He was in the same class as us. Do you remember him?"

"I see."

Michele drove around the Navigli area, randomly choosing side streets to go down whilst Chiara looked out of the window, feigning interest in the people and buildings. After fifteen awkward minutes, Michele drove her back to her apartment, and she got out. He wound down the window.

"Nice to see you again," he said.

"Good to see you too."

He drove to Porta Romana, parked the car near an Irish pub, went inside, ordered a scotch and found a seat in the corner. He was alone. Chiara was dating someone else, Maria was not speaking with him, and no one in the Irish bar bothered to look at him. It was as if he wasn't there. He ordered two more scotches, then went outside to a side street and prepared some hashish. After half an hour, he got into his car, reversed and switched to first gear. As he proceeded onto the main road, he saw a blur of flashing orange lights and cars moving in all directions. Everything looked hazy. There was heavy traffic, and the lights from the cars became too bright, and the sounds of the engines too loud. He was behind a line of cars, and when the traffic lights changed to green, he accelerated so quickly that he crashed into the car in front of him, severely damaging the back of the other car. The man from the car in front, whose face was as red as the traffic light, got out and strode angrily towards Michele and shouted something at him, but he couldn't find the handle to wind down the window. He rested his head on the steering wheel and listened to all the commotion outside until the police arrived and took Michele and the other driver's details. Michele got out and looked at the bonnet of his new car, which now resembled a crunched-up piece of paper. The police told Michele that he was lucky that the other driver was not injured, and charged him for driving under the influence of alcohol. He was given a hefty fine for dangerous driving and would need to find the money to pay for that as well as for the repair of the other man's car. He had no idea where the police moved his car to. When he sobered up, he took the metro and arrived home at nine o'clock.

Instead of going to his bedroom, he sat on the sofa, in tears.

"Mamma!" he said.

"What is it?" she said without looking at him.

Michele sat on the sofa.

"I've done some really stupid things. I don't know what to do," he said, sobbing.

"Are you drunk again?"

"No, I mean, yes. I was. I'm okay now."

"I've given you all the help I can give you. You never listen. Why should I help you? You're always rude to me, answering back. You never speak to me."

"I'm sorry."

"Sorry! You say that too often. You don't mean it."

Michele stood up slowly and went into his bedroom and lay on the bed, looking at the ceiling, wondering what was happening to him. Ten minutes later, Maria knocked gently on the door, came in and sat on the side of his bed and kissed him on his forehead.

"Let me make us a nice cup of tea, and we can talk about all of this."

Michele went to the sitting room.

"I didn't want it to be like this. I did try and study, but I just couldn't concentrate. I started drinking and smoking lots of hashish, so I could escape from everything. I'm jealous of Mario because he knows how to study and pass exams, whereas I can't. Then I started smoking even more hashish, and you know, it costs a lot of money. To make matters worse, I am in debt at the bank. I took a loan out to buy a car and spent most of my earnings on drink, cigarettes and hashish. I crashed the car after drinking too much. And I have to pay for that as well."

"I'll tell you what we can do," she said softly.

"I've been thinking of this for some time. I asked Nicole and Ben about it. When you were little, you were curious when you saw the seeds in the greenhouse in Garda. Do you remember? How would you like to stay there for a few weeks and help with the gardening and study at the same time? Nicole is happy to help you with your reading. And there would be no hashish."

Sixteen

As they approached Courmayeur, Adam said how much he adored the view of the glistening mountains and hoped that one day he could climb to the top. Michele was so pleased when he called him at the last minute to say he could visit them for five days during Easter. After they unpacked, they meandered around the town, relishing the fresh air. They stopped at a small café, and Maria asked the waiter for a table for three people and ordered some tea.

"You've been very quiet in the car," said Maria.

"Sorry!"

"I'm just joking. You must be very tired after the flight. Tell us about what you've been doing. How is your family? Are you doing well at university?"

"My family is fine, thank you. I joined the Italian society at the university, and we get together once a week with Italian native speakers and watch films and cook pasta. They taught me how to make it al dente! I've got used to pasta now. At the weekends, we go for day trips to the countryside or other cities, and we are only allowed to speak in Italian. We've just started studying 'Inferno', which is extremely hard but I suppose you can't get a degree in Italian without Dante. What have you been doing?"

"I'm still at university, and I passed five exams so far. I lived with a friend for a month, but it didn't work out well."

"Yes, that was a real disaster," said Maria.

"Anyway, we've missed you," said Michele.

"Me too. I'm so happy to be here again."

"We've arranged some proper skiing lessons for you tomorrow, and we'll be putting lots of sunblock on you before you go," said Maria.

Michele introduced Adam to the skiing instructor before gathering his equipment and going skiing with other friends. The instructor showed Adam and the other four beginners how to put the skis on, and then they practised walking. Then he demonstrated how to move forward, slow down and stop, and when they became more comfortable moving in the snow, they took it in turns to ski down a small gradual slope. They fell several times during their first attempt, and the instructor taught them how to stand up by themselves. Later in the morning, Adam descended the slope without falling, and in the distance, Michele was watching him. After the lesson, Michele and Adam went to a trattoria for lunch.

"What are we going to do this afternoon?" asked Adam.

"More skiing lessons."

"But I thought the lessons were just in the morning."

"Yes, that's right. Kind of. I'm taking over this afternoon. We're going to do some more practice."

They started on the same gentle slope where Adam had been practising in the morning, and Michele encouraged him to accelerate and taught him how to swerve left and right. They took the chair lift to a moderate slope, and one hour later, he was able to confidently descend without losing balance and tumbling into the snow.

****

Later in the week, Michele and Adam went to the pub and ordered two bottles of beer and sat at a small table near the coal fire.

"You did very well today!"

"Yeah. I never expected to be able to ski. I want to try some of the more difficult slopes."

"All in good time. Take it easy."

Michele stared at the bottle in front of him, something was upsetting him, and when he looked up, Adam could see his watery eyes. He took a paper handkerchief from his pocket, wiped the tears away and took a cigarette and a lighter from his shirt pocket.

"To be honest, I don't know where to start. It's like the world is collapsing around me. I told you on the phone all about what has happened recently. Mamma helped me by sending me to stay at Uncle Ben and Aunty Nicole's villa in Garda to put a stop to me drinking and smoking, and it did work. I suppose that helping to tend the garden was a kind of therapy and helped me to be much calmer. And Nicole helped me to study and thanks to her, I passed three exams in public law, sociology and economics. Mind you, the grades were not that great, but at least I passed. The effort is just too much and Gianni, Tommaso and Mario are all getting ahead with their exams, and that makes me jealous, as I'm so behind. I keep thinking that university's not for me."

He gulped down the beer and went to the bar and ordered another two bottles, and went to the washroom.

"Anyway, where was I? Ah yes. So now I'm living with Mamma again, and I'm back to my old ways. She got mad with me when I admitted that I'd been smoking hashish again, but I just can't stop. To get away from it all, I drown my sorrows at a bar after university and I usually get back home at two o'clock in the morning, completely stoned. I know she's waiting for me, as soon as she spots me in the courtyard, the lights in the apartment go off, and she goes to bed. In the morning, there's the usual row. I know she doesn't deserve this, but it's become a vicious circle, and I don't know what to do. I wish you lived here. I feel that you know me better than anyone else even though we don't see each other that much."

Adam listened intently, and Michele paused and drank some more beer.

"And then, there's my real mother, that's my biological mother, who wrote to me say that she's happily living with her husband, Antonio, in some God-forbidden place in Portugal and she's missing me. Does she expect me to believe her?"

"Do you write back?"

"Sometimes but it's always a brief letter just to say I'm doing well."

Michele finished drinking the second bottle of beer and ordered a third one. Adam was thinking about what he had said and gave him a warm smile.

"Why don't you go away for a bit? Get a job in a different country for a few months."

"How can I do that with a Cape Verdean passport? It's very difficult."

"Very difficult doesn't mean impossible. What do you think?"

He considered the prospect of leaving all his problems behind and starting a new chapter.

"Yes, I like the idea." He brightened up. "But where and what?"

"Well, you like sport, and you've always talked about working in hospitality and tourism."

"Yes, that's true, but I can't exactly be a manager without a degree."

"There are other jobs."

"Like what?"

"I don't know. Barman, waiter, sports instructor, entertainer. In England, there are agencies, which organize four to six-month contracts for sport teachers and entertainers. Surely, there must be something like that in Italy. And you speak good English, and you're very likeable."

Michele saw a light at the end of a long and dark tunnel. On his return to Milan, he visited an agency, which specialized in entertainment in hotels across the world. He applied for the position of 'entertainer and sports instructor' in a hotel in Hammamet, Tunisia and was accepted.

Seventeen

The airport terminal in Tunis was heaving with passengers trying to overtake each other as they rushed towards passport control, many of them tried to jump the queue, which infuriated the security guards so much that they sent them to the back of the line. Michele was overwhelmed by the stuffy and sticky atmosphere and thought that the heat probably caused some of the outbursts from impatient passengers.

After waiting in the queue for two long hours, Michele finally reached the desk. The guard looked at him, examined his documents, turned to his colleague and said something in Arabic to him. The colleague shrugged his shoulders, and the guard gave his passport, visa and letter from the agency back to him, and let him through. He picked up his large brown suitcase from the carousel and went through customs.

In the arrivals' hall, Michele ignored the five men posing to be official taxi drivers, offering to take him wherever he wanted at a good price. Eventually, he found a small man with a moustache and thick beard holding a placard with his name.

"Hello. Michele? I'm Mostafa. Welcome to Tunisia."

They shook hands.

"You're the last one. The others are waiting in the van. Let's go!"

Mostafa led the way, and Michele followed with his suitcase and rucksack to the car park. The intense humidity made Michele feel dehydrated, so he asked Mostafa for a bottle of water, but his voice was drowned by the noise of car engines and the klaxons as the cars competed with each other to leave the airport. When they got to a dusty old white van parked under a shelter, Mostafa helped him put his luggage in the boot, and Miguel jumped inside. Mostafa lit a cigarette, turned on the engine and drove out of the airport towards Hammamet.

Michele asked Mostafa again if he could have a bottle of water, and he replied that he would have to wait a couple of hours until they arrived in Hammamet. Michele greeted the other people in the van, who were also Italian, then put on his headphones and slept for most of the journey, occasionally opening his eyes to look at the desert on each side of the motorway.

The hotel was a massive white complex which was close to a glorious beach with white sands and a clear sea. As they pulled up to the front entrance, Michele took a quick look at the different shaped swimming pools with shades and deckchairs and thought this was an ideal place for him to work, meet people and start a new life. When they stepped out of the van, a large man with thick gelled bleached hair, probably in his late fifties and doing his best to look younger than he was by wearing a Hawaiian t-shirt and bright orange shorts, came to meet them.

"Welcome! Welcome! So, who have we here?" he boomed excitedly.

Before they had the chance to introduce themselves, Mostafa, who was standing beside them, looked at his clipboard and in a military-like manner, reeled off the names: Michele, Filippo, Cristina and Vincenzo.

"Good afternoon. I'm Tony! And I'm going to be looking after you for the next few months. Now you must be exhausted, so if you go and see Fatima in the lobby, she'll give you the keys to your room and you can have a rest. We'll meet at the lobby at six o'clock and then we'll have some dinner together."

Fatima told Michele and Vincenzo that they would be sharing a room. Michele was hoping to stay in a luxurious bedroom with a view of the sea, like the ones he had stayed in when he had been on holiday with Maria, but that was not to be. Inside there was an old stained brown carpet, the mirror in front of the basin in the bathroom was slightly cracked, and the blue and white chequered shower curtain had a large tear in it. And there was only one small towel on a railing next to the toilet.

"Well, it's not exactly the Ritz," said Michele.

"I don't know what the Ritz looks like? Do you?"

"I think I stayed there in Paris. Or was it New York? I can't remember.

"You're kidding me."

"No, I'm not! My mother has taken me all over the world."

"You're lucky! This is my first time I've been outside Europe."

Vincenzo was a tall thin boy with blonde hair and a dark complexion, and he was wearing a navy-blue t-shirt and dark brown shorts. He told Michele that he had just graduated in engineering from Pisa University, and he was planning to take a few months off to enjoy himself and earn some money. He had been on the university basketball team and was looking forward to teaching young children how to play. When Vincenzo asked about Michele, he was reluctant to share his recent troubles, he wanted to forget them.

"I'm still studying political science at university, and I've been working at a hotel at the same time. I'm interested in politics, but I want to go into tourism or hospitality in the future. So, all in all, this is a great opportunity for me."

"Well, this sounds ideal for you!"

At six o'clock, they met in the lobby with their new peers, and Tony guided them to a boardroom on the ground floor, where each place had a name tent and schedule for each person. There were periods allocated for coaching and refereeing football, volleyball and basketball matches on the beach and performing sketches in the evening after dinner. Tony switched on the overhead projector and gave a presentation about etiquette, policies and how to prepare for sketches. Afterwards, they had dinner together and then went to bed.

In the afternoon on the following day, Michele was tasked with teaching a group of early teenagers to play volleyball on the beach, so he asked them to sit in a semi-circle on the sand, and showed them how to perform a forearm strike, set and spike. He asked them to practice these techniques in pairs and then organised a game. One of them reminded him of Adam, as he kept dropping the ball, so he went up to him and encouraged him to keep trying. After one hour, Michele blew a whistle, indicating the end of the game, but they didn't want to finish so he promised them he would be back tomorrow.

Michele enjoyed the sports with the teenagers and children much more than the sketches and games for the adults in the evening. They were given scripts, and they had to shamefully dress up as brainless characters and act out ridiculous slapstick comedy scenes, which Michele didn't find funny at all. Fatima told him that most of the audience was made up of over-sixties from England on a 'Golden Tours' holiday package. The talent contests seemed to be the most captivating as many couples competed for a prize for being the best dancers or singers. As one of the judges, Michele had to mask his despair by complimenting them on their stunning performances, and expressing astonishment that they weren't already famous stars. On a couple of occasions, Michele overheard a few of them saying that they would apply for a real competition when they returned home.

****

On one of his days off two months later, he saw two attractive girls step out of a car. He had been on a long run on the beach and was sprinting towards the hotel entrance when he saw the concierge helping them out of the taxi and carrying their suitcases to the lobby. Covered in sweat, he avoided bumping into them by using the side entrance to the hotel and the stairs to get to his room, where he saw Vincenzo sitting on his bed reading a book.

"Two girls have just arrived! One of them is really hot!" Michele said, out of breath.

"Did you speak with them? Do you know where they're from?"

"How could I? I don't want them seeing me like this!"

"Yeah. You better have a shower."

It was the first time that Michele had seen such good-looking girls since he started work in the hotel. He had to go and find them immediately, so he put on his favourite t-shirt and shorts and sprayed some cologne on his chest and neck. He went everywhere, the bars, the two restaurants, the lobby and the swimming pool area but they were nowhere to be seen. After a thorough search of the entire hotel, he came to the conclusion that they must have been tired after their journey and were resting in their bedroom, or bedrooms. He went to one of the restaurants, had some couscous and salad, and then went back to his bedroom.

"Have you not eaten anything?" asked Michele.

"Not yet. I've nearly finished my book. I'll go down in a few minutes."

"I didn't find them."

"I thought not. Otherwise, you wouldn't be here!"

"Yes, I suppose."

"How do you know that she's hot? You only got a glimpse."

"It was enough. There's something about her, and I just can't put my finger on it. She's attractive and beautiful. Do you know what I mean?"

The following evening, Michele was finishing a tedious sketch, dressed as a cleaner, and one of his fellow entertainers had to pour a large glass of water over his head when he wasn't looking. This was the climax of the scene, and everyone laughed, including the two girls, who Michele saw in the corner of his eye. They were sitting around a small table with a bottle of champagne and two glasses. How embarrassing was that! He dashed upstairs, had a shower and put some different clothes on, so they would not recognise him, and rushed downstairs. He had become accustomed to being perhaps too overconfident with girls when he met them for the first time, but this time it was different, he was nervous and anxious. He went to the bar and ordered a vodka and orange and drank half of it, and then went up to them.

"Excuse me. Sorry to disturb you. Have you just arrived?"

"We arrived yesterday," said the girl on the left, with a heavy French accent.

She had beautiful silky blonde hair, oval brown eyes and her smile showed a perfect set of teeth, and she was wearing a light pink blouse. The girl on her right had thick brown wavy hair, blue eyes and was wearing a white blouse.

"I'm Michele,"

"I'm Fabienne, and this is Camille," replied the girl on the left.

"Why don't you sit down?"

Michele took a chair from another table and sat down opposite them, with his back to the stage.

"Are you celebrating something?" asked Michele, looking at the bottle of champagne.

"It's my birthday!" exclaimed Camille.

"Happy birthday!" said Michele.

Camille stood up and went to the bar and brought back a champagne glass and poured a glass for Michele.

"Where are you from, Michele?" asked Camille.

"Milan. I've come to Hammamet for work, so that I can get some more experience with hospitality management and tourism."

"Yes, we know you work here!" Fabienne teased him.

"Oh no. Don't tell me you saw me in that sketch!"

"Of course, we did! And you saw us looking at you as well. You looked so embarrassed," said Fabienne.

"That was terrible. I made a fool of myself," said Michele, looking down in shame.

"You didn't at all. It was really funny, wasn't it, Camille?"

"Yes, it was very funny," confirmed Camille.

Although Michele would have preferred that they had not seen him on stage, he was mildly relieved that they, unlike him, found it amusing.

"How long are you here for?" asked Fabienne.

"Six months. I have about four more months to go. Then I go back to Milan and continue my degree in political science."

They sipped their champagne.

"Where are you from?" asked Michele.

"Monaco in France. It's very beautiful. Have you been?" asked Fabienne.

"No, but I would love to go," he replied, hoping not to sound too presumptuous. "And what do you both do? Are you working or studying?"

"I'm a senior nurse in the accidents and emergencies department. Believe me, I've seen everything. People even get their hands caught in photocopier machines. Some of them are drugged up to their eyeballs and are dumped at the entrance to the hospital at two o'clock in the morning. The list goes on," said Fabienne.

"I'm a primary school teacher. It's nowhere near as interesting as Fabienne's job."

At that moment Vincenzo tapped Michele on the shoulder and grabbed another chair and introduced himself to Fabienne and Camille. Michele told him where they were from and what they did.

"I'm sorry. We've just finished the champagne, Vincenzo," said Camille.

"That's no problem. Shall I get us a bottle of red wine?" Vincenzo suggested.

"That would be very nice," replied Camille.

"I'll come with you," said Michele.

Whilst they were waiting for the barman to serve them, Michele wanted let Vincenzo know that Fabienne was out of bounds.

"Vincenzo, just to let you know…"

"It's okay. I already worked that out," interrupted Vincenzo.

They returned to their seats and Michele poured the wine into four glasses, and they toasted each other.

Michele was pleased when Vincenzo started to talk with Camille leaving him to get to know Fabienne better. After half an hour, the deejay appeared and played 'Tainted Love', and they stood up and went to the dance floor.

After the last dance, Michele looked around and couldn't see Vincenzo, so he assumed he had gone to bed. Michele accompanied Fabienne to her bedroom, gave her a kiss and wished her good night. He opened the door to his room quietly and crept into bed, without switching the light on, so that he wouldn't wake Vincenzo.

In the morning, he woke up and saw Vincenzo's untouched bed. He showered and took the elevator downstairs to breakfast and found Fabienne, Camille and Vincenzo sat around one of the tables, eating omelettes and bread. Fabienne saw him and beckoned him to sit with them.

"You're up late," remarked Vincenzo.

"Yes, I slept in. And I have to go in a few minutes."

"Ah yes. You're refereeing."

Michele turned to Fabienne. "Good morning. Did you sleep well?" he asked tenderly.

"Yes, thank you. Did you?"

"Too well!"

He looked quickly at Camille and Vincenzo sitting opposite them, now knowing that they had spent the night together. He ate a piece of bread, drank a glass of milk, wiped his mouth with a napkin, and as he was about to leave, Fabienne took his hand and kissed him on his cheek.

"I'll see you later," she said.

Halfway through the soccer match, Fabienne came to see Michele refereeing. She laid her beach towel on the sand, sat down and removed her top, revealing a black and white striped bikini. Michele saw her and wondered if she too supported Juventus. No, it must be a coincidence, he thought. She took a tube of sun cream out of her bag and lavishly rubbed it all over her body and fitted her large sunglasses carefully around her ears, and then gave a little wave to Michele, and he waved back at her.

"Is she your girlfriend, Michele?" asked one of the boys.

When the other boys started to laugh, Michele became uncomfortable and wished that Fabienne had not come to watch him.

"Never mind that! Let's get back to the soccer," he said.

"Yeah, but is she your girlfriend or not?"

"Maybe. Come on. It's your shot."

"Maybe," the boys chorused.

"I think 'maybe' means yes," said one of them.

After the game, Michele and Fabienne had lunch together by the pool, and Michele decided not to bring up her watching the soccer match. Instead, he wanted to find out more about her.

"I had always wanted to work in a hospital, even since I was a little girl. Don't ask me why. I think it was because my mother was admitted to hospital when I was very young to have gall stones removed. I remember being with my father and younger sister, and we saw all these doctors and nurses taking care of her. I was a good all-rounder at school, but I preferred the sciences. We had amazing biology and chemistry teachers, and they inspired me to study these two subjects at the university in Lyon. I am planning to study for a doctorate in the future so I can work on a research project. You're probably wondering why I am so passionate about working in accidents and emergencies. I have done rotations in dermatology, paediatrics and neurology, but in accidents and emergencies I'm under a lot of pressure to save people's lives when they are close to death, and that is rewarding."

She finished eating her salad, and Michele thought how Maria would be so impressed with her.

"My father's a highly reputable barrister, specialising in criminal law. He always seems to be on call so he can be very busy and gets back from work late sometimes. He also belongs to a chess club and takes part in competitions. He taught me how to play, but I'm nowhere near as good as him. My mother works part-time at a little patisserie just around the corner from where I live, and she occasionally does embroidery work for some of our friends. My sister, Françoise, is twenty-three years old, two years younger than me. She's doing a Masters' degree in business in London. I miss her being in Monaco as we get on very well. We often played tennis together. My parents gave me a beautiful new camera for my last birthday, as they knew I was interested in photography, so during my time off, I go to the countryside in the south of France and take stills of the landscape. Last year, I saved enough money to buy a small apartment not so far from the sea and close enough to my parents. It's very cosy. You should come and visit sometime. It's not so far away from Milan!"

Michele was mesmerized. She was beautiful. She had a good family. She was intelligent. She was stable. She was perfect. He wanted her. He needed her in his life. Michele could think of nothing else apart from being with her. He dreamt of becoming engaged, getting married, building a home together and having children. Maria would be proud of him, and they would be the happiest couple in the world.

During the next two weeks, she watched him referee every soccer game and admired how he coached the children playing volleyball. They regularly went to lunch and dinner together and went for long walks along the beach.

On her last day, they dined at the poolside and then went for a walk along the shore, treading in the crystal blue water. The light from the two floodlights gave the beach a romantic glow.

"You don't suppose that we…," began Michele.

"Keep in touch?" Fabienne finished the question.

She stopped, took his hand and faced him.

"You are very shy. I like you very much and I would love to see you again. We'll write to each other. Time passes quickly. Then you can visit me in Monaco, and I'll visit you in Milan. Then we can take it from there."

Michele took her hand, and they dived into the sea. The transparency of the water and the floodlights made it easy for them to see each other under the water. He wrapped his elbow around her neck and they kissed passionately for as long as they could. They then went back to the shore. He found a secluded area where no one could see them, removed his t-shirt and her bikini, and they made love.

Eighteen

Maria was managing her accounts at her grand wooden desk in her office, a large showroom with merchandise displayed on small tables dotted around the room, whilst her secretary was daintily placing jewellery in small grey bags and tying them at the top. She closed the ledger, went to the opaque window and watched the people passing by.

Two weeks after Michele's return to Milan, Fabienne had come to visit him for the day, so Maria had the chance to meet her. She thought it was too good to be true that Michele had fallen in love with such a beautiful and intelligent girl. Nevertheless, she was dismayed that he had taken on a job as a night porter again at a hotel far from the centre and forfeited his studies at the university. If only it had been the other way round. She sat down again and thought about offering him a job with her, and she would bring this up with him when she met him and Fabienne for lunch. Maybe this would enable him to complete his degree. Fabienne had already arrived in the morning, as it was Michele's birthday, and was having a walk with Michele near the Duomo, and Adam would be arriving at five o'clock in the afternoon. She asked her secretary to give her one of the small bags of jewellery so she could give it to Fabienne, and then glanced at her watch, took her fur coat and left.

Michele and Fabienne were holding hands and looking at the artwork in a shop window in the galleria whilst they were waiting for Maria. When she arrived, they went into a restaurant, the waiter took their coats, guided them to a table near the window and handed them the menus.

"What have you been up to?" asked Maria.

"We went for a long walk along the canal in Navigli, then we've been looking at shops!" said Michele.

"We were just talking about the first time we met. You should have seen Michele's face when he was refereeing a football match. As soon as I sat down to watch, the boys tormented him about us being together. He was so embarrassed!" said Fabienne.

"Well, I've never seen him embarrassed," said Maria.

"There's a timidity about him. I mean, he seemed so nervous when we met, even at the bar, weren't you, my darling?"

"I would love to have seen that!" exclaimed Maria.

"It wasn't like that at all. I wasn't nervous," said Michele.

"Yes, you were!" Fabienne pinched his cheek.

They opened the menus and ordered their meal.

"We still need to think about what you're going to do. You can't go on working as a night porter forever," said Maria.

Michele abruptly put his knife and fork down on his plate, he didn't like Maria telling him what he could and couldn't do, and he was about to retort when Fabienne placed her hand gently on his arm, no doubt to calm him down.

"We've already talked about this. He's going to come and live with me. He speaks some French, so we may be able to find him a job in Monaco."

"What kind of job?" asked Maria, surprised.

"There's a lot of tourists in Monaco, so I could find a job as a tour operator or work in a tourist agency," replied Michele, who was enthralled about the prospect of moving in with the love of his life.

"In any case, this is my second time in Milan. It's time Michele came to Monaco!" said Fabienne.

Fabienne described her perfect apartment near the sea and painted a rosy picture of what they would do and where they would go. And of course, Maria would be welcome to visit them at any time. Once they had finished eating, Michele stood up and went to the bathroom.

"Listen, Fabienne. I want to thank you for giving such an opportunity to Michele. But I also want to give you some money for Michele's upkeep."

"You don't need to do that at all. We'll be fine. Thank you anyway," she said.

"But I insist." Maria put her hand on top of Fabienne's as though they were sealing a deal.

After dessert, Fabienne reached into her handbag and took out a small gift-wrapped box. "Happy Birthday, sweetheart!"

Michele opened it immediately and inside was a beautiful silver necklace.

"Here, let me put it on you!" said Fabienne. "What do you think?"

Michele looked delighted. "I like it! Thank you!"

They left the restaurant and Maria told them to be ready at three forty-five, so they could go to the airport to pick up Adam. She hurried towards her car and drove back to her office.

Adam arrived half an hour late, and Michele saw his panic-stricken expression as he entered the arrivals' hall and saw them waiting for him.

"I'm sorry to have kept you waiting! There was a delay," said Adam, out of breath.

"Well, it has been very inconvenient for us!" said Michele.

"Stop teasing him, Michele!" said Maria.

"Happy birthday, Michele!" said Adam.

Michele introduced him to Fabienne.

"Finally! Pleased to meet you! I've heard so much about you," said Adam.

"Likewise. I've heard a lot about you too!"

"Come on, let's go!" said Michele. He looked at Adam's enormous heavy suitcase.

"Good grief! You're only here for one week. How long were you thinking of staying?"

Michele got into the driver's seat and asked Adam to sit next to him.

"How's the teaching going?" Adam had found himself a job as a lecturer and researcher in life sciences at the University of Manchester.

"It's fun! We get to meet people from all over the world."

"You know, I never imagined you as a teacher. But that's nice. I would love to have a job like that."

At home, they sat down in the sitting room, and Michele opened gifts from Maria and Adam. He received a soft brown leather briefcase from Maria and a couple of ties from Adam.

"You better start getting ready," said Maria.

They had booked a restaurant with Mario, his girlfriend, Gianni and Tommaso that evening.

****

Michele wasn't too happy about Fabienne staying for just one day. Maria had presented her with a pearl necklace before Michele took her to the station, and she remained at home with Adam. In the kitchen, Maria prepared some tea, and they sat down at the pull-out table.

"What do you think of Fabienne?" asked Maria.

"She's very nice."

"She's been very good for him. He's lucky to have her. I'm just hoping it will last. You know Michele. He even talked about marrying her a couple of months ago."

"Really? He never said anything."

"They need to get to know each other better, so when he goes to live with her, they will have that chance. She could give him a future if he behaves and gets a proper job."

When Michele returned home, he took the metro with Adam, and they walked through the Castello Sforzesco and sat on a bench in Parco Sempione.

"So, you're leaving," said Adam.

"Yep!"

"For good?"

"I don't know. I hope so. Hey, that doesn't mean that you can't come and visit me in Monaco!"

"That's fantastic. I'm happy you've found the right person."

"Well, it's not all fun and games. I wrote to you, do you remember? She's the hottest girl I have ever met. But sometimes she behaves like Maria. You know, going on about studying and getting a proper job. That's probably why they get along so well. That can be a bit aggravating, but on the plus side, we are in love and I want to marry her. I talked about it with Maria and she agrees."

****

One week later, Michele departed for Monaco by train. He would miss Milan, his friends and Maria but would not miss working at the hotel and going to university, this was a new chapter in his life and he was looking forward to it. After a long train journey, Fabienne met him at the station and whisked him off in her bright red mini to her apartment.

Inside Fabienne's small and clinical apartment, everything was spotless. After Michele removed and placed his shoes sporadically on the mat, Fabienne bent down to straighten them.

"Come! I'll show you around!"

The kitchen was the same size as Maria's, but with modern white cupboards above a stainless-steel basin. Fabienne opened one of them, and there were ten small jars neatly next to each other with the labels showing.

"This section here is for the herbs and spices."

She opened another which had identically sized packets of Corn Flakes on the left and five unopened cylindrical biscuit packets on the right.

"I like to call this the breakfast cupboard!" she continued.

Michele was speechless. They were like museum artefacts that you weren't allowed to touch, in fear of moving them out of place.

"I won't bore you with the rest!" she said.

In the sitting room, there were two sofas, a small glass coffee table and a television in the right corner. The bedroom had shiny brown wooden floorboards and an immaculate bed with a white cover, matching the walls and wardrobes.

"This wardrobe is mine!" Inside, her dresses, suits and blouses were arranged as neatly as the herbs and spices in the kitchen.

"And this one is for you." She pointed at the drawers. "The bottom one is for socks, and the top one is for underwear. You're looking worried. Maybe it's the long journey."

"No, no. It's just that I've never seen anywhere as orderly as this."

She laughed.

"Come on, don't worry. It's not as though I've got any disorder if that's what you're thinking. I just like keeping everything tidy, that's all. Then it's easier for me to find things and I feel much more comfortable in a tidy home. Let me rustle up some dinner for us whilst you unpack. I've got some lovely salmon and a salad," she said, leaving Michele looking dumbfounded in the bedroom.

He surmised that her obsession with cleanliness and tidiness came from working in a hospital, so there was indeed nothing to be worried about.

After dinner, they went to the bedroom, and Michele lay down on his back looking at the ceiling, whilst Fabienne drew circles on his chest with her forefinger.

"Honey, look at me. Everything's going to be all right," she said soothingly.

At that very moment, the doorbell rang, and Fabienne hurried to the door and opened it to find her parents looking eager to come in.

"This is a nice surprise. I thought we were going to see you tomorrow," said Fabienne.

"Your mother couldn't wait," said her father, a large man with grey wavy hair and an overgrown beard. He was wearing a casual tweed brown jacket, a burgundy shirt and a pair of light green trousers.

"We won't stay long, I promise!" said her mother, a petite lady with black hair, a pale complexion and she was wearing a red dress.

Michele buttoned up his shirt and came into the sitting room.

"You must be Michele," said Fabienne's father.

"Michele, this is Denis, my father, and Patricia, my mother," said Fabienne.

"I'm pleased to meet you," said Michele.

"Isn't he good looking?" said Patricia.

"Don't embarrass him!" said Fabienne.

"We've been dying to meet you! Ever since Fabienne returned from Tunisia, she has never stopped talking about you!" said Patricia.

They sat down on the sofas in the sitting room.

"Are you working tomorrow, dear?" Patricia asked.

"Yes, you know I am."

"I meant, are you working the night shift or the day shift?"

"Day shift for two weeks and then back to the night shift.

It had never crossed Michele's mind that she would be working night shifts and this would mean that he would hardly see her, especially if he found a job in a travel agency during the day.

"What are your plans for tomorrow, Michele?" asked Patricia.

"I don't know yet. I'm going to look for a job."

"Michele, sweetheart, I've already prepared a list of travel agencies. It's on the table in the kitchen with some envelopes and stamps, so you can write to each one tomorrow and send them a copy of your curriculum."

At four o'clock in the morning, Michele awoke to the loud alarm from Fabienne's bedside alarm clock. She kissed him on his forehead, went into the bathroom, got changed into her nursing uniform and had breakfast.

"See you later," she whispered and left.

Michele found it hard to get back to sleep again, but he did eventually manage to doze off and awoke at ten o'clock, went into the kitchen and made himself some tea and ate some biscuits. He looked at the list of fifteen travel agencies in Fabienne's handwriting, which, he noted, was not joined up and each letter was the same size. Before he left Milan, Maria had translated his curriculum into French and had it photocopied thirty times. She had also composed a compelling cover letter, so it was now a question of him copying it fifteen times.

He had a wash, got changed, took the key, which Fabienne had left on his bedside table, left the apartment and descended onto the main street. He didn't know where the post box was, so he decided to wander round in the hope he would come across it by chance. As he was walking, he heard Patricia call out to him from her patisserie. She had been in one of her never-ending conversations with her customers when she caught site of Michele, so she interrupted them and invited him in.

"Didn't I tell you how good looking he is!" said Patricia.

"Oh yes. He is very handsome. Your Fabienne is very lucky indeed."

"This is what we thought," Patricia said.

"What are you doing?" asked one of the ladies.

"I'm trying to find a post box," Michele said quietly.

The six ladies offered to take him to the nearest post box, but Patricia wouldn't let them.

"Lola, you mind the shop! I'll take him. After all, I'm going to be his mother-in-law one day!"

The ladies squealed in excitement at the prospect of attending a wedding, and it would give them something to talk about with their friends and family in the evening.

Patricia took him out for a light lunch, a baguette ham sandwich and a glass of white wine, and then he went back to the apartment. Having nothing to do, apart from wait for Fabienne, he lay on the sofa and watched an episode from an old French detective series after failing to find a football match. He had no idea what time Fabienne would be back. After the programme, he fell asleep for a couple of hours and realised it was half-past five. He looked in the fridge to see if there was anything to eat, and pulled out some cold chicken pieces and some ready-made salad, and prepared dinner for himself. After dinner, he went back to the sofa and watched more television.

At eight o'clock, he heard the sound of Fabienne returning. She put her bag in the hallway and sat next to him.

"I know it's late! Have you eaten?"

"Yes, I had some chicken and salad."

"That's wonderful!"

Michele wanted to tell her how bored he was, that time passed slowly, and he didn't like eating by himself. He wondered how long regular sex could compensate for being alone all day. He kept all this to himself. She snuggled up to him and changed the television channel so she could watch the news.

After breakfast on Saturday morning, Denis and Patricia picked Fabienne and Michele up from their apartment, and they went to their holiday home in the countryside. There was a lot of traffic on the road, so it took a good hour to reach it. When they arrived, Patricia, who was wearing her favourite pink top and brown shorts, took the food and drinks from the boot and put them in the fridge in the kitchen. She went into the cupboard and took out two orange woollen blankets, which were used for an extra layer of warmth on their beds during the winter months, and lay them down on the lawn. She then went back inside and came back with an assortment of food and drinks: chicken pieces, prosciutto, salad, nuts, rice, bread, prosecco and homemade lemonade.

Fabienne and Michele joined them.

"The drinks go on the right!" said Fabienne.

"You'll have to excuse our daughter, Michele. She likes to have things the way they were when she was a little girl," said Denis.

"That's not true. It's just easier to get the drinks if they are together."

"Okay darling, whatever is good for you," said Denis.

"Papa, can you please sit over there next to Maman," said Fabienne.

"Yes, of course, darling."

"And Michele and I can sit opposite you both."

"Is this your summer house?" asked Michele. "It's very beautiful."

"It's a summer and winter house. We call it a holiday home," said Denis.

Patricia, an only child, had inherited a substantial amount of money from her parents when they passed away. So, they invested in a property, which would become a holiday home during the school holidays and a place where they could entertain many friends, which was not something they could do in their smaller apartment in the centre of Monaco. They spent Christmas and Easter at the home, and they had used it as a venue to celebrate Fabienne and Françoise's twenty-first birthdays. With the glorious views of the bay, Fabienne was able to practice her photography, and it was an ideal place for Françoise to draw and paint. Fabienne's parents had met at a friend's dinner party when they were twenty-four years old. It was love at first sight. Patricia had always been interested in baking, so she set up a patisserie, and she has made many friends from regular customers. They and their families often visit them at their holiday home. Denis graduated in law at the University of Basel and set up a legal practice fifteen years ago.

"Would you like some prosecco, sweetheart?" asked Fabienne.

"Yes, please," said Michele.

Fabienne poured some prosecco into a glass and handed it to him.

"It is the weather for prosecco," said Patricia.

"It is indeed, Maman," said Fabienne.

"Anyway, tell us more about you, Michele," said Denis.

Michele let his guard down and talked about where he came from and what he had been through. It was the first time he had talked about it in so much detail, he wished he had the power to erase parts of his past from his mind. Patricia cried when she heard about his time in Vialonga, and she cuddled him.

"You're a part of our family now," said Denis.

After lunch, Fabienne's parents packed everything up, and Fabienne and Michele went to play tennis.

When they returned, Fabienne's parents had prepared some tea and cakes for them, and they sat around the large round oak table in the kitchen and played Denis' favourite card game. At eight o'clock, Patricia took some bread and cheese out of the fridge, and they watched the news and then a film on the television before going to bed.

That night, Michele couldn't sleep, he tossed and turned whilst Fabienne slept soundly, so he eventually sat on the side of his bed for a while, and then went to the window to look at the clear night sky. Why on earth had he told Fabienne and her parents about his past? He had never put his past into words before, what was done was done, what was said was said, revealing these intricacies made him feel vulnerable and depressed. What would they think of him now? Would they treat him any differently? But these weren't secrets, they were confessions, sins even, and should remain between him and God. And now it was too late to turn back.

On Sunday morning, he woke up at ten o'clock in the morning and joined Fabienne and her parents for breakfast. Once Patricia had washed and dried the dishes, they got into the car and went back to Monaco.

****

Michele waited patiently for letters to arrive from the agencies. He had time on his hands, so he helped Patricia in the patisserie during the day, and this seemed to attract more customers, who were curious to know him better. During the third week, he received an invitation to an interview at one of the agencies on Thursday afternoon. Fabienne was delighted and helped him prepare for it.

During his fourth week, he received a polite rejection letter, stating that his nationality and not being resident in Europe made it impossible to hire him. The human resources manager added that his lack of experience contributed to him not being accepted for the job in such a competitive market. He was despondent with the response and disappointed that his nationality had stopped him from being employed. Fabienne had been on night duty for nearly two weeks, so he had hardly seen her.

His patience weakened. It became unbearable. One morning at the end of his fifth week, he decided to talk about what was going through his mind with Fabienne. She normally came home at five o'clock in the morning, would slide into bed and immediately fall to sleep next to him. This time, Michele was fully clothed, sitting on the sofa, waiting for her.

"Darling, what are you doing up at this time?"

"Waiting for you."

"What's wrong?"

"You tell me what's wrong. We never see each other. I don't have a job. There's nothing to do all day, apart from work in a patisserie!" he retorted.

"Don't blame me for not getting a job! You already know that I have to work at night. You knew all of this before you came here!"

"Not that you work at night and at weekends! And don't forget the doctorate you want to fit in."

"That's not the point. If you can't find work, then at least you could study something. But of course, that hasn't crossed your mind, has it? You just don't take the initiative to do things. Have you been to the university or checked out the library?"

"How can I study at university? I have no idea how to go about that. I'm new here."

"Don't feel so sorry for yourself. Just listen to yourself. You sound ridiculous."

"Ridiculous? You are ridiculous with all your obsessiveness with tidiness. I daren't move anything out of place. Do you think that's normal?"

Michele took his key and left the apartment.

"That's right, run away!" he heard her say.

On the main street, there was a cold breeze. He walked down to the harbour to watch the sailors preparing their boats. He was exhausted, so he lay down on a bench and went to sleep. One hour later, a sailor woke him up.

"Are you okay?"

"Yes, I'm fine, thank you," he replied.

"You don't look fine if you don't mind me saying. Would you like a ride on the boat?"

"Yes, okay, why not?"

The sailor pulled the anchor onto the boat, and Michele sat at the front end, looking vacantly at the ocean. He wanted to be alone, and the quietness helped him to think about what he would say to Fabienne when he returned to her apartment. His heart sank as he realised that there might not be such a happy ending for him and Fabienne after all. After an hour, they returned to the harbour, and the sailor helped him get off the boat.

"I hope that has done you some good!" said the sailor.

"Thank you."

He went for a long walk and had lunch at an Italian restaurant before heading back to Fabienne's apartment. She was still in bed, so he waited calmly for her to wake up and prepare herself for work. At four o'clock in the afternoon, she found him sitting on the sofa and sat next to him.

"Listen, I'm sorry about earlier. I didn't mean those things," said Fabienne.

Michele did not believe her.

"I'm sorry too," he said.

"You know I love you very much. It was love at first sight. I'm always thinking about you," said Fabienne.

Michele smiled and caressed her shoulder.

"I love you too," he said.

"But we can't go on like this, especially if you're not happy. So, I was thinking that we should have a trial separation. Things were moving too quickly for us. Perhaps if you go back to Milan and we see each other at some weekends, things might get better. It'll give you time to figure out what you want to do."

Nineteen

Michele and Adam had spent the afternoon in the Irish pub near Cadorna, watching the football and drinking beer. Knowing how Maria would react if he came home reeking of alcohol and cigarettes, Michele thought that spending an hour or so in the fresh air in the park opposite their apartment would remove the smell.

It was a quiet autumnal afternoon. They sat on a bench, watching the orange-brown leaves gently parachute to the ground. Adam had never seen Michele look so broody and lost in thoughts, so he broke the ice

"I got your letter," Adam said quietly. Michele had written a long letter to Adam, describing his time in Monaco and his dream of a better life with Fabienne. It was because of this that Adam had taken a flight to come and see him. Michele sighed and put his head in his hands.

"I've been thinking about a lot of things recently. Trying to find answers, do you know what I mean?"

"Answers to what?"

"I don't want to sound philosophical or anything, but I'm looking for answers about who I am. And I thought that if I managed to find my father, things would become a bit clearer."

"Your father! Have you ever met him?"

"No, I've never met him. My mother, Ana, never talked about him. I asked her on a couple of occasions, and she either ignored me or shouted back that she didn't want to talk about him. As far as I know, they were never married, but I get the feeling they didn't get along, which doesn't surprise me."

"I'm so sorry to hear this, Michele."

"It's okay. It's just that I don't feel that I fit in here. Think about it. I was born on a small, primitive island, São Nicolau and lived there for four years. Then my mother, who was working as a cleaning lady for Maria's brother and wife, brought me to Milan. They loved me whereas my mother detested me, so imagine how I felt after one year, when she took me away from them to some unearthly shantytown on the outskirts of Lisbon to be with her family. I was so scared of her, and I will never forget the cigarette burn on my hand when I went out to the woods for too long. Anyway, when we came back to Milan, one thing led to another, and Maria ended up taking custody of me. You'd think that was a good thing, and at the time, I was overjoyed, but over the last couple of years, we've always been fighting, mainly because she thinks I'm lazy and do the wrong things. Then I disclosed all of this to Fabienne and her family, which I regret. So right now, it seems that the two people I love the most have given up on me."

"It'll be all right," said Adam and he put his arm around him.

The hour in the park had not expelled the scent of cigarettes from his clothes, so when they returned to the apartment, Maria was sitting on the sofa, looking displeased.

"You've been smoking again, haven't you?"

"It's none of your business."

"It is when it's my money!"

"Give me a break, please."

"And another thing. The manager at the hotel called and told me that he had invited you back to your old job. And you refused! What on earth are you going to do all day, if you're not going to study and not going to work?"

Adam was invisible, standing behind him.

Exasperated, Michele shrugged his shoulders, went into the kitchen with Adam and prepared some pasta.

"Fabienne is just like her," he whispered.

****

Michele and Adam spent the next five days walking around the city, going ten-pin bowling, ice skating and visiting the Irish pub. On his last day, Adam persuaded Michele to accept the job offer as a night porter again, and emphasized that it would at least give him some money. The atmosphere in the apartment had reached icy levels, and when Michele tried to appease Maria by letting her know that he had accepted a job as a night porter at a hotel, she looked away and didn't reply. Whilst he was having a bath, Maria beckoned Adam to sit down next to her.

"He's getting worse. I'm so worried about him," said Maria.

"Well, at least he's going back to work," Adam said.

"Yes. But how long will it last? I wish you were here more often. He listens to you."

****

After dropping off Adam at the airport, Michele came back home, parked the car, and took the metro to Cadorna. From there he walked to his favourite bench in Parco Sempione, took out a notepad and a pen, and started to write down some of his memories of his life as a child. After half an hour, he stopped writing and watched the passers-by, immersed in thoughts about finding his father, who could surely help him in some way, although he didn't know how.

"Hey man, you're looking a bit down. Is everything okay?"

Michele looked up and right in front of him was a short, muscular man with short black hair and large brown eyes. He was wearing a light blue shirt, a beige jacket, navy blue trousers and shiny black shoes. Michele thought that he must be a businessman and on his way home from work, and he was pleased that someone had noticed him.

"Not really," Michele replied. "It's just one of those days."

"Can I sit down?" the man asked.

"Okay. I've got to go in a minute. I'll be late home," said Michele.

There was a pause, and the stranger took a pack of cigarettes and a lighter from his shirt pocket and lit a cigarette.

"Do you want one?"

"Okay. Thanks." Michele took out a cigarette, and the man lit it for him."

"What's your name?"

"Michele. And yours?"

"I'm Damiano. Pleased to meet you. Where are you from?"

"I'm from Cape Verde, but I've been living in Italy for most of my life. What about you?"

"I was born in Naples and brought up in Milan. So, I work for the mafia."

He laughed, and so did Michele.

"You're kidding me, I hope," said Michele.

"Yeah. The mafia wouldn't take me on. I did apply, though. They said I was too young and needed to be a godfather before I could join."

Michele liked Damiano's sense of humour.

"Do you live close by?" Damiano asked.

"No, I have to take the underground. It's two stops on the green line."

"I see. And do you live alone?"

"No. I live with my mother. It's just the two of us. She'll be wondering where I am. She doesn't like it when I'm late. Do you live near here?"

"Yes, I have an apartment just down the road. I live with friends, so basically I can do whatever I like!"

"I wish I had my own place."

"You don't look okay, Michele. Can I ask what's wrong?"

"The biggest problem I have is my passport!"

Damiano laughed. "Is that it?"

"No. I still haven't got Italian nationality, and so I'm stuck in dead-end jobs like a night porter in some crumby hotel outside Milan. All my friends have degrees and good jobs. On top of that, I'm broke, and my girlfriend suggested a trial separation a couple of months ago. So, a crap job and no future."

"Sorry to hear that, man. Sometimes these things happen all at the same time."

"You know, my big dream was to become a professional soccer player, and play for Juventus."

"That sounds like a great dream!" said Damiano.

"Yeah. I still play occasionally, but they're friendly matches. I didn't have much training. I was just naturally good at it at school."

"Juventus is a good team. Alessandro Del Piero is my favourite player. I go and see the match sometimes," said Damiano.

"Lucky you!"

"I've got an idea. I could get you a ticket for next Sunday, and we could go together."

"I told you. I'm broke. I'm starting to get some money with the job at the hotel."

"No problem. You can have this one on me!"

"Are you sure?"

"Yes, of course, I'm sure. Don't worry. Leave it with me. Listen. I don't want to interfere, but I can see that these things are still bothering you."

"Yeah. I suppose. I'm not sleeping very well at the moment. I keep waking up thinking about things."

"You know, I used to be like that, and then I came across something that made things better. At least it gave me some direction."

"What's that?"

"Oh, nothing big. I can't explain it now. Basically, it's a group which helps others to be better people."

"Do you need a degree? I don't have any qualifications."

"No, you don't need a degree."

"Okay, so what exactly is it? How did you hear about it?"

"All I can say is that I created this group. It's a kind of committee. Anyway, I think you have to get going. It's getting late, man. You did say you had to get home."

He took a pen from his jacket pocket and a small piece of paper and wrote down his name and telephone number and handed it to Michele. Damiano stood up to leave.

"Hang on!" said Michele.

"This group. What's it called?"

"I'm afraid I can't explain it at the moment. I'd need more time."

"Would there be room for me in this group? I like the sound of helping people."

"Okay. I can't promise we'd accept you. Here's what we can do. Give me a call during the week, and we can go to the match in Turin together. I'll pick you up. Then we can talk more about it."

"Thanks. I'll do just that."

"I've got to go now. Speak to you during the week. And go home. Everything will be fine, man. Trust me."

Twenty

There was something enigmatic about Damiano's elegance and suave conduct. It was obvious that he was a man of well-being, with the high-fashion clothes he was wearing and the new black BMW he had driven to Turin to watch the match with Michele. The only things that he had revealed about himself were that he was an only child, and that he had a part-time job in a bookshop, which could not possibly give him enough money to buy an expensive car as well as expensive clothes. He probably had affluent parents who spoiled him, Michele thought.

One week after the match, Damiano called Michele and invited him to go for an aperativo on Thursday evening. In the early afternoon, Michele, not wanting to stay at home, went for a meander near the Duomo, and in his tracks, he came across a small tattoo shop. He admired the intricacy of the designs in the window, so he stepped inside, and saw two tattoo artists with their arms and necks covered in colourful tattoos.

"Good afternoon! Welcome."

"Good afternoon!"

"Are you thinking about having a tattoo done?"

"I'm not sure."

"What kind of tattoo would you like to have, if you could have one?"

Michele surveyed the shop walls, which were covered in posters displaying so many different tattoos, that it was difficult to decide which one he liked the most. One of the artists handed him a large dog-eared book with a collection of designs, and after sifting through them, there was one which resembled a blag cog that caught his eye.

"You like that one?" asked one of the artists.

"Yes, it's very nice!"

"Would you like it?"

"Yes, I think I would!"

"Where would you like it?"

"On my right shoulder."

The artist applied the stencil transfer onto his shoulder, and after the shading and colouring, he dressed and bandaged the tattoo and gave Michele some aftercare instructions. It took a lot longer than Michele had anticipated, but he didn't mind, having the tattoo made him more confident and lightened his mood. Michele paid the artist and left and walked to the Duomo to meet Damiano.

"What have you been doing today, my friend?"

"I got a tattoo!"

"That's fantastic! Can I see it?"

"It's all bandaged up."

"What is it?"

"It's a black cog. You find them in mechanical clocks."

"It must be very beautiful. Congratulations! You must show it to me when it's ready."

They walked into a nearby bar. Michele sat down next to a small table, whilst Damiano went to bring the cocktails and bruschetta.

"I hope you like cocktails, Michele. I got you a strong one, it's my favourite!"

"Thank you. That's very kind of you. I can't wait to try it!"

Damiano prepared a cigarette for himself and Michele.

"Can I ask you a personal question?" asked Damiano.

"Yes, fire away," replied Michele.

"Do you believe in God?"

"Yes, of course. I mean, it's been a while since I've been to church. Mamma used to take me to midnight mass when I was younger."

"That's good, that's good. I'm pleased to hear that."

"Why do you ask?"

"You know the group I was talking about, the day we met. They are all worshippers of God, and our aim is to help each other by doing God's work."

"I see," said Michele politely but he was none the wiser.

"You're confused, aren't you. Don't be. Think of it as a charity. Basically, what we do in our daily lives is in accordance with what God wants, so we don't sin, and we help and protect others who are in need. It's not a full-time job, it's more of a way of being. Like me, the others all have part-time or full-time jobs."

"So, you are the leader of the group?"

"Yes, I am indeed."

"So, what do you get out of it?"

"Nothing at all, apart from the satisfaction of helping others in the group. You see, all of the group members have suffered or been through some kind of trauma, and I've helped them to get to a better place. And now they're much stronger. We're always on the lookout for other lost souls so we can all help them. Of course, I charge a nominal fee for therapy, but it's just to cover costs."

Michele didn't know what to think, he had never heard of such a group in his life, and in all honesty, he didn't understand what Damiano was talking about. On the one hand, it seemed weird, and on the other, he might find some solace and new friends, who had been in the same boat as him.

"I can see that it doesn't make complete sense at the moment. Why don't you come and visit us at the weekend? Let's say Saturday afternoon? That will give you enough sleep after you return from work."

They finished their aperitivo. Damiano said that he had urgent business to attend to, and Michele agreed to meet him on Saturday.

When Michele arrived home, Maria was not there, so he went into the bathroom and took off his shirt so he could see the bandage on his shoulder. He didn't hear the front door open, and he was taken aback when he saw her looking at him.

"What's happened? Have you had an accident?" she asked.

"No, I didn't have an accident. You're not going to like this. I had a tattoo done."

"You had a tattoo done! How can you waste all your money on a tattoo? Are you an imbecile?"

"But it looked nice and I …"

"I've heard enough. I don't understand you. You can do what you like."

They had fish and potatoes for dinner, Maria read the newspaper whilst she was eating. When they finished, Michele went to his room, put his suit on, and as he was about to leave for Damiano's, he heard Maria call after him.

"And don't forget that Fabienne is coming on Sunday," said Maria.

"I know," he replied and closed the door behind him.

"I hope she knocks some sense into you," she murmured to herself.

At five o'clock, Michele arrived at Damiano's apartment. Damiano opened the door and greeted him warmly and introduced him to the other eight people who were lingering in the doorway. He led Michele into the sitting room and invited him to sit on the armchair, and the others sat on the floor and on old and dusty sofas. Michele looked around the room. It was stuffy, the large rectangular window, above which hung a small wooden crucifix, mustn't have been opened for a long time. Why was that? The whitish paint was peeling from the walls, and there was a single, shadeless light bulb hanging from the ceiling. There were two pictures on the wall: one of the Last Supper with a thick golden frame around it, and the other was an oil painting of Mary with the newly-born Jesus in her hands. To complete the room's religious aura, there were two tables with candles on them. There was no television. Michele was dumbfounded, every aspect of the room showed age and parsimony, especially for one who dressed in designer clothes and owned a high-end car.

"Would you like an espresso or maybe some tea or water?" asked Damiano.

"An espresso, please."

"Katia, go and get Michele an espresso."

Katia was in her late twenties. She was a tall girl with frizzy mousy hair, huge eyes and a long thin nose, and she was wearing a baggy woollen dark green jumper which hung over her grey trousers.

"Do you all live here? Michele asked.

"Yes, we do," replied Damiano. "And it's very comfortable, isn't it?"

The others agreed. Michele looked at them one by one, their bags under their eyes, their strained smiles, their old scruffy stained clothes. One of them had a small tear on the right sleeve on his shirt.

"You're probably wondering where you are and what we do," he said in the same mellow tone.

"Yes, you're right," said Michele.

"Let me explain. When we look at today's world, it's full of materialism, greed and jealousy. And there is no place for God," said Damiano, and he raised his arms above his head, to show despair.

The others hummed in agreement.

"We do what is right, so that we can live an eternal life in heaven. In other words, we make sure that religion plays a part in our daily life by having Bible readings in the mornings and the evenings, and saving others' souls by inviting them to join our group. We encourage our members to confess their sins to me. This might be an immoral thought or action, or it may be something you have said to hurt someone."

"Do you go to church on Sundays as well?" asked Michele.

"This is our church. Why would we need to go to another one?" asked Damiano assertively.

Katia brought the espresso in and placed it on a coaster on the side table next to him. The more Damiano talked, the more perplexed Michele became. It was hard to take in that the sitting room was a designated church and Damiano, a proxy priest. It appeared that way, but he wasn't too sure as Damiano was never explicit.

"Katia, why don't you share your story with Michele? Then he will understand the purpose and benefits of the group."

"I used to live with my mother and stepfather. My stepfather was not very nice to me, always shouting at me for no reason, and my mother would take his side. He stopped me from going to school, and then kept banishing me from the house. I started to go out and get drunk. I met Damiano by chance, whilst I was waiting for the bus, and he invited me to join his group and to stay at his home. Now, I'm much happier because I'm surrounded by people who love me," said Katia mechanically. It sounded as though she had learned and rehearsed this short speech several times.

"Well done Katia. That can't have been easy for you. Katia's had a traumatic time, and you can see how much better she is with us. As a group, we have helped her to find love and happiness through Lord Jesus."

Michele felt sorry for Katia. If belonging to this group has helped her, surely it could help him as well. Damiano was a strange and mysterious man, yet his words were reassuring and comforting enough for

Michele to want to come back. He finished his espresso and stood up.

"This has been an amazing experience, and I'm so lucky to have met all of you. I have to go to work now."

"Of course," replied Damiano. "We all hope to see you again very soon."

He escorted Michele out of the apartment, down the steps and onto the street.

****

The following day, Fabienne arrived, dressed in a cream suit, and she had a faint tan, which made her look so beautiful. Michele saw her descend from the train, and when they met, Michele gave her a bunch of white roses. He took her luggage and walked down the platform with her towards the car park. Michele did his best to veil his uneasiness as he didn't know what Fabienne wanted. It was her who had suggested a trial separation, yet here she was coming to visit him.

"How was the journey?" he asked.

"Very pleasant. I was able to catch up with my reading."

"Oh yes. How is that going?"

"It's very hard work. My professor has given me plenty to do. To be honest, I'm not sure how I'll get through it all, given the tight deadline for the first draft of my first few chapters."

"I'm sure you'll manage it."

"And how are you, Michele? It seems ages since we've spoken."

"Not much has happened. I returned to my job as a night porter, as you know."

"That's right. Well, I'm sure that you'll find something more exciting soon."

They went left at the entrance to the station where Maria was waiting in her car. When she saw them approach, she jumped out to greet Fabienne and looked ecstatic to see her.

"How long are you staying?"

"Only three days."

"Never mind. I wish you could stay longer. Listen, we've decided to take you to Courmayeur."

Michele sat in the back of the car, looking pensively out of the window, whilst Maria and Fabienne talked with each other, like best friends, about costume jewellery, nursing, the weather, the economy, books and films. He was fed up as not once did they say anything to him. When they arrived, Michele took the luggage out of the car and into the apartment, and as he unpacked, he wondered if there was any slight chance that he and Fabienne could be together again. He didn't have much hope, especially as she had ignored him all the way from the central station to Courmayeur. Unlike him, she was ambitious, always busy at work and with her doctorate, and she would never disrupt her career and come and live in Milan just for him. And as he had experienced, the possibilities of being employed in Monaco were few and far between. He recalled the moment that he thought she was perfect for him when she left Tunisia, but it never occurred to him that he was inadequate for her. This short holiday would answer this question once and for all.

They made love in the bedroom, whilst Maria went into town to meet one of her friends. They had a shower together, got changed, then sat down in the sitting room, and he listened to her passionately reeling off her work achievements and describing what the next year and the year after that looked like. He was happy for her for she had her future all mapped out, but she never mentioned him in her plans.

"I know it's hard now, but it will pay off in the end," said Maria during dinner.

"Yes, I know. That's what my parents keep saying!"

"You've done remarkably well."

They woke up late the following morning, had breakfast and spent most of the day reading, visiting coffee shops and going for walks. Maria bought some steak and salad. Michele was dreading another painful dinner.

"So, what are your plans, Michele?" asked Fabienne.

"I wish I had some concrete plans, but I don't."

"What about finishing your degree? It's not too late! That would surely open doors."

"I'm not interested in political science anymore."

"He's not interested in anything," Maria added.

"Yes, I am. I'm interested in tourism, but there aren't any opportunities. My nationality keeps stopping me from getting employment, even as an intern."

"Come on, you can't keep using that as an excuse," said Fabienne.

"It's not an excuse. What do you know about it? I tried and tried to get a job in Monaco."

"It seems you didn't try hard enough," replied Fabienne.

"He's lazy, that's the problem. He gives up too easily," said Maria.

Michele looked at them, he couldn't contain himself any longer. This was the last straw. He wiped his mouth with his napkin, and without saying a word, he left the apartment in high dudgeon, and went for a long walk outside.

"You black guys need to go back to your country," a boy shouted behind him.

Michele ignored him and kept walking until he came to a bar. Inside he glanced at a sleek blonde girl in the corner. She was reading a magazine.

"Hi! Can I join you? Would you like a drink?"

Twenty-One

The daily commute was beginning to take its toll, he had to take two buses to reach the hotel, and with the delays and waiting time, it took just over an hour to get there. The highlight was checking in late guests, but from midnight until five o'clock in the morning, he had to endure the slow passing of time. He tried to stay awake by completing puzzles and reading magazines. This worked for a couple of hours, then he would fall asleep in the revolving chair.

Michele crashed on his bed when he arrived home at seven o'clock in the morning and awoke at five o'clock in the evening. He had some broth and a piece of white fish and salad, which Maria had left for him. He couldn't take his mind off those stilted conversations with Maria and Fabienne the morning after he had left them in a huff during dinner. On the platform before leaving, Fabienne had told him how selfish she had been, how lovely it was to see him again, and that she didn't want to lose him. Michele didn't know whether to believe her or not, but what he did come to realise was that since Tunisia, every time they met, there was always some confrontation. Perhaps Damiano could help him with his relationship.

At half-past six, Michele arrived at Damiano's apartment, he had just returned from the bookshop.

"Brother, I am so pleased to see you again," said Damiano.

"Good to see you too," replied Michele.

"Let me show you the rest of the apartment," said Damiano

Just like the sitting room, the kitchen on the right of the entrance looked old and dilapidated, there were two cupboards with broken hinges, the hobs were all rusty, and the wooden table had a dent in the corner. Damiano took him further along the corridor to a bedroom on the right. The door was closed. Damiano quietly opened it so that Michele could have a peek inside. Someone was sleeping on a single bed at the end of the room next to the window, and next to it were seven sleeping bags neatly lined up next to each other.

"Is this where everyone sleeps?"

"Yes, it is. And they sleep very well. It's very comfortable."

Michele turned towards the door opposite him, but Damiano intercepted him.

"Sorry, my friend. I'm afraid that this room is out of bounds," he said.

"But you've…"

"All in good time, brother. All in good time."

Damiano put his arm around Michele and led him to the sitting room, which was full of people, not just the ones he had met on his previous visit. Michele calculated that there must be around fifteen of them, and the strange thing was that no one was talking. Katia got up from the armchair and asked Michele to sit down.

"So, what brings you back here?" asked Damiano.

"I don't know really," replied Michele. He didn't want to reveal his troubles in front of fifteen strangers.

"Are you interested in joining our group?"

"Please say yes," pleaded Katia.

"Okay yes! Why not?"

"Congratulations Michele!" said Damiano and embraced him. "You've made the right decision."

The others applauded Michele and Damiano moved to the middle of the room.

"It's not as simple as that, as we all know. First of all, I need to have an intimate conversation with you, Michele. I'm going to be asking questions about your past, your opinions about things and people in your life. It's just to help us to help you to feel better. You can handle that, can't you, Michele?"

They went into the kitchen, and Damiano closed the door behind him. They sat down, and Damiano put a cassette recorder and clipboard on the table.

"Before we start, I want to let you know that some of the questions may appear to be a bit weird but rest assured, you're safe with me, and everything you say will be between you and me. The important thing is that you're honest. Are you ready?"

He pressed 'record' on the cassette recorder.

"Interview with Michele at seven o'clock in the evening on Friday, the fifth of December 1997."

Damiano asked Michele to talk about where he was born and his childhood. It took him about twenty minutes to tell him about his past in a similar fashion to the way he had described it to Fabienne and her parents when they went to their holiday home. Damiano scribbled everything down on his notepad.

"What makes you happy?" asked Damiano.

"Girls!"

"Don't they just!" exclaimed Damiano. "I remember you saying that you had a girlfriend."

"Yes. Fabienne. We're on a trial separation. I told you that when we met. She came to visit me just recently."

"Ah yes, I remember. What do you like about her?"

"Well, she's really hot! I mean she's great in bed. She's ambitious, got solid plans for the future, intelligent, funny."

"Why are you not living together?"

"We tried, but it didn't work out. I went to live with her in Monaco for a bit, but I couldn't get a job there, and she was working nights as a nurse."

"That's a shame. I can imagine that must have been tough for you. Is there anything you don't like about her?"

"Well, she can be quite arrogant and snobbish. I don't think she intends to be, it's just the way she is. She thinks she's better than me, and she's right."

"You know, I can't stand arrogant and snobbish people. And don't put yourself down! It's probably her that has made you feel inferior. Have you ever been unfaithful to her?"

Michele paused and looked down.

"Come on. It's okay," said Damiano.

"Yes. It happened recently. As I said, she came to visit last week and we went to Courmayeur, but both she and Mamma were having a go at me about me being lazy and not thinking about the future, so

I stormed out of the apartment and went for a walk to cool down. I stopped by a bar and got talking to a girl, and we went back to her hotel and had sex."

"I see. She probably drove you to it. Did you tell her about this?"

"No way! Why would I tell her?"

"Indeed. What was this girl like, the one you met in the bar?"

"Slim, young, beautiful. Dark hair. Extremely good looking."

"How long did you spend talking with her at the bar."

"About half an hour."

"After half an hour, she invited you to go back to her hotel room and have sex with her."

"Well, yes. I mean, it wasn't quite as simple as that. I mean, there was a price to pay."

"You paid for sex with her?"

"Yes, you could put it like that."

"And how much did it cost?"

"Two hundred thousand lire."

"That is a lot of money! But worth it, I'm sure! Who was the best person you had sex with?"

"Isabella. She's a girl I met in Brazil after we went to the carnival."

"What did you find attractive about her?"

"I think it was her tight black miniskirt and her dark skin which made me go up to her."

"Okay, it sounds as though you liked her a lot. Moving on to other things. What do you do to relax?"

"Football, swimming, skiing, most sports, going out with friends, eating, drinking."

"What about smoking? Have you ever smoked marijuana?"

"Yes, a few times!"

"Nice! It really calms you, doesn't it? I just love the feeling you get when you take in the first drag. Have you tried any other drugs?"

"No."

"If you had the chance, would you try them?"

"I don't know. I don't think so."

"But maybe you would. Now tell me what makes you unhappy?"

"Arguing with Mamma and Fabienne. The fact I have no future, my nationality, racist comments."

"Yes, I thought as much. Well, I can assure you that you do have a future, and a very bright one with us. You work in a hotel, right? What's it like?"

"It's boring. As you know, I do the night shift. It's a crummy three-star hotel outside Milan. I'm surprised anyone stays there, to be honest."

Damiano looked up from his notepad and smiled at him.

"Let's talk about the group. What do you think about Katia? Do you find her attractive?"

"She's a nice person, but I don't find her attractive."

"So, she's ugly?"

"Well yeah. But I wouldn't put it quite like that."

"Would you sleep with her?"

"No."

"And what do you think about me?"

"Well, you're charismatic, very sociable, friendly, trustworthy."

"That's very nice of you. But tell me what you don't like about me. Something I need to improve."

"Hmmm. Well, you seemed a bit intrusive at first, a bit pushy but then you seemed so nice when you took me to see Juventus."

Damiano stopped the cassette recorder, reviewed his notes and looked up at Michele.

"Michele, we're going to stop here. Thank you so much for answering all these questions. I'm sure you are exhausted! Anyway, there's nothing to worry about, but it does seem that you have mild depression and you resort to making impulsive decisions when things aren't going well for you. Nothing we can't fix. You're lucky that you came to us because we can help to cure you of these disorders."

"Really? I had no idea that I had them."

"Most people don't."

Michele looked at his watch.

"I need to go in a minute as I have to go to work."

"Okay. Just give me two minutes."

Damiano went out and came back with a thick-stapled document.

"Listen, brother. If you want to be part of our community, we're going to need you to sign this contract. Nothing in life is for free, unfortunately, so we expect you to pay thirty thousand lire a week to support our mission and group. This will give you access to my special therapy sessions, so you become a better person, free from anxiety and sins, and it will help you prepare for judgement day when you die. The contract expects you not to disclose what we do here to anyone and that you swear your allegiance to us. You have nothing to lose."

Michele stood up, took the pen and signed it.

"Just one more thing. Please could you add your mother and Fabienne's contact details so we can contact them in case of an emergency."

****

Michele started going to daily Bible readings in the evening before he went to work. The first time he went, he was asked to read from Luke V.

"You see, Michele, how everyone in this room feels uplifted, listening to parts of the Bible, praying for the needy and thanking God and Jesus for all the good things they have brought to humanity," said Damiano.

After one of his therapy sessions with Damiano, Michele had a renewed interest to re-enrol in university. He was certain that the thirty thousand lire per week were going to help him to be happier and, despite Damiano's eccentricities, the group gave him a sense of belonging, so he felt more stable than he had been in a long time.

****

After New Year, he went to Damiano's apartment.

"Where have you been? You didn't visit us for a whole week," said Damiano.

"Come on. I had Christmas with my mother and her family, and then went out with friends at New Year."

"You should have been with us. Never mind."

In the sitting room, there were lit candles everywhere, and unlike other times where Damiano had invited his so-called extended family, this time there was just the people who lived there. Michele sat on the floor whilst Damiano read a prayer and Katia recited a passage from the Bible. Then Damiano raised his arms and looked upwards.

"Last night, I received a message from The Lord."

Michele had never seen Damiano in this way. By the expressions of awe and excitement from the other group members, it was as though Damiano was more than just a proxy vicar, he saw himself as a messenger of God. He kept his eyes shut for a couple of minutes.

"The Lord has proclaimed that we need a large donation to support our cause, so that we may prosper as His ambassadors. The Lord himself has asked me to seek other premises to continue our prayer, expand our group, and work to save sinful souls. And for this, we will need all of you to contribute by acquiring an allotted amount of money, which you will give me in two weeks."

One of the boys raised his hand.

"Yes, Salvatore," said Damiano.

"How much money do we have to get and what if we don't have it?"

Damiano looked down for a few seconds, and then walked slowly towards Salvatore, who was sitting on the floor next to one of the armchairs. He grabbed him by the collar of his shirt, and hauled him up against the wall, his face turning from pale to red.

"You dare to question The Lord? You dare to question me? If you don't get me the money, you break your contract! And you know what that means!"

He released Salvatore, who was struggling to breathe. Damiano looked around.

"And that goes for all of you!"

He went into his bedroom and brought out some slips of paper. Each slip had the name of the group member, and next to it was the amount of money required. After distributing them, he returned to his bedroom and locked the door behind him.

When Michele looked at his slip, he gasped when he saw ten million lire next to his name.

"There's no way I can get hold of his!" he said.

"You have no choice. Take a bank loan, that's what I'm going to do," said Katia.

"Otherwise we risk eternal damnation. You heard Damiano, this was a message from The Lord," said Salvatore.

Damiano's outburst had shocked Michele. And so did the group's blind obedience to his instructions. He didn't believe for one minute that Damiano had received a message from God, even though everyone else did. On the other hand, Damiano's therapy sessions were helping him to be stronger, and he was sure that he had good intentions. He knew that Maria stored surplus cash in her safe, and she never touched it, so he thought he could take the money without her knowing. It was the only way he could get the cash within two weeks. The safe had a padlock attached to it, so he would need a clench to open it, and then he could buy a similar padlock to replace it.

When Michele arrived home at his usual time at seven o'clock in the morning, he forced himself to stay awake and waited for Maria to leave. As soon as the front door closed, he took the mini-ladder to the hallway and climbed up to the cupboard, which was attached to the ceiling between the two bedrooms. He opened it and used the clench to break the padlock but failed, and made a big conspicuous dent on the front of the safe. On the third attempt, he successfully broke the padlock and opened the safe, inside there were hundreds of notes in different currencies. He found the American dollars and threw them onto the floor, and put the replacement padlock on the safe. As he was descending, he lost balance and clung onto the right cupboard door, and after dangling for a few seconds, he fell onto the floor with a thud. He picked himself up and saw a few bruises on his left arm. He then put the ladder back into the storeroom near the kitchen, took the money, put it in his briefcase, set his alarm clock and went to bed. He didn't sleep well at all, he kept waking up. He was torn between feeling guilty about stealing from Maria, the only one who cared for him, and Damiano's religious agenda.

At three o'clock, he got up, washed his face in cold water and heard the telephone ring.

"Hello sweetheart. I didn't want to disturb your sleep. I imagine you're up now. Anyway, I just wanted to let you know that I'll be back later tonight as Sabrina has invited me to dinner," said Maria.

"Okay, that's fine."

"There's some pasta sauce in the fridge."

"Okay, thanks."

"See you later."

It was a long time since she had called him sweetheart. Despite all the things he had done, she still loved and cared for him, and this made him feel even more culpable. Stealing was indeed a sin, but

Damiano never mentioned that. On the slip of paper, he had written that they should take any means to obtain the money. Did this include stealing? Damiano must have known that no one could afford these amounts of money.

When he arrived at Damiano's apartment, he found two of the group members busy in the kitchen preparing boiled potatoes and peas. Salvatore was cleaning the toilet and bathroom with a small brush and cloth.

"Salvatore, it's not clean enough!" shouted Damiano.

"I'm doing my best. I've been doing this for hours."

"Don't answer back," said Damiano and kicked him in the chest.

"Salvatore has sinned. He questioned the Lord and so, I'm sure you'll agree, he needs to be punished. It's much better that he's punished here on Earth rather than in the afterlife," Damiano told Michele.

When Michele showed Damiano the money, he laughed hysterically as he counted the notes frantically before depositing them in his bedroom. He called everyone to attend an immediate house meeting in the sitting room. Michele looked at Damiano's face, it was red, his pupils dilated, and he seemed to be possessed by a tonne of nervous energy. Damiano asked Michele to stand next to him.

"Today, I want to talk about loyalty. This new member of our family has shown loyalty to God and me. He has found all the money I asked for him and has given it to me in cash today. And one week earlier than I asked for. Michele is a hero. Not like Salvatore, who questions God's will. Michele is an example, and if you follow him and learn from him, then you will all be triumphant, and your place in heaven will be secure. You are all amazing people, and I love you so much, and I know you can do this for God and me."

He kissed everyone on the forehead and returned to his bedroom.

On his return from work at seven o'clock in the morning, Michele unlocked the door of Maria's apartment, but the chain stopped the door from opening properly. Maria came to the doorway with the chain still attached so Michele could see her through the gap.

"Did you take the money?" she asked him solemnly.

"Yes, but let me explain."

"Come back here at four o'clock, so you can collect all your things. You don't live here anymore."

Twenty-Two

Michele left the apartment and went to the nearest telephone box. This was all Damiano's fault, he wished he had never met him. His hand was trembling as he took the coins out of his right pocket. Annoyingly, most of them fell on the floor. He picked them up, inserted them into the slot and dialled what he thought was Gianni's number, only to be told by an automated voice that the number didn't exist. After uttering some profanities at the telephone, he ran to the metro, punched the ticket into the machine and ran down the steps. He paced up and down, impatiently waiting for the train to arrive, and as soon as the headlights appeared, he stood as close to the edge of the platform as possible. He slipped through the opening door of the carriage and, even though there were many empty seats, he remained standing so he would be ready to jump off. When he arrived at his destination, he sped through the moving doors, up the stairs onto the main road, and sprinted towards Gianni's apartment.

"You're looking very smart," said Sandra, having never seen Michele in a suit before. "Are you okay?"

She could see that he had been crying and let him in.

There were open books scattered everywhere in Gianni's bedroom, and there was barely anywhere

Michele could sit down, so Gianni removed some of them from his bed. He would take an exam in five days, so he was revising every day.

"I've really messed up this time."

"What have you done?"

"I took a lot of money, five thousand dollars, from my mother."

"Why on earth did you do that?"

"I can't say at the moment. I'll tell you another time. The thing is that Maria has kicked me out for good and wants me to collect my things at four o'clock."

"I see. Don't worry. You can stay with us for the time being. I can help you to collect your things."

The first thing Maria did, as soon as the shops opened, was to arrange for a blacksmith to change the lock on the front door of her apartment. She then went to her office, where she spent most of the morning trying to finish her bookkeeping and preparing an order for a new client. Unable to concentrate, she made a few errors in her calculations, and had to rewrite them. Her fury with Michele had turned to fear. She was desperately looking for a logical reason for why he had purloined so much money from her. Had someone perhaps forced him to steal the money? She telephoned Ben and told him that she needed to talk with him.

Nicole, wearing a pencil grey suit, took Maria's brown fur coat and hung it on the coat stand in the hallway, and led the way to the sitting room. Inside, the windows were wide open to let in some fresh air, they had had guests the previous evening. She was upset to see Maria looking so distressed, so she called Ben, who was in his office.

Nicole closed the windows, and they sat down on the sofas.

"So, what's the matter?" asked Ben. "You're looking terrible.

"It's Michele," said Maria.

Nicole gave a 'I knew this would happen all along' look at Ben.

"He stole five thousand dollars from the safe."

"How on earth did he manage that?" asked Ben.

"He must have used some kind of clench to break it, and he tried to hide what he had done by replacing the padlock with another one. But it had gone horribly wrong for him because when I got home, I saw one of the cupboard doors off its hinges and a dent in the safe. When he got home, he admitted doing it, so I told him that he can't live with me anymore, and I changed the locks this morning. I don't know if I've done the right thing or not. He must have been desperate for money. I don't know who he is any more and I can't trust him."

Nicole passed Maria a paper handkerchief, and she dried her eyes. She held her hand to comfort her.

"Would you like some tea?" asked Nicole.

"Yes, please. That would be very nice."

Nicole went into the kitchen.

"I'm sorry to hear this, darling. I know he means a lot to you, and I can see that you care for him," said Ben.

"Maybe I was too strict with him."

"Don't blame yourself, Maria. You did all the right things. You gave him opportunities that he would never have had."

"I know. I know."

"You remember that we were a bit uneasy about taking custody of him, and we did warn you that this kind of thing could happen. He's reckless, and he does seem to be showing some of the traits of his real family."

Nicole came in with a china teapot and teacups, went to the shelves, took a box of dark chocolates and put them on the table.

"What do I do next?" asked Maria. "I don't want to go to the police."

"And I'm not suggesting you do. But you need to leave him to fend for himself," said Ben.

"That's a bit cruel," isn't it?"

"You need to think about yourself. I can see that you still love him, but think of the consequences of him moving back in with you. You'll end up being a nervous wreck."

Maria didn't reply, she looked at the magnificent books and imagined what it would have been like if Michele had graduated from university, obtained an Italian passport and found a good job. But no, that was never going to happen, she quashed the idea, tearing out the last pages of a story with a happy ending. She knew Ben was right, but she hoped he would have said that Michele's conduct was venial and invite him to come back and stay with her. After all, any decent mother would do that regardless. That is what unconditional love is all about.

"I told him to come back at four o'clock to get his things."

"That must have been very hard for you. Would you like me to be with you when he comes?"

Ben and Maria put all Michele's possessions in bags and put them in the hallway. At four o'clock, Gianni and Michele took them downstairs and threw them in the back of the car. They drove back to Gianni's apartment and put them in the storeroom. Then Michele had a shower and went to work.

When Michele arrived at the hotel, he was worn out and hungry. He sat on his chair behind the reception desk and replayed what had happened in the last twenty-four hours. Maria had not given him the chance to explain himself. Instead she had thrown him out, and if Gianni hadn't been able to accommodate him, he would have been left on the streets. His resentment towards Damiano started to diminish, so he decided that he would resume his daily visits as this was the only way he could achieve redemption for lying and stealing.

Gianni's father owned two other apartments in Milan, and he rented them to students from the south of Italy. One of the tenants had recently given notice, having finished her degree, and so a one-bedroomed, newly renovated apartment on the fourth floor overlooking the main street had become available for Michele.

He stepped through the open door and squinted his eyes as the sun's rays struck his face from the two large square windows directly in front of him. On the right, there was a kitchenette and a small table, and on the left, there were built-in shelves, a cupboard and a wardrobe. In the middle, there was a sofa bed, an armchair and a television. The bathroom was behind him, next to the front door. Gianni helped him take his possessions upstairs and left, as he had arranged to go out for dinner with his girlfriend. Michele spent the next hour unpacking. He didn't feel like eating, so he collapsed on the sofa and watched television until he drifted into a deep sleep half-way through an old film. At two o'clock in the morning, he woke up sweating and looked at the fuzzy television screen. He stood up, went to the bathroom to have a shower, then pulled out the sofa bed, put the sheets on and went back to sleep. It was fortuitous he wasn't on duty at the hotel that night.

****

Fabienne invited Michele to visit her in early October and suggested bringing Adam with him. It took a while to convince Adam, Michele told him time and time again that he would not be in the way and that he would stay at one of Fabienne's friend's apartments whilst she was away on holiday.

When they arrived in Monaco, Fabienne took them to one of her favourite cafés in the old town, and they had tea. Michele was bored with her endless talk about work, but he did his best to look interested, he was glad when they finally finished their tea, and she proposed going for a long walk along the quayside. She took Michele's hand, and Adam followed them.

"Once I have enough money, I'm going to buy one of those beauties," she said, admiring the luxurious boats.

Michele let go of her hand and strode ahead of her until she caught up with him.

"You're looking a bit down, my darling. Is everything all right?" asked Fabienne.

"You know it wasn't easy coming back here. To be honest, I don't know where we stand. I'm really confused," replied Michele.

She took his hand again, and looked at him.

"You think too much. Just enjoy the moment. We can talk about all of this later."

Fabienne drove to her friend's apartment and let Adam in so he could rest for a couple of hours before coming for dinner. As soon as they got home, they ran to the bedroom, undressed and made passionate love. Michele eventually turned the light on, sat next to her, and caressed her silky hair. Did she love him? Did he love her? She was in love with her career and just needed sex now and then, why would she want to spend the rest of her life with a dropout like him?

"Are you asleep?" he asked softly.

"No, not yet."

She opened her eyes and sat opposite him, cross-legged, and held his hands. He looked at her melancholically.

"Listen you're doing my head in, and I can't handle this anymore. First, you want a trial separation, then you and Mamma hardly talk to me when we go to Courmayeur, then you accuse me of being lazy, and for some bizarre reason, which I still can't understand, you invite me to come here. What's going on? Just be honest with me for once in your life."

"I want to be with you."

"Well, I'm not exactly a perfect match for you, am I? I'm always in trouble. I don't have any qualifications, no prospects. Why would you want to stay with me?"

"I don't care about your qualifications, you silly silly boy. I love you, that's all that matters. Here's what I think. When you get back to Milan, you should concentrate on getting your Italian nationality. I spoke with Maria about it a few weeks ago, and she said it was possible but would take some time. At the same time, you can work or study, whatever you like, and I'll wait for you, no matter how long it takes. Then you can come back here, and it'll be easier to find a job."

"Do you really mean that?"

"Yes, of course, I do."

"Do you think we may get married one day?"

"I don't see why not."

"And have children?"

"Come on, stop rushing things! But yes, I would love that."

Michele was relieved and surprised, he leaned forward and kissed her.

After a late dinner, Michele and Adam went in search of a bar, which was not easy because of the lack of parking spaces. Eventually, they found a small, chic bar on the outskirts of the city, inside there were black walls, and the only light came from the tall circular shades which hung from the ceiling onto the countless bottles of wine and spirits. They sat on two adjourning stools in front of the bar. They turned around and saw three women looking at them. It was hard to make out any of their features or their age, and when one of them beckoned Michele to sit down next to her with her hand, he ignored her and ordered two bottles of beer.

"Michele, do you think we're in some kind of brothel?"

"I think we are! But I don't trust them. And they might not even be ladies, if you get what I mean! Anyway, how have things been? You've been very quiet."

"Everything's okay. The commute was becoming a nightmare, so I moved closer to the campus, so now I walk to the university. At the weekends, I've been visiting family and friends. I saved enough money to go to Madrid, and I spent about five hours in the Prado national museum, I had always wanted to go there."

"Yes, I can imagine you doing that!"

"To be honest, I've been getting a bit restless recently. I've been in the same job for nearly five years, and I was thinking of finding something in Milan."

Michele's eyes lightened up. With his best friend in Milan and a life with Fabienne, he would have a future, after all. He just had to make amends with Maria.

"What about you?" asked Adam.

"I take it you read my letter. It's been pretty bad. My mother threw me out of the house for stealing money from her. Don't ask me why I did it. But she practically left me on the street without giving me a chance to explain things. I know she doesn't deserve all of this. But thankfully, Gianni's father rented me an apartment, so that's where I'm living now. Everything's okay with Fabienne, but I have no idea how long it will last. We talked about marriage and children today, and she appears to feel the same way as I feel about her. She thinks that getting an Italian passport will help, so I'll apply for it when I get back to Milan. I don't want to sound pessimistic, but I have moments when I'm really low. It would mean a lot to me if you moved to Milan. We could share an apartment," said Michele.

"You've had a rough time, haven't you? I hope things work out between you and Fabienne, and getting a passport would make life easier for you. By the way, I meant to ask you, did you manage to find your father?"

"No, I gave up on that idea. I don't think it will make any difference whether I see him or not."

They spent the next two hours chatting and drinking, and observed the women in the back making acquaintances with single men and then leaving the bar, hand in hand. Michele looked at his watch.

"It's three o'clock! Fabienne will go crazy with me."

The barman gave the bill to Adam, and he showed it to Michele.

"I had no idea it would be that expensive," said Adam. "Let's go halves."

After paying the barman, Michele dropped Adam off and drove back to Fabienne's apartment. He crept inside and found her fast asleep.

On Monday afternoon, they went to the station, and they parted on good terms. Michele now had a plan, he would return to Milan and start the process of obtaining Italian nationality, and this would solve all his problems.

****

When Michele and Adam arrived back at the central station in Milan at six o'clock in the evening, they went to the metro and took the green line to Sant'Ambrogio. They walked for about ten minutes and just as they were about to enter Michele's apartment, two boys stopped right in front of them. Both of them were taller than Michele and Adam, the one on the left had small eyes, short black hair and a tattoo of a dragon on the back of his right arm, and the one on the right had a shaved head, and his face was covered in acne. Michele tried to walk past them, but the boy on the left blocked him. Michele looked down.

"Look at me!" screamed the one on the left, so Michele looked at him.

"What's the problem?" asked Michele.

"You don't belong here, that's the problem! This is a country for white people. Do you get that?" said the one on the right.

"We know where you live, so get your things, get on a boat and get out of here," said the one on the left.

The boy on the right turned to Adam. "What are you doing hanging out with a negro?" he asked rhetorically.

The boys walked away, and Michele opened the door to the apartment block.

Inside, Michele sat on the sofa.

"Shouldn't we call the police?" asked Adam

"What good will that do? The police won't do anything."

"Then what are you going to do about it?"

"There's nothing I can do," replied Michele.

After breakfast the following morning, Adam created a timetable for Michele to show how he could balance studying and working at the hotel. Even though Michele had tried it many times, he wanted to try one last time, and having talked about it with Adam over dinner the previous day, he was determined to make it work. From ten o'clock at night until six o'clock in the morning, he would work at the hotel. From seven o'clock in the morning until two o'clock in the afternoon, he would sleep. From three o'clock in the afternoon until seven o'clock in the evening, he would attend lectures and study. And from seven o'clock until ten o'clock he would relax. Michele attached the timetable to the wall, to show that this was official and he would comply to it. Adam then packed his suitcases, and Michele accompanied him to the central station from where he would take a bus to the airport.

"Are you sure you'll be okay?" asked Adam.

"Yes, of course! Just think about coming over to live here. In the meantime, I'll try and come and visit you," said Michele.

When Michele returned to his apartment, he took the Bible from the shelves and opened it at a random page and started reading it. After an hour, he had lunch: mozzarella cheese, salsiccia, tomatoes, bread and a glass of water, and then checked the timetable. It was time to go to university.

Michele arrived at the lecture hall early and selected a seat at the front and took out his pen and notepad, ready to listen to two hours on the political economy. The black walls, the mustiness, the heat and the lecturer's monotonous voice would induce sleepiness to even the most eager of students, he thought. Maybe the uncomfortable seats and sitting at the front would keep him awake. In any case, it was better than sitting on the stairs, which was reserved for latecomers, as the lecture halls were always overcrowded. As he waited, he pictured himself on the day he received his Italian passport, then graduating from university and being photographed with Maria on his left and Fabienne on his right, then marrying Fabienne, he in a dark suit and she in a magnificent wedding dress, and Maria looking proud.

These images dissolved as the crowd swarmed into the lecture hall, just like ants finding their way to a new food source. The lecturer walked in, switched on the overhead projector, went to the pulpit and proceeded to drearily read aloud his notes without looking up. Michele tried to concentrate, but it was hard because of the chatter and laughter coming from clusters of friends, who were using the lecture hall as a meeting place to gossip. He took notes but was lost in the long, complex sentences and unfamiliar vernacular, so after two hours he was none the wiser, the historical context and theories made no sense to him at all. The lecturer looked up briefly and informed the students that they should read a particular book in preparation for their next tutorial. There was then a speedy exodus of students, leaving the hall and heading towards the numerous bars for a much-needed and well-deserved aperativo.

As Michele walked towards his apartment, he saw a figure leaning against the wall next to the door. When he got nearer, he saw it was Damiano.

"Damiano. What are you doing here?" asked Michele, taken aback as Damiano had never visited him before.

"Come on, buddy! That's no way to greet me!" he said, and looked at Michele's briefcase. "Have you been to university?"

"Yes, I've just been to a lecture," replied Michele.

Damiano embraced him tightly and kissed him on his cheeks.

"That's amazing! I'm so pleased for you. I told you to go back to university, didn't I? It's a good job you came to us, isn't it?"

"I suppose so," said Michele. What Damiano said wasn't entirely true. He had attempted to study many times, but this time, it wasn't because of Damiano, it was more because he wanted to be with Fabienne, and Adam's official timetable would help him to fit everything in.

"Aren't you going to invite me in?"

Like an excited puppy, Damiano followed Michele up the stairs and into his apartment and sprawled out on the sofa.

"Can you make me a tea?" he asked.

Michele boiled some water and took two cups from the cupboard, whilst Damiano looked around the apartment. He got up and walked to the table and found the Bible open.

"You're reading the Bible as well. That's impressive. You know, I've noticed a big change in you since you joined us."

Damiano returned to the sofa and Michele placed a large cup of black tea on the side table.

"What do you mean?" asked Michele.

He breathed in thoughtfully and looked at the ceiling.

"You just seem to be much more stable than you were when I met you for the first time. I mean, look what you've achieved. You're employed, you've returned to university. And you're turning to your faith to help you get through your challenges."

"I don't know about that."

"Of course, you have."

Damiano sipped some tea and looked at him with a warm smile.

"You've come to our meetings. You've contributed financially to a better cause. Don't think that hasn't gone unnoticed. You'll be rewarded for this when you get to heaven. Anyway, tell me how you got on with Fabienne."

Michele sat next to him on the sofa

"It was great. It seems that she hasn't ruled out the possibility of us being together, maybe getting married and having children."

"That's wonderful!" he gleamed. "But you still feel a bit awkward about it. Am I right?"

"A bit. I just need to figure out how I can fit in with her lifestyle, I suppose."

"I thought so. You're feeling a bit inadequate, aren't you?"

"Yes, probably."

"And I'm right in thinking that you don't want to feel that inadequacy."

"Yes, you're right."

"I could offer you some additional therapy to help you build that confidence so that you can still be yourself and fit into Fabienne's world. How does that sound?"

"That would be great."

"Leave it with me!"

He leaned forward and patted Michele on the shoulder.

All of a sudden Damiano clasped his hands together and looked tearful.

"What's the matter?" asked Michele.

"It's nothing. It'll pass."

Damiano took a handkerchief out of his pocket and wiped his eyes and looked at Michele with a forced smile.

"It doesn't look like nothing," said Michele.

"I better go," said Damiano.

"Okay, but please tell me what's wrong."

Damiano stood up.

"I'm so sorry. It's not good that you're seeing me like this."

"Come on, we're friends, aren't we?"

"Okay. I didn't want to bring this up, especially with you, as you have already helped us so much. I'm afraid we still need more cash to pay for the new apartment as well as books for therapy sessions."

"Books?"

"Yes, there are expensive books that I need to buy to keep up to date with modern ways of helping others."

"Are there others in the group on therapy?"

"Yes, all of them."

"I'm sorry Damiano. I don't have any cash."

"That's okay. Is there anything you can sell here?"

Before Michele had the chance to reply, Damiano darted over to the tennis racquet and picked it up. At light speed, he took a wristwatch from the table, a cashmere pullover from the chest of drawers and the necklace which was lying next to a glass of water on the kitchen table.

"No, not the necklace!" shouted Michele.

"This should do," said Damiano. "Thank you so much. I don't know what I'd do without you."

He opened the front door and hurried down the stairs, leaving Michele open-mouthed.

Michele sat on the sofa, taking a minute to think about what had just happened. He looked at the empty spaces where the tennis racquet, watch and necklace had been. According to his timetable, this was the time to have something to eat and relax, but he couldn't. Instead, he put on his navy tracksuit trousers, white t-shirt, white socks and trainers and went for a run. As he was running, he couldn't take his mind off what Damiano had just done. It was Damiano who had caused the rift between him and Maria, and stolen his things, including a special gift from Fabienne. It was Damiano who made some people believe that he was some kind of messiah. He was a fake, and Michele was determined to show the other group members what sort of a person he really was, and he would get his things back.

As he was running back home, he saw the same two boys who had tormented him the other day, just before Adam had left, so he crossed the road and pretended not to notice them. But they also crossed the road, and the one with the dragon tattoo pushed Michele's shoulders with the palms of this hands. The one with the shaved head went behind him, gave him a dead leg and pushed him to the ground. Michele felt two brutal kicks, one on his right side and one on the left of his head.

"What are you still doing here?" asked the one with the tattoo.

"We told you to go home," said the one with the shaved head.

Michele grabbed the leg of the one with the tattoo, unbalancing him until he fell to the ground and punched him hard in the stomach, and then pushed the shaved head one onto the ground and kicked him in the chest. He looked at them choking in agony. He wouldn't let people take advantage of him anymore, they both deserved it.

"Don't mess with me!" shouted Michele.

As he opened the main door and went inside, he heard one of them say, "You're a dead man!"

In his apartment, he went to the bathroom and dressed the cut near his ear, it was much less severe than he thought. He had unfinished business to attend to with Damiano, but not right now, he would visit him before he went to work the following day. He called Maria and, to his surprise, she didn't put the telephone down on him and asked him if he would like to come for dinner after university tomorrow.

"Come in! Come in! It's nice to see you," said Maria, who was wearing a grey suit. "I've prepared some pasta with pesto sauce for us."

Michele took off his shoes and accompanied her into the kitchen.

"What happened to your ear?"

"Someone hit me on my way back from running."

"That's terrible. Do you want me to take a look?"

"No, it's okay. I dressed it last night."

Maria looked at his saturnine face and felt sorry for him.

"Are you okay? I worry about you," she said.

"I'm okay. I have ups and downs. I'm back at university yet again, but I find it incredibly hard. At the same time, I'm still working nights at the hotel to earn some money."

"At least that's something."

"And talking about money, I realise what I did was unforgivable, so I would like to pay you back in instalments. I know it will take me a long time, but I still want to do it."

"That's very sweet of you. Anyway, I have some good news for you. Your Italian citizenship has been approved, and your passport will be ready in February."

"That's a relief! What have you been doing?" he asked.

"Business is going well. I have some new customers in New York, so I'll be going there in December. I've been to Garda with Ben and Nicole a few times. It really so lovely there, as you know. The family is doing well. David and Robert are both married and are living in London. By the way, I was going to ask, would you like to come to Courmayeur with me for Christmas?"

"Yes, I would love that? Can we invite Adam?"

"Of course. He sent me a letter. He's coming here for a week's holiday next week."

"Yes, I know. He's coming on Saturday, and then he's taking the train to visit one of his students in Florence, and he'll be back here on Sunday, so we can talk about it with him then."

They finished their dinner, went to the sitting room and watched television for another hour. In the hallway, as Michele was about to leave, Maria gave him a big hug.

"No matter what you have done, I still love you," said Maria

"I love you too, Mamma."

As Michele strode towards Damiano's apartment, his breath was galloping, he couldn't get there quickly enough. He banged on the door, and Katia opened it.

"You're early!" she exclaimed. "Would you like me to take your coat?"

"No, thank you. I'm not staying long."

Michele looked at the other group members, busy cleaning the apartment, and peered into the kitchen.

"Salvatore is cooking some boiled potatoes. Would you like to have some with us? You're more than welcome," said Katia.

"Is that all you're having?"

"Yes. Damiano has prescribed us some very simple meals, so we can learn the importance of not being greedy, and it's good for our health. Damiano has warned us about eating foods such as pasta, meat, desserts, sweets and biscuits."

Michele couldn't believe how obedient these people were, and was flabbergasted at Katia's choice of words, Damiano was also a doctor, prescribing food.

"That's ridiculous!"

"I beg your pardon," said Katia.

"I said, that's ridiculous," said Michele.

"I sense you're a bit nervous. Damiano told me about you needing extra therapy, so I'm sure he'll sort all of this out for you. He always does. Why don't you sit down? I'm sure Damiano will come out shortly," said Katia.

"I'm okay. I don't want to sit down. Can I just ask, do you only eat potatoes?"

"Yes, for about a month now. They're really good for you."

Michele shook his head. "That's not healthy. That's crazy!"

"I think the Devil is within him," said Katia.

"I think you might be right," said Salvatore.

"Only Damiano can cure him. I'll have a word with him when he comes out," said Katia.

"Have you just heard yourselves? How on earth can Damiano cure me? I don't need curing," said Michele, raising his voice.

This heated conversation had stirred the other group members, so they stopped cleaning and hovered around him.

"Where's Damiano?" demanded Michele.

"He's in his room. He's not to be disturbed," said Salvatore.

Michele was not going to listen to any more nonsense, so he knocked on Damiano's door loudly.

"Damiano! This is Michele. I need to talk to you right now," he shouted.

There was no reply, so Michele tried the door handle, but it was locked.

"Please stop, Michele," pleaded Katia. "You're not doing yourself any good. You'll only bring Damiano's wrath on you. And believe me, you don't want to see him when he's angry."

Michele had already seen Damiano lose his temper with Salvatore, and he wasn't scared of him at all. His rage got the better of him, so he used his right shoulder to break down the door in five swift blows. He stood in the doorway, gasping at what was in front of him, whilst the others cowered in the corridor in fear of seeing the inside of Damiano's forbidden room. Unlike the rest of the apartment, this was a five-star bedroom, clean, tidy and well painted. On the right was a four-poster bed with golden poles, a beige blanket and fluffy pillows. In the right corner, there was a door to an en suite bathroom. In front, there were two large windows and a white wardrobe with open doors revealing designer shirts and trousers, all neatly hung up on wooden clothes hangers. In the left corner, next to the wardrobe, there was Michele's tennis racquet, a baseball bat and two Louis Vuitton bags. There was a large television perched on a table facing the bed. And there was Damiano, sat down next to a large wooden black desk, on which there were some paper, a Mont Blanc pen, a small paper tube and a line of white powder.

Michele turned his head to talk to the group members.

"Come in and have a look inside Damiano's bedroom," said Michele, but none of them moved.

"You don't want to have a look? Well, in that case, let me describe it to you."

Michele moved back into the hallway and, out of Michele's sight, Damiano quickly snorted the remaining powder and came out of his room.

"Shut up!" Damiano said deliriously. "Michele's gone insane! This is what happens when the Devil possesses someone. He's dangerous so all of you, please don't go near him. God help us all!"

"Do you honestly believe he's a messenger of God? Do you know what he has done with all your money?" asked Michele, but Damiano spoke over him.

"Katia, do you know that Michele thinks you're ugly. He's a loser. Just listen to him! He goes with prostitutes! He smokes weed! Can you take this person seriously? And now he's trying to destroy our group. We must be strong, my brothers and sisters!"

Michele went into Damiano's room and took his tennis racquet, his cashmere jumper and his watch, but he couldn't find the necklace.

"His bedroom is full of luxurious goods! And drugs! And all the things he has stolen from me!" said Michele.

"Don't listen to him! He's deluded! My bedroom is sacred, it's a private place for worship. Does anyone dare to enter this room?"

"I want my money back, or I'll go to the police," threatened Michele.

Damiano laughed hysterically. "You go to the police. Do you think they'll believe a sick negro like you?"

"You've all been brainwashed. You need to get out of here. I'm leaving!" said Michele.

"Do Fabienne and Maria know what you are like? Maybe I should call them, or pay them a visit. I think Fabienne deserves to know what you really think about her," said Damiano.

"That was personal, between you and me! Don't you dare go near Fabienne!" he said.

"There's nothing personal about the Devil! And I shall do what I like, you can't threaten me!"

Michele walked past the group members to the front door and walked out, and Damiano rushed after him.

"You're going to tell others about what you've seen? The police? Your friends? Maria? Fabienne? Don't forget, I know where you all live. You've just made the biggest mistake of your life."

Michele ran to the bus stop, shaken by his confrontation with Damiano. Damiano was disturbed, deranged, and this terrified him. When he got to the hotel, he checked in two customers and then called Adam.

"Hi Adam. I know it's late. How are you?"

"I'm okay, thank you. What about you? You don't sound so good."

"I'm fine, just trying to keep awake with the job. I just want to check that when you come and visit on Sunday, you'll be staying in my apartment, and not Maria's. I'll pick you up from the station when you return from Florence." Michele couldn't stop his voice from trembling.

"That's okay. There's something wrong, I can tell."

"No, not at all. I'm just a bit tired. By the way, have you made any further progress on coming to live here in Milan?

"No, not yet. I applied for a couple of jobs, so I'm waiting to hear from them."

"I see. Well, I hope you can come soon. Anyway, I'll let you go and get some sleep."

"Thank you. I look forward to seeing you next week."

Twenty-Three

The heavy fog blanketed the entire city leaving the buildings with a colourless shape and blurry outline. The only sign of life came from the small brittle leaves, which rattled as the slight wind passed by. Milan was a bustling, noisy city, especially on Friday and Saturday nights, but Sunday mornings were reserved for sleep and stillness. Even the cars slept.

On the street where Maria lived, a small elderly man wearing a cap, broke the silence with the opening of the grey metallic shutters, which revealed his small tabaccheria, where he served different coffees, cakes and newspapers. He switched on the light and put the newspaper stand outside. He looked reluctant to open the shop so early as there would be no customers for at least another hour, but this had become a routine that he just couldn't break, so he propped himself on a stool behind the till and read one of the newspapers. He and his shop were invisible to the world.

In spite of the unwritten rule that there should be no noise on a Sunday morning, there was a faint sound of an alarm in the distance. Could a thief have taken advantage of the quietness and attempted to burgle someone, thereby triggering an alarm? Except, it wasn't an alarm, it was more like the shrilling sound of a siren, which was slicing its way through the silence and doubtlessly waking thousands of people from their sleep and dreams. Then came the source of the noise: the blazing headlights and the circling blue light on top of a police car bringing the first ounce of colour to the otherwise monochrome streets.

A small elderly lady with a walking stick stooped over a body, which was lying on the ground with his face looking to the sky. A pool of blood surrounded his head and had started to clot in his curly, knotted black hair. A police officer asked if she had seen or heard anything. She pointed at the wide-open window on the fourth floor. She told him that she lived on the same floor and hadn't seen anyone, but had been awoken by loud music coming from the apartment from where the boy had fallen. Two ambulance men arrived, one of them checked the boy's pulse, then they placed him on a stretcher, and put him in the ambulance.

The policeman went inside the apartment and saw that there were some splashes of blood on two of the walls closest to the windows. He took out his camera from his bag, and took photographs of the whole apartment. Notably, there were no sheets, blankets or pillows on the bed. When the policeman saw a pair of trousers, a jumper, and t-shirt hung over the back of a chair, he put them all in a white plastic bag and put them into the back of his car. He then proceeded to knock on the door of every apartment on the same floor, but no one was able to give any evidence of what had happened.

The lady was still outside when the policeman came downstairs. She asked him if the boy was all right.

"He's conscious. He'll be in accidents and emergencies, so let's hope he'll pull through," the policeman said.

She waited until the police car had vanished, and looked down at the blood and then up at the window again and went back inside. And the street, having been interrupted, went back to normal: sleep and stillness.

Maria was having breakfast when she received a telephone call from the police, who told her that Michele had had a serious accident and was now being treated in hospital. She left the hot tea and two biscuits lying on a small plate, took her car keys and ran out of the door and down the stairs, the elevator would have slowed her down. Being a Sunday, she didn't have to wait in any long traffic jams. Her heart was pumping as she drove over the speed limit towards the hospital, cursing the traffic lights when they turned red. In twenty minutes, she reached the hospital and rushed into the accidents and emergencies ward and demanded to see Michele and the doctor in charge of him. The lady at the reception asked her to have a seat, but she refused.

"I'm sure everything will be all right. I'll ask the doctor to come and speak to you as soon as possible."

The doctor, a slim young man with straight brown hair, wearing thick black glasses, came out of the ward after half an hour and put his hand gently on her arm. He spoke softly to her, but she couldn't hear a word he was saying. She was numb, unable to speak and think. Eventually, the doctor put his arm around her, took her to a waiting room and asked one of the nurses to bring her some water and tea. Maria sat down, breathed deeply, and sipped some of the water. Then Ben and Nicole arrived.

Before going to bed, Maria went into Michele's bedroom and sat on his bed for a while, and then went to her balcony and looked at the stars. She remembered Michele arriving in Milan for the first time, she had been the one to get him to eat a banana. She remembered watching him play football, visiting the family for Passover, him making friends in Courmayeur and Camogli, enjoying the carnival in Rio de Janeiro, meeting Fabienne. They were good times. She couldn't bring herself to think of all the mishaps that had happened, all the arguments they had had. Looking down, she saw people arriving in cars, walking to their apartments or leaving for a night out, knowing that the world would go on, but without her son.

Epilogue

Adam goes to São Nicolau
September, 2013

I look at my watch. It's half-past three, and my flight from Lisbon to Mindelo leaves at half past four, so I run to the gate, only to find that my boarding pass isn't in my jacket pocket. I run back to the café where I stopped to have a coffee, and the waitress is waiting for me. Out of breath, I take the boarding pass, go back to the gate and get on the plane.

The previous evening, I went to see Maria. Her apartment looks exactly the same as it was all those years ago, Michele's room has the same blanket, the same books and the same ornaments. She was pleased to see me and she had prepared a vegetable broth and some fried chicken and potatoes. Just as I was about to start a new term as a lecturer in life sciences at the Università Cattolica, I arranged to go on a five-day hiking tour of São Nicolau during the wet season to get an idea about where Michele came from. Maria had always wanted to go there, and she asked me to take lots of photographs. After dinner, we sat down in her sitting room, and I listened with fascination as she recounted her life story and how she eventually took custody of Michele.

There's a three-hour wait at Mindelo airport before the flight to Preguiça airport in São Nicolau, so I take out my bulky weekend newspaper and finish reading the science section. When the lady announces the boarding of the aircraft, I put the newspaper in my rucksack and board the bus, which takes me to a tiny aeroplane, the type you would see in periodic and historic dramas. Normally I select an aisle seat, but this time I choose a window seat, so I can get a good view of São Nicolau, but sadly it's so foggy that I can only see blotches of green protruding from the clouds.

I collect my suitcase, which has somewhat been damaged in the hold, it now has large patches of black oil on the grey surface. Outside I feel the rain sprinkling on my forehead, and the humidity makes me start sweating. Carlos, the tour guide, is waiting for me outside the airport and takes me to a small family-owned pension in Ribeira Brava. On our arrival, the mother makes us some capucha for dinner. I tell Carlos how I met Michele, and he asks me for his full name and date of birth. Carlos is thirty years old and set up his own tourist company. He tells me that São Nicolau doesn't have any sandy beaches so it doesn't attract as many tourists as the other islands, such as Sal, Boa Vista and São Vicente. Tourists usually visit São Nicolau for one-day trips where they can go hiking or scuba diving.

The following morning, I put my t-shirt, trousers and hiking boots on and go down to the grocer's shop and buy two bottles of water, which I put in my rucksack. I go up the slope back to the pension and wait for Carlos to arrive.

We go hiking from Campo di Porta to Porta da Lapa, which was the first village established in São Nicolau, and then onto Morro Alto. Carlos tells me that it will be a moderate climb, but it is incredibly steep. I look in admiration at the beautiful and dramatic volcanic terrain, and by the coastline, I see how the erosion over time has given parts of the mountainous landscape a unique artistic quality.

As we are hiking, Carlos tells me that he gave Miguel's name and date of birth to the town hall, and they were able to trace where his relatives live. On the way back to the pension, we stop by Fajã de Baixo, the village where Michele was born and lived for four years. We go into a small grocer's shop and meet Angelo, who invites Carlos and me to visit his wife in their home. The house is tiny, and there are flies everywhere. Carlos does all the translation for me. Angelo's wife says that she knows that Miguel died from a car accident, travelling from Monaco to Milan. I don't contradict her because shortly after Michele had passed away, Maria asked me to call Ana and let her know that Miguel had had an accident on a motorway. Angelo's wife tells me that Ana died in Portugal six months ago, and that José died in the United States two years ago.

Angelo arrives and takes Carlos and me to see the house where Michele was born, and it's still very much the same as it was during the early years of his life. I pick up three stones near the house, I'll give one of them to Maria when I return to Milan.

Five days later, after strenuous hiking and a diet consisting only of capucha, I take the plane back to Mindelo. It's funny to see the written passenger list and boarding card.

I return to Milan, and on the following Sunday, I visit the Duomo and light a candle in memory of Michele before going to Maria's for lunch. I share all my photographs with her, and I tell her about Michele's parents. She's moved when I give her one of the stones, and she places it on the glass coffee table. In the afternoon, I take the tram to the cemetery and place one of the other stones next to Michele's gravestone, and say a prayer. On the way back to the centre, I look out of the window and smile, thinking of all the happy memories I had with Michele.

Acknowledgements

Madeleine Grunberg for her friendship, for sharing her own story and helping me construct the main events in the novel.

Antonio Joao Lopes Rosario for being an amazing guide, interpreter and friend on my visit to São Nicolau in 2013.

Hipolito Soares for helping me with translations into crioulo, and providing me with the historical context of emigration pre-independence of Cape Verde.

Fábio Sacoman for his help with the chapter set in Rio de Janeiro.

Luz Mercurio, my former colleague and dear friend, for designing the stunning front cover of this novel.

Jonathan Webb for his support editing and reviewing selected chapters from Part One.

Diane Miller, my mother, for being a soundboard on phrasing and use of language.

And to my late father, *John Miller*, for having so much faith in me.

In memory of
Mateus Dos Santos Duarte